THE SUNSHINE STONE

Foster Henderson

ISBN: 1548676721
ISBN 13: 9781548676728

Dedicated to Myrbims

1

My life began to fall apart in Year 9.

It started in October, when about twenty police officers battered down our front door at 5 in the morning and dragged Dad away. I'll never forget how utterly miserable he looked when they handcuffed him and pushed his head into the police car.

The officers smashed their way through the house, ripping up expensive carpets and pulling treasured possessions apart. Then they confiscated all our computers, tablets and mobile phones and removed them in large, transparent bags. We never got them back.

Dad was released on bail the next day, shaken, pale and silent. He refused to answer my questions and Mum just dismissed the whole episode as a huge misunderstanding.

If only.

Nine months after Dad's arrest, I was called into the living room. Oh, boy, I could tell it was serious *straight away*. Dad kept looking down and Mum's eyes were raw from crying.

She asked me to close the door and sit down. By the way, when anyone asks you to close the door and sit down, always brace yourself. You're about to receive some *seriously shit news*.

Dad was going to prison. They started explaining what he'd done wrong but it didn't make much sense. I couldn't really concentrate anyway. Something involving *laundering* money at my Dad's law firm and Dad *taking the fall* because he was the compliance partner.

A few days later, he was sentenced to five years and ordered to pay an enormous fine. It was big news and the tabloids loved it. *A lot.* Mummy didn't want me going to school for a few days but I did anyway.

School was High Mount for Girls. I took their entrance exam but was always going to get in. Dad's mum, Granny Strictness, was the previous headmistress and there was a bloody oil painting of her in the school lobby! Of course, no one mentioned this but the only way I wasn't getting into High Mount was if I went on a killing spree in the middle of Purchester and got banged up in the same cell as Dad.

I was doing all right at High Mount, quite popular. My favourite subjects were art and gym but I really hated maths. I don't get maths.

A few days after sentencing, Mum started selling everything as quickly as possible because we had to pay this massive penalty. The house got sold to our neighbours and I think they paid a bit extra for the contents. Mum sold the cars online and her jewellery in Hatton Garden.

We called it the *purge.* By the time it finished, we were just left with a small TV, a few bits of furniture, an ancient clock radio and some old clothes. Even the new computers and teddy bears went to the neighbours.

At the end of August, we departed Purchester, for the final time, and moved into a tiny, flat in Rotney. Then, in early September, I commenced Year 10 at my new school.

Rotney High.

Oh, God. I barely slept the night before my first day. In the morning, when I put on my new uniform, it was like dressing for a funeral.

The jacket and tie were all black and the woollen skirt and shirt were leftovers from High Mount. No more decent school shoes, by the way, just flimsy, black sneakers.

Mum set off for work and I took the bus to Rotney High. I sat on the top floor, looking and feeling like I'd swallowed poison. There were quite a few other kids sitting right ahead, chattering loudly and screeching with laughter.

When we reached the school's bus stop, they clambered down the spiral staircase, still gossiping excitedly. I followed slowly, maintaining a respectable distance.

But as soon I got out the bus...*WHAM!!!* The most ear splitting, savage noise, you've ever heard. One thousand six hundred kids bellowing at the top of the voices. I felt dizzy, disorientated and intimidated. Combined with the immense, surrounding walls, it felt like I was approaching the gates of hell.

Assembly was a horrid, cold affair. Just a massive gathering of unwelcome faces. I desperately missed High Mount and my head and stomach throbbed with tension.

My class, 10E, was much bigger than my class at High Mount. There must have been at least 20 kids more in class, the majority black or Asian. They were universally unfriendly and I continued feeling about as appreciated as an outbreak of Ebola.

Miss Patel, my new form teacher, took a register of names and introduced me briefly. A few pairs of eyes flicked in my direction but soon found something else more interesting to focus on. Then, the maths lesson began.

At lunch, I bought a ham sandwich with my token card and sat at the edge of a wooden bench, in an enormous, grotesque hall feeling alienated and frightened. Countless, talkative kids passed by and everyone seemed to know everyone else. I wondered briefly if this was how Dad felt on his first day of prison.

After finishing my sandwich, I walked through the hall's exit and wandered aimlessly through the school's grounds for a few minutes. Eventually I stopped at the very back of the school, barred by an imposing wire fence. Turning around, I noticed a large black girl. She was trailed by three sullen, mixed-race girls, all chewing gum.

She walked right up and stuck her face into mine.

"Who the *fuck* are you?"

"Antonia," I said, simply.

She stared at me with disgust and sneered. There was a bit of a pause so I continued the conversation.

"What's your name?"

"My name? *My name?*"

She grinned at her mates, then dropped her smile and turned back.

"My name's *Fuck You,* as in *Fuck You, I ask the questions.* OK?"

One of her cronies spat at my feet and a slimy piece of gob missed my Primark sneakers by a few inches.

The black girl prodded me backwards. "You look like a little bitch and I fucking *hate* little bitches. How about I cut your throat, you piece of *shit?*"

I didn't reply. To be honest, this kind of thing didn't really happen at High Mount. Instead, I just gawped ahead, hoping I didn't urinate down my school tights.

She pushed me backwards, again. "Well?" she demanded. "*Well?*"

"Please...don't..." I whimpered, pathetically.

"Ooooh...please don't" mimicked one of the stooges, "please don't slice my pretty white throat!"

The black girl reached into her jacket and pulled out an object. She snapped it open – *click* – and held it up, glaring.

"Shit," I stammered and stepped backwards.

"Fuck...yeah!" hollered the black girl. "Flick knife, sister. How about I slice you open?"

I stumbled further backwards, but her pals closed in quickly. The girl on the far right picked at her nose ring and breathed loudly in my ear.

I tilted my head back. The knife approached my face, slowly, *slowly* and I closed my eyes, "don't...please don't..."

I braced myself for searing pain but there was no impact. I blinked my eyes open and glanced down. The blade hovered above my throat, tickling it.

"Hey!" The black girl raised my chin and stared calmly in my eyes. "Little. Fucking. Whore. You got any money?"

"No, absolutely nothing. Seriously..."

"Liar!"

No, *really!* Nothing!"

"Wrong fucking answer!"

"No, I promise you, I swear, I swear ...please. *Please!"*

The black girl smirked and shook her head. "Just shut the fuck up!" Then she closed the blade.

"Since you asked, my name is Demi. And if you fuck with me, I will take your life. Slowly. So, I'll be seeing you around, *Antonia*." She turned around and swaggered off. Her little gang followed obediently for a few seconds, then wheeled round and jeered at my distress.

I shook my head and closed my eyes again. *Welcome to Rotney High,* I thought.

2

The first thing I noticed when I got home was someone had erected a large painted sign at the back of the corridor.

DON'T FEED THE RATS

I thought this was a bit comical, not least because there wasn't much food in our flat.

Mum wasn't back yet so I made myself a cup of tea and switched on the television. There was nothing on apart from a cookery shown on BBC2 but I gawped at the screen anyway.

The walls of the flat must have been paper-thin because I could easily hear things banging around upstairs and all sorts of voices yelling and crying. It wasn't cold outside but I was really shaking. I could still sense Demi's knife tickling my windpipe.

Eventually, Mum got back. She normally left her secretarial job in Baker Street at 4 in the afternoon

She seemed cranky and unhappy, complaining about her chronic back problem. I made a few sympathetic noises, hoping she couldn't see my trembling. Then she asked a few cursory questions about my first day at school.

I didn't tell her about Demi – poor Mum had enough to worry about – instead I just said everyone seemed quite friendly and helpful.

Mum then disappeared into the world's smallest kitchen returning, a few minutes later, with a couple of cheese sandwiches and a packet of ready salted crisps.

I could hear boys kicking empty beer cans outside, bawling and swearing, dogs yelping, doors slamming and a constant yacking in foreign tongues. And the noise never stopped – not once - even as it became darker.

Meanwhile, Mum turned in early, complaining of exhaustion and I carried on watching television. Pretty soon, I could hear Mum snoring, adding to the unpleasant racket outside.

ℒ

And so, began a pattern.

I replaced talk with homework, television, reading free papers and listening to my clock radio. There was no money for make-up, clothes, books, mobile phones or computers so I was constantly battling boredom and loneliness.

When we lived in Purchester, I was quite proud of my dark, cookie hair and spent far too much time brushing it in front of my bedroom mirror. But I stopped caring. I stopped looking in mirrors, or even sneaking a quick glance in a shop reflection. It just wasn't important anymore.

Once a week, we visited Dad, surrounded by grim tables, sinister inmates and watchful guards. The prison was a wretchedly cold place, in every sense, but an oasis of calm compared to Rotney High.

Night times were the worst. I could easily hear Mum sobbing into her cheap pillows. Although we both hated Dad for being such a dick and getting himself into such trouble, we missed him desperately and yearned for our former life.

But my biggest problem was Demi.

She kept cornering me during school breaks and after school, demanding money, swearing and menacing. Always surrounded by her nasty, little gang, revelling in my fear and discomfort.

Then there was that menacing click. The click I heard closing my eyes, walking down the street, running for the bus, watching the news, eating my sandwiches, listening to the radio, even dreaming. The *click*. The sharp sound of Demi's flick-knife snapping open before it scratched my throat.

Then the usual, repeated threats. She knew where I lived. If I ever reported her to anyone, she would cut me, kill me, murder Mum, pour petrol through the letterbox and set my house on fire.

Got it? Got it, bitch? Fuck. You.

Then...BAAAM! Nose ring would punch my ear. SLAM! Demi would smack my face. OOOMPH! Kick in the shins. WHAAAM! Knee in the crotch. BANG! Have another. BANG! Another. BAAAM! Shoulder punch.

Sinking to the floor. World swirling, swirling, pain, pain, jutting, spiking, screaming. Laughter. Gobbing. Another kick, more laughter and then trailing off. Just me, alone, clutching myself.

Then it *really* hurt getting up and moving around, especially reaching for things. But no one noticed what was going on. Not even at home.

I often got back to the flat sporting large bruises but Mum rarely commented. She seemed so wrapped up in her own misery and paralyzing back pains.

I tried keeping in touch with my friends from High Mount but it became increasingly difficult. I couldn't email, text or message them and we could only use the landline very sparingly.

But the overall problem with my old pals was simple. My whole situation was just plain *embarrassing*. It was no secret my Dad had gone to prison. Although I pined for friendship, it was always awkward communicating with girls from my former life. We now inhabited entirely separate worlds. They had comfort, money and loving families. I had a broken family, poverty and Demi.

Two weeks into my first term, I lay in bed, fretting and turning. The neon red digits of my clock blared 01:47. Meanwhile, Mum was in great form.

Grrrrrrrrrrrr...hawwwwwwwww!

Then again. Wait for it.

Grrrrrrrrrrrr...hawwwwwwwww!

She'd obviously drifted off watching television because I could still hear BBC News. I pulled off my blankets and padded into the living room. She was slumped across our tatty couch, head tilted back.

I squeezed next to her and stared blankly at the screen. My shoulder pounded from where Demi had punched it earlier and I rubbed it slowly. Even though it was late, Mum looked peaceful so I let her slumber on. I stretched my legs out instead and pointed my toes.

I half watched the television presenter. He was pointing to a graph, which kind of resembled my life. Basically, the line wavered up slightly, then dropped down sharply. Then the picture cut to a city riot, angry bodies chucking missiles at police shields and cars being set alight.

I dropped my head and stopped pointing my feet. I tried sitting still but the agitation just shifted into my stomach, clawing and nagging away. Pulling at my insides.

Then I found myself *aching* for Dad. I mean, where the was he? He was supposed to care for us, right? Not *abandon* us, for God's sake.

But even before the police snatched him away, he was never around. Maybe he was a good provider but he was always working. Always at the office. Even at the weekends. Two holidays in ten years.

Then when he was at home, he barely showed any interest in us. He was constantly babbling on his iPhone or responding to emails. Never quite there. Maybe now he was in prison, he could grow a long beard and reflect on his parental failings.

The television faded into the background.

Two days ago, my form teacher, Miss Patel asked me how I was getting on. I couldn't exactly tell her I was being harassed by a psychopathic student with a fondness for weapons, arson and gobbing so I simply replied, "Fine, Miss." She strolled off, mumbling something about her door always being open - not a great idea in Rotney.

Unlike Mount High, no one seemed to know my Dad was a prison inmate. Well, nobody ever spoke to me so the subject never arose. But I bet half of the pupils had parents behind bars, anyway.

I glimpsed at Mum. Still deeply asleep, probably dreaming about Land Rovers, nannies, jewellery, holidays in Florida, respectable husbands and oodles of money.

I stared blankly at the television for a few more minutes, then went back to bed.

The next morning, during the school break, I really needed a wee. However, as usual, this was a potentially severe problem.

The primary aim of my school day was very straightforward. *Avoid Demi.*

But it wasn't easy. The most dangerous areas were the back of the school grounds - where we first met - the hall and lockers behind the science labs and - of course - any of the school toilets.

The girls' toilets were particularly treacherous. I always tried sneaking in discreetly but she often caught me. God knows how. She must have used informers.

I clenched my lower abdomen muscles as hard as possible – but it didn't help.

I was *desperate*. Worse than desperate. I quickly calculated that the nearest - and probably safest toilet - was on the third floor of the Left Block. It was just a sole cubicle with a good, firm lock.

I was sitting at the back of the English classroom on the second floor of the South Block. Not a dire situation. The toilet was less than two minutes away if I sprinted. I stood up, walked slowly out the classroom, glanced around casually then bolted towards the staircase.

I swerved twice to avoid groups of raucous kids and reached the toilet in about ninety seconds. Then I hurled myself inside, slamming the door shut and whipping the bolt through.

God, the relief was exhilarating. My heart was smashing into my lungs but I'd *made* it.

I checked my watch. Six minutes to lessons. Even being a couple of minutes late could get you a Room 18 detention so I had to be careful. I decided to wait three more minutes before risking the return.

I wiped myself, flushed and stood up. Then I placed my ear on the door, straining to identify anything unusual. But it was a waste of time. All I could hear was my uneven breathing and kids rushing to lessons. I straightened my skirt, washed my hands, inhaled deeply and pulled the bolt back. Then I opened the door cautiously.

Suddenly a rude, external force yanked the door open and Demi burst inside, the usual gang tagging behind.

"Little bitch, you think that'll work?"

I shook my head, shaking, cowering. Nose Ring tutted and waved a reprimanding finger.

"Well?"

"No...I..."

"Huh?"

"I..."

Demi grabbed her ear with an exaggerated gesture and leaned in. "Yes?"

"I..."

"Yes, *Antonia*?"

"I needed the toilet. Sorry."

She pulled away slightly and glanced at her cronies. "*Antonia* needed the toilet," she explained. They sniggered like cartoon characters. Demi smiled too, glancing down. Then she whipped my face. It was so fast and hard I didn't see it. It stung and screamed, throwing me backwards.

I stayed down, blood seeping from my lip.

"Get up," ordered Demi.

I raised myself slowly, only to be hit even harder and faster. The cronies screeched with pleasure. This time I stayed down.

Flick. Oh, here we go.

The knife closed within a centimetre of my left eye, looming ominously.

"Now, see, this is how it's going to do down, *Antonia*. You're a rich, white bitch and you're holding out on me – because I know you got money. Haven't you?"

I didn't reply.

"Haven't you?" She kicked me in the ribs. Hard.

"No," I groaned.

"Wrong answer, *Antonia*. Wrong. Fucking. Answer." She slammed her foot into my ribs and spat on me. "Fucking whore. Don't you ever say *no*, I'll cut you open! You hear me?"

I nodded.

"What's that?"

"*Yes...*" A tiny whisper.

"I can't hear you. Louder."

"Yes."

"Louder!"

"Yes!"

"Hell...yeah!

She bent down and whispered in my ear. "Ten pounds tomorrow, or I'll kill you and burn you so bad, Mummy won't recognize her baby girl. This ain't no game, girl. I'm for real, *Antonia*. And you tell anyone about this, I will fucking find you and rip you to pieces. Real slow. Real. Fucking. Slow. Know what I'm saying?"

I nodded.

Demi pulled herself up and raised her tone. "Tomorrow. Here. Quarter to eleven. Ten quid or you are fucking dead. Got it?"

I nodded.

"Sorry what was that?"

She leaned in.

"I get it...I get it."

She patted me gently on the head and retracted the blade. "Good girl. I knew you would." Then she kicked me again in the same damned spot.

3

I stole the money from Mum's purse, crying as I did it. I felt so ashamed.

Then I listened to her searching for the note all evening, cursing herself.

I paid Demi the next day and she thanked me by punching my jaw. Then she vanished for a few days but I knew it was only a matter of time before she returned for more. I had confirmed her mistaken belief that I was wealthy.

It turned slightly colder. I developed a sore throat although sadly not severe enough to keep me off school.

Mum started suffering with severe back pains and spasms. When I was four years old, a small lorry ran into the back of her car and her airbag didn't expand properly. Part of her lower spine was crushed and she had spent several weeks in hospital. From then on, she suffered from intense, periodic back muscle spasms. These crippled her for days and could only be calmed by powerful, stupefying painkillers.

It was horrible watching her in so much pain. Apart from fetching the odd cup of tea, helping with groceries and repeating the same soothing phrases, there was nothing I could do.

Then, in the third week of September, Rotney Fair arrived. It was a one-day event and advertised as a celebration of home grown produce and talent. *Celebration?* You know, as if we were in the middle of

the country and had competitions for who could grow the biggest tur-
nip. Local artists demonstrated their wares; local poets recited their
verse and the pubs exhibited "local displays".

Intriguingly, the pub at the bottom of my road was advertising an
evening magic show and I felt drawn. It offered a brief escape from
my claustrophobic flat, although venturing into any part of Rotney
outside daylight was a dangerous game.

Mum passed out from all her painkillers and sedatives just after
eight o'clock. I didn't have any homework so I left her a brief note
saying I was popping out for a few minutes. Then I grabbed my jacket
and slipped away.

I turned left and pounded briskly down the street towards the pub,
shivering as I passed a couple of idling hoodies. Then I increased my
pace as sinister yells and laughter echoed in the near distance. Every
step was difficult, though, as my shoulders and stomach pulsated with
pain from recent beatings.

I arrived at the pub a few minutes later and edged inside. I didn't
have any money for drinks so just hovered at the back.

The floor was packed with punters, slurping pints and guffaw-
ing loudly – but always tinged with edgy aggression. To be honest, if
crotch-kicking Demi suddenly sauntered through the front door, it
would have felt just like school.

I waited several minutes but there was no sign of the magician.
Not that anyone seemed particularly bothered. Meanwhile, apart
from a couple of white boys in Puma tracksuits, it appeared I was the
only young teenager in the pub.

I checked my watch and shook my head. Quarter past eight. The
show was already running fifteen minutes late! I decided to give the
magician five more minutes, then head home.

There was a small, makeshift stage at the front of the floor and I
watched it anxiously. More customers teemed through the front door,
squawking crudely and forcing their way through impatiently.

I glanced at my watch *again*, one of the few things Mum didn't
sell off a few weeks ago. The second hand dragged lazily over the dial

and the minutes passed at an elderly snail's pace. Then suddenly, at twenty past eight, there was a muffled round of applause and the world's most unconvincing magician appeared.

I almost bit my lip because it was so funny. He was a very tall, old boy, sporting a long, false beard and pointed wizard's hat. This barely complemented an ill-fitting, purple gown and tight, leather trousers.

He looked worse than the BBC presenter. And then he spoke.

"Hey, people," he bellowed, in an American accent, "I am *The Great Cornelius!*"

This was greeted with a collective snort of derision, then someone chucked a bun. I think it was a bun, or maybe it was a doughnut, but - anyway - it sailed leisurely through the air and smacked Cornelius on the forehead. This pub burst into a huge wave of mocking laughter. Another bun sailed by but it missed.

Cornelius seemed unperturbed by this attack on his decency and waved his palms at the audience. "Thank you, very kind," he said, "but I had my dinner a few minutes ago."

This amused the crowd and the magician continued.

"Tonight folks," he announced, "you are in for a hell of a treat. Right here, in this Rotney drinking establishment, you will witness the most unusual thing. *True magic.* Not a mirage, or an illusion, or smoke and mirrors. No. You will see *true magic.* Maybe you won't believe it, maybe you will but I can promise you this. I am the greatest magician in the world and I will perform true miracles before your very eyes. I am *The Great Cornelius!*"

He paused and - for just a second - he had the audience mesmerized. Then someone in the front row belched loudly and the pub dissolved into another wave of rowdy laughter.

However, *The Great Cornelius* remained unfazed. He gave a bit more talk about how his act was truly unique, then he started performing his magic.

The first thing he did was pull a white rabbit from his hat. This was just about the corniest thing a magician could do and the crowd hated it but I thought it was quite impressive. The hat wasn't a top hat or anything. It was a silly, crumpled pointed thing so I couldn't see how he could pull a fat bunny out. But the Rotney knuckleheads jeered with disdain.

Cornelius raised a left palm and pulled out a large, empty birdcage. He placed it on a small round table and covered it in a glittery sheet. Then he whipped off the sheet and revealed a large, white dove.

Then he replaced the sheet and repeated the trick several times. Soon there were six doves cluttering the cage, beating their wings. Cornelius raised a finger, draped the sheet over the birdcage with a theatrical gesture and threw it back to reveal two brightly coloured parrots. I grinned like crazy but the audience were underwhelmed. Another bun smacked into the birdcage, startling the poor parrots slightly.

Cornelius dropped the sheet theatrically over the cage, then snatched it back. Just *empty space*. No sign of any animals! I clapped in delight but the punters glared angrily in my direction and I stopped immediately. God, I was so *embarrassed* but Cornelius winked in my direction and I felt saved. The first friendly gesture since I'd arrived in Rotney.

Then it got better. The magician did something remarkable. I'd seen it a few times on television but performed live; it was a very different experience. He asked for a female volunteer and eventually an obese, drunken creature with short-cropped hair and a nose stud was pushed forward by her equally obese partner. The woman giggled and looked uncomfortable. Cornelius asked her to lie on a pub table and she complied awkwardly. For a *horrible* moment, I thought the table would fall apart under her bulk but it just about held steady.

Cornelius laid the old glittery sheet over her body so you could only see her head. He motioned slowly with his hands and after a few seconds, the woman levitated upwards and kept rising. She rose at least three feet in the air but the spectacle was ruined by her startled screeching.

Cornelius lowered the body, thanked her graciously and sent her back into the crowd. I thought it was a fantastic trick but the audience seemed distinctly unsatisfied. In fact, they were growing restless.

A young man in a Fred Perry shirt stood up, suddenly.

"Oi Cornelius!" An uncouth, beckoning shout.

The magician looked up. "Yes?"

"Can you make my cock bigger? It's about ten inches long but I could do with another yard!"

The crowd hooted merrily but Cornelius just smiled and raised a bony finger.

He commenced an unwieldy bobbing dance with his glittery sheet. It looked absurd but succeeded in quietening the crowd as they wondered what the hell he was doing. The dance continued for maybe thirty seconds before he suddenly stepped backwards and flung the sheet aside.

"Behold," he announced and pointed to a chimpanzee in a large cage, which had appeared from nowhere. "Magic," he continued knowingly and opened the cage door. The chimpanzee shrieked and jumped out the cage into the magician's arms. It hugged him tightly before turning towards the audience.

For a second, the chimpanzee stared at the knuckleheads and the knuckleheads stared at the monkey. Then a beer bottle rifled through the air and whacked Cornelius on the forehead. The old man collapsed with a groan and dropped the chimp as he sank to the ground. The monkey screeched in fear, darted back into the cage and covered its eyes. Then all merry hell broke loose.

The bartender vaulted over the bar and ran towards the stage. He held the crowd back from the prostrate magician as they surged forward. Someone smashed a wooden chair into someone else, a person at the front got head butted and then, suddenly, the whole pub dissolved into an enormous brawl. Rotney was like the Wild West except the cowboy hats had been replaced with nasty tattoos and missing teeth.

A beer glass missed my ear by millimetres, shattering spectacularly on the wall to my left. Then screams. Time to leave.

Fortunately, I was positioned right next to the fire exit. I wheeled round, slammed through the double doors and sprinted back towards my house. Obviously, I was concerned about the chimpanzee and old magician but I sincerely hoped all the pub customers killed each other by the time the police arrived.

After I was halfway down the street, I glanced behind my shoulder. No one following. I half expected to start hearing police sirens but there was nothing like that. No doubt this kind of thing happened all the time in Rotney.

I accelerated frantically, arriving at my building, gasping, breathless and shaken. I unlocked the front door. The familiar stench of urine. Battered stairs. Empty corridor. DON'T FEED THE RATS.

Then I halted. For a mad second, I felt like turning back. The magician, the parrots, the doves, the chimp. Especially the chimp. It seemed so frightened.

Then I shook my head. Much too risky. I'd just pop into the pub tomorrow afternoon, on my way back from school.

4

There was still no sign of Demi.

I'd avoided the usual places and traps, hiding in a small classroom in the South Block during the lunch breaks. I hated feeling constantly hunted and frightened but what could I do?

Just thinking about Demi made my bruises pound and swell, acting as an additional reminder. It seemed extraordinary that she could walk around with a flick knife with impunity but I suspected that the teachers were also afraid of her.

The real danger was after school. She had cornered me twice on the turning into Rotney High Street and dragged me behind the chemists.

Now I was taking extra precautions, leaving at varying times and keeping within the mass of pupils. But I soon learnt there was no safety in numbers. If Demi appeared, they just separated and walked straight on.

And yet...for the fifth day in a row, I appeared lucky. I hadn't see her in assembly or during the lunch break and now, turning into the High Street, I was breathing easier.

I scanned the road quickly. Left, right. Still not there. I began accelerating, picking up speed. There were no buses around so I kept going. Quicker. Cars, shops and people flew by, faster and faster.

Then I tripped up heavily. The world tumbled upside down and I slammed into a post box.

Sharp pains jutted through my forearms and legs as I bounced off the box and hit the ground. For a few seconds, I just lay there, utterly dazed, before there was a familiar voice.

"Not so fast – *Antonia*."

I raised my head up, slowly. Vehicles and pedestrians passed fleetingly but no one noticed. I was on my own again.

Demi crouched down and patted my head. "Ooooh…I bet that's gonna hurt tomorrow. See that flick, though? What a fucking flick! I should be playing for them England lionesses with my fancy footwork. That is fucking *class*, baby!"

More footsteps approaching. The *gang*. I heard Nose Ring gathering up phlegm in the back of her throat, then she spat viciously. Her cold gob struck the back of my neck, trailing down slowly.

Demi crouched over. "Don't even think about trying to get away from me. I can find you whenever I want to. Don't you know that? Hey, maybe I'll come over and slash you while you're sleep. Cut you into little, tiny pieces. Then burn you, baby. Burn you *real slow*."

She patted my head again. "See, I really fucking *hate* you. Hate everything about you. You piece of fucking shit. But maybe I won't kill you. Not just yet, anyway. Not if you give me twenty pounds tomorrow. Yeah, maybe then I'll think about it."

She leaned into my ear. "I don't want no fucking excuses and no fucking games. This ain't a game! Twenty pounds. Third floor, Left Block, quarter to eleven. And if you're not there, with the money, I will come and get you. I will stick my blade in your heart. And you will die. OK, *Antonia?*"

I nodded, shaking.

Demi leaned in, even closer, whispering now. "You say anything. I'll kill you. You tell anyone, I'll kill you. You don't show. I'll kill you. You fuck me around, I'll kill you. OK?"

I nodded again.

"Good girl. "She kissed me.

Then she stood up. "Let's go, ladies!"

They walked off, leaving me trembling on the floor. Numb with fear and shock. Sobbing. Numerous people walking by, ignoring me.

Eventually, I checked my injuries. My arms and legs were badly scraped from the fall but it wasn't too bad.

I picked myself up and carried on walking towards the pub, limping slightly.

I was in serious trouble. There was no doubt I had to appease Demi with another payment but I had no further source. It was a miracle Mum had ten pounds in her purse, last time, but there was no way I taken could steal more money.

Poor Mummy. She *really* didn't have two pennies to rub together and I was too young to hold up the post office. I couldn't run just away or report the problem. And the police were *out of the question*. Their filthy gang was far larger and more sinister than Demi's.

So basically, I was screwed.

A few minutes later, I arrived at the pub. I hoped the magician would be there, or failing that, his chimpanzee.

I pushed opened the front door and glanced around. I suppose I expected to see broken chair legs everywhere and bloodstains on the carpet but the place appeared remarkably calm and tidy. Normal, even.

I recognized the barman. He was the guy who had vaulted over the bar, trying to break up the impending fight. I gawped at him and he shot me an unfriendly glance.

"Can I help you?"

"Is the magician from last night here?"

"Maybe."

"Can I see him?"

"Why?"

"Just wanted to say hello and see if he's OK."

The barman raised his brows. "Don't see why not." He scratched his chin, still considering my request. "You're probably his only fan, you know. Hang on..."

He turned around, "Frank!"

"I thought his name was Cornelius?"

"Nah...Frank's his real name"

"Oh."

There was some rumbling behind the bar, then a door opened and the magician appeared. He'd exchanged his false beard and leather trousers for a grey sweatshirt and jeans but still looked markedly different from the usual Rotney residents.

"Yeah?" The voice from last night.

The barman nodded in my direction. "The girl wants to say hello."

Frank looked up at me, "hey." He grinned, then cocked his head. "You been in a fight?"

I stepped back, defensively. "No. Why?"

"You look kind of shaken up, Miss."

Miss, I liked that.

"No, definitely not."

"OK." He grinned pleasantly. "So how you are doing?"

"Fine, thank you." I paused. "I came to your show last night, I thought it was really good. But I had to leave when people started throwing things."

Frank nodded understandingly. "I understand – and thank you."

No reaction or excuse from the barman. He just stared ahead impassively, then looked away.

I carried on. "Are you OK? You look OK."

"Me? Couldn't be better. But thanks for asking."

It was true. I couldn't see a mark on his forehead, or anywhere on his face. It was odd because the beer mug hit his head with enough power and speed to floor him.

"How's the monkey? He seemed scared."

"Cheetah! Yeah, he's fine. Just got a bit of a surprise, that's all."

"Can I see him, please?"

"No, sorry, I'm afraid he's gone back home now."

"Oh," I looked downwards.

"But you can meet Brian if you want?"

"Brian?"

"Yeah."

"Who's Brian?"

"Come and meet him, He can be a little shy, though."

I glanced at the barman but he was fiddling with something behind the counter, ignoring the conversation.

I looked back at the old man. He didn't seem particularly threatening. Besides, I was probably going to be dead in less than 24 hours. I shrugged, "sure."

"Great. Well, this way."

He led me back into the small room behind the bar

Once inside, it appeared even smaller because it was so full of boxes and crates. In the centre were a couple of saggy chairs and a battered coffee table. An even more battered bowler hat rested on the table.

I looked around.

"Where's Brian?"

Frank motioned towards the hat. "Under there."

"Really?" I walked over to the hat and picked it up. Then I put it down.

"There's nothing there."

"Really?"

"Yes, really."

"Huh? Try again."

I raised the hat. There was a fat, white rabbit underneath it.

I gasped. "*Huh...!*"

Frank smiled. "Magic."

"That. Is. *Amazing.*"

I looked down at the rabbit that was wrinkling his nose. "Can I? Please?"

"Sure."

I picked it up and held it tight, clasping its warm, furry body.

"I like his name - *Brian*. It suits him"

"Thank you – but I don't think you've told me yours."

I exhaled, slowly. "It's Antonia."

Then I burst into tears. I kept crying and crying, then found I couldn't stop.

Frank seemed quite shocked by my sudden outbreak of tears. He removed Brian gently, sat me down on a saggy chair and fetched a glass of water. He kept repeating, "hey, it's ok...it's ok." Then produced tissues, bless him.

I sipped the water but couldn't stop crying. Frustration, anger, fear and confusion seeping out my eyes. Unfortunately, there was a huge amount of it so it was taking a long time. I dabbed my cheeks with the tissues and occasionally blew my nose loudly.

The old man sat down opposite, waiting patiently. Eventually I cried myself out and blew my nose for a final time. My face flushed with embarrassment.

"I am *so* sorry. I think I got Brian wet."

"Brian's fine, Antonia. I'm more worried about you."

I sniffed and nodded.

"Do you want to talk about it?"

"Not really. Sorry."

Frank nodded. "Try, though. It might help."

I exhaled, then sniffed again, louder.

"Go on. I won't bite."

So, I told him - not everything, of course, but still an awful lot. I told him about Dad, prison, selling everything, moving, the flat, school and of course, Demi. Nose Ring, too. I went into *plenty* of detail about them. It was odd but I felt I could trust him straight away. Meanwhile, Frank listened quietly until I finished.

"How old is this girl, Demi?" he asked, eventually.

"I'd say sixteen but she looks about thirty."

Frank didn't say anything. He seemed to be thinking hard.

"She's figures she's a gangster. But she's just a bully and a coward," he said quietly.

I nodded in agreement.

"You ever hear of a guy called Bruce Lee?"

I laughed at this. "Are you going to teach me karate so I can beat up Demi? Then maybe win a karate competition or something."

Frank grinned. "Not quite."

"So why are you asking me about Bruce Lee?"

"Just a foolish notion. But you've heard of him, right?"

I nodded.

"Well, that's great. You know who he is. So, let me tell you a story about Bruce Lee. What many people didn't realize was that Bruce Lee was very near sighted. Back in the day when they were cutting-edge technology, Lee was one of the first to wear contact lenses -- but they were expensive, difficult to replace, and uncomfortable. This meant that much of the time, he wore thick, coke-bottle glasses -- nerd-glasses, if you will.

"Anyway, the story goes that Lee had returned to Hong Kong for a visit, walking along with a friend of his. This was before he'd started serious strength training so he didn't have the muscular build we remember today. He wasn't famous then so he wasn't dressed particularly well. Basically, he was slender, wore thick glasses, and dressed in a non-descript way. Easy pickings for a bully.

"Sure enough, a bully starts verbally harassing him, beginning with verbal insults and then moving into pushes and shoves. Bruce, never one to suffer this kind of treatment, lets loose with this awkward, effeminate persona, complete with nervous giggles, whines, and pathetic entreaties for the bully to stop and so forth. And with that as a disguise, he let loose with two quick strikes, one to the groin and one to the head -- and down goes the bully. To any untrained, casual observer, it looked like the nerd got lucky.

"As they walked away, Bruce's friend asked him, "What the heck was all that stammering and giggling and pathetic bullshit about?"

"And Bruce replied: "A bully can accept being beaten by a superior fighter. *But that asshole is going to remember for the rest of his life that he got the crap beaten out of him by a weakling.*""

I stopped sniffing and stared at Frank. What was he saying?

"You know," he said, looking at me intently "I could help you but you'd have to obey some ground rules."

"What kind of rules?"

"The rules of engagement."

I gawped at him.

Frank smiled, "don't worry, it'll all make sense. Play by my rules and we'll put Demi out the picture very quickly."

"What do you mean *put her out the picture?* Are we going to kill her?"

Frank laughed again, "Why? Do you want to?"

I thought about this, it was a good question. I winced, "well, maybe not kill her but just send her to a hospital for a few weeks. Make a statement."

Frank nodded approvingly. "Sounds good," he said. "OK, well, let's just put her out the picture for a while."

I bounded forward. "You serious?"

"Absolutely."

"*Really?*"

"Really." Then a slow, reassuring grin.

"But *how?*"

Frank raised his hand slowly in the air and clawed his fingers.

"With these."

5

F rank straightened up in his chair.

"I've met people like Demi before, throughout my life, actually. Bullies, villains, cowards, scoffers, criminals – world's full of them. Sometimes you can ignore them, sometimes you can't."

He sighed. "In *your* case, you can't. You've got to make your stand; otherwise she'll do something terrible. And if you report her, it'll make it worse. But don't worry, kid, you have something, she doesn't."

"What's that?"

"Me."

He stood up and started rummaging in one of the larger boxes. "You're going to need to take out Demi, slowly and Nose Ring, quickly.

"Nose Ring?"

"Yup."

"Why?"

"Just give me a second. I need to find something."

He carried on searching. "Hey, here we go...." He reached lower into the box and produced a white ball, roughly the size of a football.

"What's that?"

"*Ah-hah!*" Frank sat down in the chair and grinned. "See, many years back, I used to be in the military and they taught us a few mean tricks. And mean tricks are my profession, you know? I'm going to show you something that will make Demi think long and hard before speaking to you again."

I tilted my head. "But what about Nose Ring?"

"Nose Ring? Right. Well, what's going to happen is this. You'll take down Demi nice and slow and when Nosey gets over her shock, she'll lurch forwards, try and hit you. So, you'll disable her. Fast. Then the other two will beat it"

I tensed. "Beat it? Or beat me?"

Frank laughed. "Hell no, they'll beat it! They'll run back to their mummies so fast, Antonia, you won't believe it."

I shook my head. "How do you know this?"

"If you fight a gang of five or six, you rarely need to take out more than three of the gang. First, you take out the leader. He's the hardest. Then the next two in the chain will have a go. You beat those guys and the others won't challenge. They'll run away."

"The chain?"

"Right, like the pecking order. In your case, from what you say, you need to humiliate the leader, disable the number two and the rest will make scarce."

I raised my palms. "How do you *know* this? I'm sorry. I'm *sorry*. I really don't mean to sound rude but...I mean..."

Frank leaned in. "I'm 81 years old but like I said I was in the American Army and those boys taught me how to fight pretty damn well."

"Wow." I dropped my palms. "So, what do I do - please?"

"Just listen carefully. I'm going to show you a couple of party tricks but I need you to solemnly promise that Demi and Nose Ring will be the only recipients – save in the case of an emergency. These are tools of combat. *Dangerous* tools. We clear?"

I nodded.

"Good. Now close your eyes."

I obeyed.

"I want you to think about this place. *Rotney*. Everything about it, everything associated with it, maybe picture your typical day. But just take a moment."

I nodded again.

"Now. Antonia. What's your overwhelming emotion?"

I exhaled. "Fear."

"What kind of fear? Describe it."

"Suffocating. Choking. Crushing. Overwhelming..."

"Excellent. Now, pay attention. What lurks under the fear? Just beneath the surface. Hovering."

"Anger," I mumbled.

"What's that?"

"*Anger.*"

"Anger! You're damn right. Open your eyes."

They flicked open.

"Fear has its place, in fact, it's an essential component of living. But right now, it's *unhelpful*. It's crippling you. Instead, you need to access your anger, control it, channel it, *use* it."

I nodded slowly. "OK..."

"Good. Catch the ball."

He chucked it over and I caught it easily.

"We start with Demi. Now let's imagine this ball is Demi's face. Put your thumb on her right cheek...just here...and your four fingers above your thumb...just here, here, here and here."

I grasped the ball as he asked.

Frank waved his right hand, shook it and produced a black pen from thin air. He marked around my fingers. Then flexed his right wrist again and the pen vanished.

"I want you to squeeze the ball with everything you've got. Put all your anger, your frustration and your hatred into it. Concentrate all that negative energy and rage so it burns and shoots through your fingers. Crush it! Crush the ball! Do it!"

I started squeezing. My eyes narrowed. Then I squeezed much harder.

"Outstanding. Keep squeezing! Keep squeezing! Keep squeezing! Now close your eyes again. Imagine her laughing, mocking face. Think about everything you've lost, every little thing. That horrible stinking flat and school. Why you? Why always you? Squeeze! Squeeze that ball!"

By this time, I was squeezing so hard, it felt like my wrist was about to break off. But funnily enough, it felt great clearing out all that negative stuff and forcing it into Demi's face. My hand pulsating with rage.

"OK, stop," said Frank.

I released the ball.

"That was great, Antonia."

He sat back. "You'll see I've marked where you need to grip. When you get home, keep practicing, again and again, squeezing in the correct areas. Also, practice grabbing the ball so your fingers land neatly on the target areas in a lightening quick motion. Keep doing it again and again until its second nature. If your Mum catches you, just say you're doing some wrist exercises. Got it?"

"Yes."

"Good. Tell me again, what time is Demi expecting you?

"Quarter to eleven in the Left Block."

"Uh-huh. And what time does your break start?"

"Half past ten, tomorrow."

"Fifteen minutes, plenty of time. So, get there early. Sit in the little toilet, take slow, deep breaths and concentrate on your breathing. Calm yourself as best as you can. I say again, focus on your breathing - not on what's going on inside your head, or outside the door. Right?"

I nodded. "Right."

"Good. Now listen very carefully, I'm going to tell you exactly what to do."

And then he did.

6

I skipped home, clutching Frank's ball in my pocket.

Mum made baked beans on toast, then I watched a bit of television and did some maths homework. Tough, as always. Then I spent a few hours practicing with the ball before turning in.

But when I woke the next morning, there were sinister shadows in my bedroom and my heart thumped a dark rhythm. *De-mi, De-mi, De-mi...*

On the bus, I found myself praying intently. To who? I don't know. But still I prayed. Please let me be courageous, give me strength and help me. *Help me. Please!*

Don't let me fail...

In the morning we had double English, followed by Maths. As always, I sat quietly at the back, ignored by everyone else. You would have thought that, after almost three weeks, someone would have said hello but I remained a complete outsider. My classmates just looked through me as if was entirely hollow.

At the school break, my insides were beating so wildly I thought they'd explode through my rib cage. But I tore my mind away from these sensations and concentrated carefully on Frank's instructions. I knew I could do this.

I walked slowly up the stars and turned towards the Left Block toilet. Kids flew by me, mouths open, pushing, shoving. But I'd stopped listening. Just kept on walking, eyes narrowing, staring dead ahead.

I entered the small toilet and shut the door quietly, ignoring the lock. There was a stale fragrance of air freshener and a couple of empty cardboard rolls lying on the floor. I sat down slowly on the toilet seat and adjusted my posture. Then I closed my eyes and breathed deeply and rhythmically. Inhaling and exhaling deliberately, focusing on the calm flow of oxygen. Then I opened my eyes and stared ahead. The anger seeped upwards, spreading outwards and transforming. I clenched my fists and blinked deliberately. Waiting.

Waiting.

❧

Demi slammed the door wide.

"Where's my money, bitch?"

I stood up. "I've got it, I've got it all," I said, rapidly. "But please don't hurt me, please don't, please don't, I can't take it anymore. I can't take it. I can't take the pain." I grabbed her sleeve. "Please, I'm begging you, Demi, I'm begging you."

Nose Ring grunted.

Demi winced and took a step back. "Don't touch me, you piece of shit. And quit your fucking whining!"

"Please, Demi, please. Please, don't hurt me. I'll do anything for you. Look, look, I didn't get twenty pounds." My eyes blazed. "I got fifty pounds, have it, please have it, anything. I'll do anything for you."

I had her attention. "*Fifty?*"

"Yeah."

"Show me."

I waved a loose fist.

"I'm holding it. Look."

She leaned in. Closer.

Then I grabbed her face. I hit all five targets perfectly and pressed with *intense* ferocity. The anger was already there, boiling and screaming inside. Powering through my fingers, snapping them in.

For several seconds – it was difficult to tell – all I was aware of was Demi's startled face and the unwavering determination of my iron grip. I kept increasing the pressure until I began realizing she was in terrible pain. Her face turned bright red and then blue. She tried producing a sound but could only emit tortured gagging noises. Then she started choking.

I gripped and gripped, like I was possessed by a demonic force, enjoying the sight of her losing consciousness. Her eyes rolled back, lost focus, then became vacant. She stopped moving or responding in any way.

I released her limp body and she dropped heavily to the ground, her head smacking the bathroom floor.

Nose Ring lurched forwards but I punched her savagely in the throat. One, clean, strike. Just as Frank showed me. She crumpled onto the floor, gasping. Then I turned to the other two girls, smiling. They reversed slowly, then fled rapidly. I didn't bother chasing and walked away.

Then something changed. Slowly.

Kids in my class started checking me out. Just for a moment but I still noticed it, a flicker of acknowledgement. Then they *even* started greeting me. A few cursory, stumbling exchanges. Awkward but not unwelcome.

Then, not just the kids in my class, other pupils too. Sometimes during a break, or at lunch, even after school. Two days after the incident, a large black guy sauntered over and I started getting nervous. I thought maybe he was a member of Demi's extended family. For a second he stared into my eyes and sized me up. Then he clenched a ringed fist, mumbled *respect* and walked on. It was bizarre.

Even the teachers began talking to me. Suddenly friendly and inquisitive. Never mentioning Demi, or her cronies. Always unspoken.

Meanwhile, Demi and Nose Ring just vanished, disappearing like the doves in Frank's stage act.

⤵

Irritatingly, I couldn't report my success to the old man. At least, not immediately.

Frank had told me he was staying in a room over the pub for a few weeks and I could usually find him there. But when I dropped into the pub after school, bristling with excitement and gratitude, the joyless girl behind the bar said he'd gone away for a few days. She didn't know where, of course and suggested I came back over the weekend.

It was very frustrating but what I could do?

When I returned to the pub on Saturday afternoon, I found him immediately. He was sitting at the bar by himself, dressed in the same plain clothes as before, sipping from a glass of water. I *think* it was water, anyway.

As soon as he saw me he started grinning like his missing chimpanzee.

"Hey, whaddya know! It's my pal, Antonia!" he announced. "Good to see you, kid. Have a seat. How you been?"

"Fine, thanks." I sat on the barstool next to him and surveyed the pub. It seemed quiet. "The people in the pub said you were away for a few days."

"Yeah, I had a few things to take care of."

"Oh, OK." I shuffled my feet.

"Drink?"

"Thanks. Gin and tonic."

Frank raised an eyebrow, "I don't think so."

I shrugged, "diet coke?"

Frank nodded to the barman who fetched my drink, then disappeared into another back room behind the counter.

I played with the glass. Rotating it slowly and staring ahead.

"So, young lady. How did it go with Demi?"

"Well…" I exhaled slowly. "I was nervous, *really* nervous but your trick was…*incredible!* I mean, it really worked. I did the whole blubbering routine – "

"Which unsettled her, right?"

"Absolutely, then I grabbed her cheek *hard* - exactly the way you showed me - pressed like mad and…"

"And?"

"It was *insane.* I mean, she went red then blue, making these weird gagging sounds, then she passed out. Literally, her head *smacked* the floor. Then I jabbed Nose Ring in the throat and she went down too."

Frank beamed wider than ever and offered me a fist. I smiled back and pounded it. Then I threw my arms around him. "Thank you so much, thank you! You saved my life."

"Hey, hey, that's ok…. thank you."

I released him.

"Yeah, the claw can be pretty devastating. I don't think Demi will give you any trouble for some time now. I take it you haven't seen her again this week."

"No, thank God. Is she in hospital?"

"Possibly. Probably."

"Hmm", I considered this. "What does it do?"

"What?"

"The claw."

Frank shrugged.

I frowned. "Frank?"

"Yeah."

"What does it do?"

"Trade secret, kid."

"*Frank?*"

"Yeah?"

"Tell me. Please."

He sighed in an exaggerated fashion. "OK, *OK*…well, as I understand it, it applies very precise pressure points to the face. You don't need to know the exact, *physiological* details but the resulting effect is a shit storm of pain and reduced blood circulation. It makes your victim pass out and wake up with a monster headache. And a helluva sore cheek. There can be some pretty nasty after effects too."

"Like what?"

"Like pain. Lots of it."

"Wow. So, I really hurt her?"

"Oh, yeah."

"Sick! Did you really learn that trick in the army?"

"Sure did."

I sipped my diet coke, thoughtfully. Then I thought of something, "Where's Cheetah?"

"I told you last time. He's gone home."

"Where's that?"

"Small sanctuary, not far from here. About ten monkeys live there. They let me borrow him for a few hours."

"*Really*? Isn't it dangerous to take Cheetah to a pub like this? I mean, in the middle of Rotney? It must be frightening for him. It's scary enough for me!"

"Not really. He likes his trips out and besides he can handle himself."

"Why - you also taught him the claw?"

"Nah! Chimps just rip off your arm if you annoy them."

"Sick! I should introduce him to Demi."

"He'd enjoy that."

I grinned. "I didn't know there was a monkey home round here."

"Yeah, it's not very well known. The owners keep pretty quiet about it."

I took another sip, considering this.

"Say, Antonia," said Frank brightly, "I'm doing a magic show real near here tomorrow afternoon. Fancy coming along? I can give you directions. It's not difficult."

I nodded. "Sure. Sounds really good."

"Great!"

"But just one thing, Frank. Are you going to wear that ridiculous get up?"

"What ridiculous get up?"

"You know the long beard, dressing gown, leather trousers...?"

"That, my dear, is a magician's robe, not a dressing gown and yes, it's an essential component of *The Great Cornelius's* act."

"But it makes *The Great Cornelius* look like a bigger monkey than Cheetah!"

Frank laughed and shook his head. "You don't understand, my dear. The magic can't work without it."

7

When I got home, there were two surprises waiting.

The first one was a present from Mum. Wow.

Mum hadn't bought me any presents since Dad was sentenced – mostly because she was so preoccupied with selling everything we ever possessed. Although it was obvious she hadn't gone further than Rotney's nearest charity shop to find something, I was still touched by her effort.

I examined it. It was a small, brass tube, dented and scratched. I imagined smacking it round the back of Demi's head repeatedly until the blood gushed out.

Well, that was Rotney for you. A few years ago, I was planning which teddies to take for a picnic, now I was working out the best way to put someone in hospital.

"What is it?"

"It's a telescope, an old fashioned one."

Old fashioned! It must have been at least three hundred years old. Something used by an Admiral on the High Seas. I rotated it slowly and tried looking through the eyepiece. I couldn't make out anything other than a vague jumble of colours so I decided to try again later in my bedroom.

"Thanks, Mummy," I mumbled, "I love it". I reached over and kissed her loudly. Then the second surprise came out of the kitchen, holding a mug.

If the first surprise was relatively pleasant, the second surprise was a distinct downer. It consisted of a creepy looking, middle-aged man with dank hair and dirty fingernails. He looked like the type of guy who had a wet palm when you shook his hand and never brushed his teeth.

I immediately suspected he was a policeman, probably here to arrest me for assaulting Demi. If he was, I didn't care.

I slid back, slightly. "Who are *you?*"

Mum smiled pleasantly. "Toni, this is Neil Huck. He's a doctor and my new friend."

So, he wasn't the police but then again...*my new friend*. What the fuck did that mean? I glanced down at the telescope. Forget Demi, I could practice using it on the *new friend* first. Here and now. Smash his nose in, then kick him in the stomach as he rolled on the ground.

I nodded my head reluctantly. Huck grinned back, flashing a couple of yellowing teeth. He probably thought I was well behaved by local standards. I mean I hadn't tried to run off with his wallet yet, or anything.

"You must be Antonia? Your Mum's told me all about you."

I shrugged, dropped onto the sofa and switched on the television. Then I sat motionless.

There was an ugly pause before Huck sipped his tea and carried on chatting to Mum instead. I stared intently at the screen, although I couldn't tell you what I was watching. Huck finally departed a few minutes later and I continued to pretend he'd never been there.

Later that night, I tried using the telescope out my bedroom window.

Mum had turned in early, as usual. Her back was still very painful and the medication didn't seem to be having much effect. God, I hoped she wouldn't require *hospitalizing*. What a terrifying thought, stuck all alone in Rotney...

I concentrated through the old eyepiece, turning the tube gradually. At first, all I could see were tiny pricks of light but as I adjusted the focus, I discovered I could make out small, luminous shapes.

Oh…there were whole worlds, stars and galaxies outside Rotney. I was just nothing compared to the surrounding universe. So infinitely large. One day, soon, I would be dead and completely forgotten and nothing would matter anymore.

I stared through that silly old tube for ages.

I didn't know if God existed - Mum and Dad were atheists – although I thought if God did exist, he didn't like me very much. But looking through the telescope that night, I really sensed something so much *grander* than myself. Maybe, even a bit of peace too.

On Sunday afternoon, I set off for Frank's magic show. He'd offered directions but I knew where he was performing. It was a pub on the other side of Rotney.

I told Mum that I was going to Rotney's Public Library to catch upon some homework. Mummy was so doped up she didn't realize what a terrible excuse this was. There was no library – at least not any more. It had been destroyed in an arson attack years ago.

Obviously, books weren't valued as highly as weapons in Rotney because the Local Authority had left the library as a burned-out hulk. Just another ugly object along the High Road.

The show was at three in the afternoon so I gave myself twenty minutes to get there.

You could hardly classify *walking in Rotney* as a pleasant, recreational activity. The streets were littered with needles, used condoms and piles of stinking garbage. Many of the shops were closed or boarded up and there was little sign of any affluence.

I passed several ghastly retail outlets, amusement arcades, charity shops, a "Domestic Violence Refuge" and a bunch of fast food takeaways. It was a busy Sunday afternoon and the streets teemed with people. This meant challenging work, continuously dodging facial tattoos, fat necks, shaved heads, aggressive stares, raucous Cockney yells, gabbling foreign accents, veering strollers and screeching children. Then, in front of the station, I almost collided with a pacing, bearded eccentric screaming about the love of Jesus.

It got worse. As I turned off Rotney Plaza, I was shoved aside by two huge thugs, dressed in black and running very quickly. They jumped on a pizza delivery boy, several metres to my right, throwing him off his tin scooter and wrestling him to the ground. One of the thugs whipped out a pair of handcuffs from his back pocket and slapped them on the boy's wrists. Then they pulled him up, hurled him forward for a short distance and slammed him into a white police van.

I *shuddered* but kept on going, arriving at the pub just before three. Again, it was very full indeed, with people sitting and standing everywhere. Still not many children around, though.

Justin Bieber blasted out of the pub's speakers and I noticed a small stage had been erected in the pub's left corner. There was no sign of Frank so I positioned myself in my usual space, next to the fire exit. I guessed it was only a matter of time before another brawl broke out and I had no intention of being floored by a flying ashtray – or monkey, if things got particularly heated.

I didn't have long to wait because soon after I arrived the barman, dressed in a white shirt and red bowtie, grabbed a microphone from behind a table and addressed the crowd.

"Right. Thank you, everybody. Shut the fuck up!"

The crowd quietened slowly.

"No stripper this afternoon - sorry guys…"

Someone shouted, "Shame!"

"Thank you but we have got something a bit different for you." Then he dropped the microphone. It smacked the ground, screeching feedback.

"Oh, fucking bollocks." He bent down, grabbed the microphone off the floor and belched loudly into it. "Excuse me."

The crowd laughed approvingly and the barman took an exaggerated bow. Then he stepped back, flinging out an expansive arm. "Give it up please, for Rotney's answer to Dynamo, *The Great Cornelius!*"

The crowd clapped again, someone wolf whistled and Frank appeared wearing his ridiculous leather trousers, false beard and wizard's hat. There was huge laughter at his costume and the crowd at least seemed to be in slightly better spirits than at his last show.

Then, unfortunately, I noticed a familiar character at the opposite end of the pub. He had a cheap suit, dank hair and a creepy face. I couldn't see whether his fingernails were dirty – he was too far away - but there was no mistaking Dr Huck.

He appeared out of place amongst the rabble and I wondered what he was doing here.

It was a problem. There was no way I wanted Dr Huck to see me. In the first place, he'd probably run back to Mum, reporting that I was hanging out in one of Rotney's seediest pubs. No doubt, forgetting it was hosting a family magic show. Secondly, I had absolutely no desire for any kind of social interaction with the man.

I stayed near the fire exit - well out of Dr Huck's field of vision - which conveniently gave me a perfect view of the stage.

Meanwhile, Frank had ridden out the initial laughter and began his *real magic* routine.

"Ladies and Gentlemen, I bring you a truly unique spectacle. This afternoon, I will be performing genuine sorcery, real magic, if you will. There will be no illusions, no smoke and mirrors. Real magic, folks!"

There was no encouragement from the crowd, just a bit of tittering at the back.

Frank removed his crumpled hat, revealing a small woolly monkey perched on his head. It looked at the audience, blinking with a startled expression. Frank replaced his hat, then removed it again. Goodbye woolly monkey. Hello yellow parrot

"Wankers!" shouted the yellow parrot at the crowd, causing some amusement, "wankers!"

Then Frank transferred the parrot from his head onto a perch on the stage. He flung his glitzy sheet over it, whipped it back and revealed two identical, blue parrots. There was no sign of the yellow parrot.

"Wankers!" screamed both parrots, "wankers!"

It was just great, Frank was putting two fingers up at the crowd which was just as well, as they were clearly unimpressed. The tittering increased and there was no applause but *The Great Cornelius* persisted. With a few more strokes of the sheet, Frank changed the parrots into a large pelican and then into Cheetah – who didn't seem altogether delighted to be back in Rotney. Then Cheetah disappeared and was replaced by two lion cubs, then, with another flick of the sheet, they also vanished into thin air. It was stunning but there was still no applause.

Suddenly, there was a slight commotion at the back of the pub. Then a white man with the fattest neck I have ever seen, emerged from the crowd and approached the stage. I could see from the way he walked he must have been drinking heavily as his movement was disjointed.

The man came right up to Frank and bellowed into his face. "Oi! Wizard! Is that a real beard?"

Frank looked at him for a few seconds, then smiled. "*The Great Cornelius* never reveals his secrets."

Fat Neck thought about this for a few seconds before deciding it wasn't a satisfactory response. "Answer the fucking question, Wizard – is your beard real?" Repeating *Wizard* had an unintentionally comic effect, making him sound like he was in a cheap Disney film.

Frank was about to give him the same response but didn't get that far because Fat Neck suddenly lunged at his beard.

For an old man, Frank dodged extremely nimbly and Fat Neck just ended up groping thin air. He wheeled round heavily, slightly confused and reached for the beard again but Frank was much too fast, evading him easily.

Fat Neck snorted like an enraged rhinoceros and after turning again, swung a massive hook at Frank's face. But the old man jerked his head back faster than Spiderman and Fat Neck completely missed his target, overbalanced and tumbled straight into the perch. Thank goodness there were no more parrots on it, although, no doubt they would have thoroughly enjoyed shouting *wanker* at Fat Neck for crashing into their home.

Fat Neck picked himself up slowly and I recognized his expression immediately. Utter hatred and fury. "You're a dead man, Wizard," he said quietly, keeping with the Disney theme.

At this, Frank did something extraordinary. He beckoned Fat Neck towards him with his fingers, inviting him to attack. There must have been at least a 40-year age difference between the two men but my money was on Frank. Aside from his army background, he seemed entirely calm whereas Fat Neck was fuelled by venom and alcohol.

Now the crowd was alert, many of them clenching their fists and urging Fat Neck on. Where was the barman?

Fat Neck rotated his fat neck. He was bleeding from a cut in his forehead – no doubt from hitting the perch at full speed. He pulled out a 4-inch knife, stepped towards *The Great Cornelius* and lunged again. Frank dodged the extended arm, kicked the knife out of Fat Neck's hand and slammed him in the face, smashing the drunkard off the stage and back into the perch.

Now the barman appeared, pushing his way through the excitable crowd. He broke clear and ran towards Fat Neck. But Fat Neck picked himself up, adjusted his stance and swung a massive right hook at the red bow tie. The barman couldn't dodge the missile as neatly as Frank and the huge blow broke his nose with a stunning crack, sending him sprawling back towards the tables. He crashed loudly into one of them, unconscious and bloodied.

Encouraged by this, Fat Neck charged at Frank again but the magician had decided to end the fight. He swivelled neatly, felled his opponent with two rapid jabs to the stomach and face, then kicked him immensely hard under the jaw. Fat Neck collapsed immediately, landing on the stage with a brutal thud.

Then everything went crazy again. The crowd poured forward and missiles started shooting through the air.

Time to go.

I jerked hard on the fire exit's handles but they wouldn't budge. *No!* What's the point of a fire exit if you couldn't open it in an emergency? I glanced around for help but there was a full-scale riot developing. I tried the fire exit again, then again but it was useless. I had to make for the main exit – but how?

I turned around. *Oh, God!* Dr Huck was approaching. How had he got over from the other side so quickly? Couldn't someone knock him out, please? He hadn't seen me yet but he would any second now. I instinctively dived behind the nearest pub table and hoped he would be too distracted to notice. There was a huge amount of movement behind me, then I heard the unmistakable sound of glass being smashed followed by further uproar. A woman started screaming.

So, this was it. I was going to die before reaching my fifteenth birthday – and in Rotney too. How *glamorous*. I just wanted to see a magic show on a sunny Sunday afternoon. Was that so much to ask for?

There was more shattering glass directly above and I crawled further under the table, curling up into an awkward ball. Boots darted around round me, left, right, thudding, more glass, fists, screams, yells. I closed my eyes and held myself firmly, squeezing tighter.

Then someone called my name. And again.

I opened my eyes and the ceiling disappeared. Strong hands grabbed under my shoulders and hoisted me up swiftly.

"You OK?" Familiar voice.

"Yeah, think so."

"Sure?"

"Yeah."

Frank grabbed my hand and headed towards the main exit. God, he was going fast for an 81-year-old, swerving faster than a spooked rabbit on speed. I suppose it helped that he'd discarded the false beard and flappy gown. He hurdled a couple of crumpled bodies and flailing fists, before finally finding the main exit barred by a gigantic, white, bald man with tattooed limbs. He stood in a taut posture, legs slightly splayed, arms folded and sporting the meanest expression you've ever seen.

Frank stalled and grinned amiably at the enormous human obstacle.

"Excuse me, pal. Young lady needs to come through."

The giant shook his head. "I don't think so."

"Excuse me?"

"You're going nowhere. *Pal.*"

"And why might that be?"

Because Barry Baines is my mate, *pal.* And you're an old cunt that needs sorting." He unclasped his arms and edged forward. "Now, I'm going to fuck you up…"

But he didn't get any further because Frank sort of prodded him in the chest from about an inch away. Well, I say prodded, it was more like a lightning fast jab that propelled the huge man through the pubs doors with incredible force. The windows in the door shattered on impact and the jab's momentum deposited the big boy onto the pavement in an undignified heap.

Frank pulled me forward, detouring only briefly to kick the bald man in the head. Then we bolted down the road, at the same crazy pace, veering left into the Plaza, past the Primark, past the countless cheap retail stores, arcades and fast food outlets, only slowing down when we turned again into Rotney High Street.

"Whoa! Time out," I gasped and collapsed onto the nearest park bench. For a few seconds, I struggled to gain my bearing and sanity, folding myself over my knees. Then I sat up slowly and craned my neck in every direction. It was just a regular street scene. No whirring ambulances. No flashing blue lights. No sign of the police. Nothing at all. Presumably, the boys in blue were still arresting pizza delivery boys and tripping over the public.

I shook my head, exhaling. Then I looked at Frank. He was waiting patiently for me to recover – but something wasn't right.

"You're not even out of breath!" I protested.

He shrugged. "I work out. Go for a run, every day. You know, keeps me fit."

I shook my head. Nothing made sense.

"Where are the animals?"

"Still fighting in the pub."

"Very funny. You know what I mean. Cheetah, the parrots, the *lion cubs* – for God's sake."

"Oh, don't worry about them. They're all safe, believe me."

"I don't believe you, Frank! There's a flipping riot going on in that pub. They're going to get hurt."

"They're safe," he repeated. "Hand to God, Antonia, they're in no danger. Let's just get you home."

I thought about this. It wasn't very satisfactory but he'd given me his word so I changed the subject.

"Who's Barry Baines?"

"Who?"

"Barry Baines."

"I have no idea."

"But that huge man seemed seriously upset with you. He said he was a mate of Barry Baines. What was he talking about?"

Frank shrugged. "I really don't know. I assume he was the guy that tried to grab my beard."

"You mean the guy you beat up? I mean the *first* guy you beat up?"

"I mean the guy who tried to take my beard and pulled a knife on me."

"Yeah…well, that might explain it. They did look like friends, or lovers, or whatever."

"I guess."

I stood up and we took a few steps forward. Then I stopped and turned.

"Frank?"

"Antonia?"

"Thanks for getting me out of that place. I think that's twice you've saved my life."

"Hey, no trouble." Then he stalled too. "You sure you're OK?"

I ignored the question. "How can people behave like that? So disgustingly. *Twice!* It was such a great, magic show too – and…like…it had no impact on them. Or rather, it did. But the wrong impact. How could they not appreciate it? *I don't understand.*"

"Hey…" He touched my forearm gently. "It was a just tough crowd, that's all. No big deal."

"No big deal?" I gaped at him.

"No."

I furrowed my brow. "…and by the way, how could you hit such a massive bloke so hard, from, like, *half an inch away*? I mean – no disrespect - you're over eighty years old."

Frank shrugged. "Pretty standard punch. Jeet Kune Do"

"Jeet Kune *what?*"

"Jeet Kune Do. Bruce Lee's martial art tactics."

"Oh, right. Bruce Lee again."

Frank grinned. "That's right. You can't beat Bruce."

I shook my head in disbelief. "Are you like a superhero or something?"

"A super-what?"

"A superhero. You know, disguised as *The Great Cornelius*, or whatever?"

Frank laughed merrily. "No ma'am. I'm just an old man."

And he carried on walking.

8

I was back at Rotney High, on Monday. Then we visited Dad on Tuesday afternoon.

The prison was like Rotney High, in many ways. It was a huge, intimidating structure, although built earlier than the school and opened in 1891. Security cameras observed you everywhere and I was always searched before and after each visit. I don't know what the un-smiling guards thought I might smuggle in. Maybe my two-hundred-year telescope so Dad could plot his escape to the moon.

Mum was also searched every time. What a joke! The most she ever brought in was a ten-pound note for Dad so he could buy some hot drinks in the prison canteen.

After we'd passed through another scanner, we went into the visiting centre. It was the coldest, most clinical, unwelcoming place in the world – apart from my school, of course. We sat round a rectangular, bare table and Dad was brought out, wearing a shapeless, grey, prison uniform. Once he'd sat down, he wasn't allowed to stand up again and we couldn't talk for more than an hour.

Daddy. He'd deteriorated so much in the last two months. I always knew hold old he was because our birthdays were exactly four days apart. This meant he was 45 years old tomorrow.

But he certainly didn't look that age. Before Dad was arrested, he always seemed stressed and distracted by his ghastly job. But he kept trim by working out regularly in a plush City gym, next to his office.

Now he looked like the oldest, most broken man in the world. I know that sounds odd, obviously he wasn't the oldest man in the world. There was probably some hermit living in Japan who was approaching his 150th birthday or something – but even that hermit would have looked better than my father, that's for sure.

He just appeared destroyed. Smashed to smithereens by the criminal justice system and tabloids. It was deeply unpleasant seeing my father like this. When he was a City partner, he was always very well groomed and owned a bunch of expensive suits. Now he looked like a Rotney tramp – with the same haunted eyes I'd seen on the street corners.

My parents chatted for a while about finances and prison diet, then Dad glanced in my direction.

"And how are you, Toni? How's school?"

"Yeah, fine."

"Settling in?"

"Yeah."

"Any problems? Other kids all right?"

"Yeah. All good."

"Learning anything interesting."

I flicked my eyebrows. "Same old…you know."

Dad nodded understandingly, then turned back to Mum.

OK, here's the thing about Dad. It didn't make sense.

The truth was I didn't really understand how he got himself into so much trouble. However, I knew certain things instinctively. I knew he was honest and hardworking. I knew he didn't need to steal or *launder* money. I knew he was responsible and took his job extremely seriously.

Yet he pleaded guilty, almost immediately, annihilating every shred of comfort and respectability surrounding him. Condemning himself to the company of rapists, paedophiles and murderers for years. Why? How could it have happened?

When I wasn't worrying about Rotney High, I was worrying about my wretched parents. *Boy, what a couple.* Mum, the cripple and Dad, the common criminal. I didn't even know if they'd stay together now that Dr Huck was sniffing around and making eyes at Mum. Not that I could talk to Mum about him. She just changed the subject when I started asking questions, or departed to the bedroom with her bottles of pills.

And everything could have been very much worse, if it hadn't been for Granny Strictness. According to Mum, she spent her life savings paying for Dad's legal costs and half the fine. And now we couldn't thank her anymore. She was still in hospital after suffering a serious stroke.

The 5th of October used to be a happy date. I loved getting presents on my birthday and in the past my parents usually treated me to a great party, or an unexpected treat.

But my 14th birthday was marred by Dad's arrest and my 15th birthday was even worse. Mum gave me a cheap card and chocolate bar. And that was it. I didn't get anything from my old High Mount friends and I couldn't check *Instagram* and *Facebook*.

In the early afternoon, I popped into the pub down the road, hunting for Frank but he wasn't around as usual and nobody knew where he was.

The old man remained an enigma. Always dodging questions. I didn't even know what he was doing in Rotney or for how long. Was he waiting for an audition on *Britain's Got Talent* or something? Maybe that wasn't such a clever idea. Judging by Frank's prior record, Simon Cowell would probably try and assault him with a microphone and end up with a broken jaw.

In the late afternoon, Mum and I visited Granny Strictness in hospital. Another sordid family chore. Granny barely responded to anything we said and just sat immobile in her hospital chair.

I told her a few times it was my birthday but it made no impact. She kept dribbling and the nurse wiped her mouth regularly with a tissue. After half an hour, we set off home, returning to the flat about forty minutes later.

The painted rat sign was still there, although, I still hadn't seen a single rat! I wondered if Frank could change rats into parrots or monkeys.

After eating omelettes, we watched Downton Abbey and then went to bed. Before turning in, I looked through my old telescope and spotted the Orion constellation. I couldn't locate a planet, though. Not even Jupiter and that was the biggest. After finally giving up on my stargazing, I lay down and listened to Capital Radio for a long time on my clock radio. They didn't play anything interesting, just the same old chart tracks and eventually I drifted off.

The next afternoon, there was still no sign of Frank.

The girl behind the bar said she didn't know where he was and they had hadn't seen him at all for the last few days. As usual, my further questions resulted in blank expressions and shoulder shrugging.

The pub wasn't particularly crowded but I didn't want to hang round. To be honest, I didn't fancy visiting another Rotney pub for the rest of my life. However, I was seized by a mad impulse. I felt *certain* I could find something juicy if I snooped around his room upstairs for a few minutes.

The problem was his room was bound to be locked and if I was caught going through his things, they'd think I was stealing – a fair assumption in Rotney. I considered the issue slightly longer and then remembered Frank kept some boxes in the small room behind the bar.

I approached the bar and adopted a coy posture. "Do you mind if I leave Frank a brief note?"

The girl behind the counter wiggled her nose, a bit like Brian. She had piercings everywhere and short, auburn hair. Tough looking, like everyone else round here.

"Suppose so. Leave it with me, I'll make sure he gets it."

I paused for a second, collecting myself. "It's kind of a surprise. Can I just put it in his room? You know, behind the bar?"

The girl looked at me closer, probably wondering if I was up to mischief. However, I hoped she was impressed I was comparatively well spoken and not an obvious troublemaker. She frowned and glanced around. "You've come in here a few times before for Frank, haven't you?"

I nodded and smiled.

"I'm not really supposed to let people behind the bar but…yeah, all right. He knows you. Make it quick, though!"

"Of course, thank you *so* much."

She let me in around the back and even gave me a pen and paper! For a few moments, I thought she would stay in the room and watch me but fortunately she trundled back to the counter. I reckoned I now had a maximum of five minutes but that was probably enough time to find something interesting. It was quite exciting although I felt seriously nosey.

The first thing I did was scribble my note. *Hi, Frank, came around to see if you were all right. Please tell the bar when I can see you next. Love, A. xx*

A bit lame but it would do. I folded the note up and put in my pocket, then I started exploring. Last time, the room was full of assorted boxes, with a coffee table and two saggy chairs in the centre. And a rabbit.

Well, Brian had gone but the boxes and furniture were still there. But where should I start?

I could discount several boxes immediately. They obviously contained stuff for the pub, like glasses, beer mats and cutlery. I kept looking. I needed to find a box that obviously belonged to Frank but I couldn't see anything resembling that. I rifled through a few more boxes and was thinking of giving up when I found a medium sized box in the corner. It held a few well-thumbed books by authors I didn't recognize and under that a heap of black and white photos.

I pulled a bunch of them out. They were tattered and worn but still fascinating. Most of them portrayed scenes of an American town from many years ago and several were stamped *Charlotte* on the back. One photo was of the inside of a theatre and another particularly battered snap was of a performer that I instantly recognized. On the back of that photo, someone had scrawled *Elvis Presley, Carolina Theatre, Charlotte, NC. February 10, 1956.*

So maybe this was where Frank was from originally? Well, it wasn't exactly a huge revelation. He was obviously from the United States. I paused for a second, slightly unsure of what to do next. I could finish looking through the pile of old photos or try another box. But I had to be very quick now.

I glanced around the room, then decided to look through the rest of the photos. I flipped through the remaining pictures – older town scenes, houses, a baseball team, the inside of a diner and then another baseball team. I couldn't recognize a younger Frank in the baseball teams, although I was looking much faster now. I put the photos back and was about to close the box when I noticed something else.

Yet I could have *sworn* it wasn't there before. How did I miss it?

Towards the bottom of the box, there was a heavy silver photo frame that had been placed face down. I pulled it out, flipped it over and gasped.

It was a photo of Frank but he looked *much* younger. He couldn't have been more than twenty-one, maybe still a teenager.

The photo was quite faded but still very impressive. Frank looked solemn – maybe even a little sad – and was dressed in a smart, military outfit. He wore a flat peaked cap with an eagle emblem in the centre and a matching jacket, shirt and dark tie. The most stunning thing about the photo was what Frank wore round his neck. It was a broad ribbon from which dangled another eagle emblem and a five-pointed star. There was some wording between the eagle and the star but I couldn't quite make it out.

Clearly Frank had been awarded something important, a medal, probably. I stared at it, doing my best to memorize it for another time. I had a feeling that if I asked Frank about it he would play it down so I'd probably have to carry out some research. I turned the frame over, searching for clues as to year, location, or even war – but there was nothing. I thought about opening the frame and looking at the back of the photo but I didn't have the heart to take it apart. Besides, I was out of time.

I hurriedly replaced the photo in the box and closed it up. Then I took the note out of my pocket, wrote *Frank* on it and placed it in the centre of the coffee table. After that, I made a quick exit, thanked the girl behind the bar – who just nodded sullenly – and ran home.

9

Mum didn't ask where I'd been. She was lying on the couch, relaxing. Although her back had eased up slightly in the last few days, she was still chomping down the painkillers like a junkie.

I squeezed up beside her and closed my eyes, mind racing.

The problem was my history was so sketchy. I knew we fought the Germans twice in the last century. The first time my great-great-uncle was injured twice - there was a photo of him in his shabby uniform somewhere. Then the second time was even worse. It was the one with the Dambusters. We fought Hitler, Churchill was Prime Minister. Loads of people got killed, especially Russians and Jews. The Americans dropped atom bombs on Japan. The French were involved, I think.

It was embarrassing, really. I was so ignorant. The other problem was I didn't have a computer so I couldn't look up anything on *Wikipedia* anymore. When I was in Purchester, I had an Apple laptop and iPhone. Mum also had an Apple tablet. We were fairly spoilt like that, I guess.

Mind you, most of the time, I was on social media. All my friends were. You only really used *Wikipedia* for homework.

But everything had been sold months ago. I couldn't even remember the last time I had been on a computer. I really didn't understand our new family finances but one thing was clear - we could just about afford food. Breakfast and lunch were usually a packet of crisps now; no wonder I was so skinny.

Anyway, if I had a computer, it would have been easy checking out what Frank was wearing around his neck, maybe even discovering what it was for. But I didn't have one and getting access to one was complicated. The local Internet Café was expensive, I didn't have any friends in Rotney and it was just too depressing going back to Purchester.

It seemed the only computers I could use were the ones at Rotney High. Theoretically, this wasn't difficult, there were plenty of computer bays throughout the school and all pupils had been issued with login details. However, most of the computers had been either ripped out their bays, or badly vandalized.

Even so, I could probably locate a computer at the school that hadn't been destroyed or stolen but I doubted I'd be able to stay on it for more than a few minutes. Working computers were so rare at the school that they were in constant demand.

Yet this was my reality. My options were so limited, I had no choice. I just had to try getting onto a school computer tomorrow. But it was about as appealing as a date with Fat Neck.

The next morning, I was greeted by the usual ear-splitting noise as I approached the school grounds. Dad had taken me to Wembley Stadium quite regularly so I wasn't unfamiliar with intense volume. But oddly that kind of noise never really bothered me. It was *exciting*.

The school's noise was different. A raw, belligerent *howl*. Sometimes when I was lying in my bed at night, I could still hear it echoing through my mind. Screeching. Throbbing. A packed football stadium was positively genteel, in comparison.

It was a dull morning's timetable. Maths, Geography, a twenty-minute break and then Science. Utter boredom had largely replaced anxiety at school, these days. There wasn't exactly very much to do at home but it was a whole lot better than being stuck in the classroom.

During the lunch break, I started exploring the computer bays, looking for a working, available computer. It was frustrating. As I expected, most of the bays were impressively wrecked. It seemed when anything got broken in Rotney, it was either ignored or repaired extremely slowly. And then when something finally got fixed, it was immediately ruined again.

The few working bays were already taken so I continued keep pacing the school corridors. Eventually, I located two bays at the end of one of the halls. Predictably, one of the bays looked like it had been hit repeatedly with a massive hammer but the second bay appeared to contain a working computer.

Amazing. I glanced around quickly, then sat inside the bay and switched the machine on.

I entered my login details and the computer's unit started burbling, considering whether to co-operate. The burbling transformed into whirring, then a slow intermittent whining. *Come on,* I whispered and peered around. I couldn't see anyone else but I could hear other pupils moving around nearby. Probably hunting for other pieces of school furniture and equipment to destroy.

I turned back and glared at the monitor. Finally, it spluttered into activity and connected to Google.

I punched the air triumphantly but my spine tingled with apprehension. I had to operate quickly. It was just a question of time before either the computer conked out or I was slung out the bay by someone four times my size.

I thought fast. I didn't know what Frank's last name was so I googled *Frank Cornelius.* The results threw up some random characters I'd never heard of, including an actor who'd been in *The Adventures of Priscilla, Queen of the Desert* in 1994. Well, that wasn't Frank.

Searching *Great Cornelius* was a similar waste of time. How did I know his name was really Frank, anyway? OK, I had to get more creative. I thought about the five-pointed star that Frank wore round his neck and searched *five pointed stars, American war medal.*

Straight away, I got a result. It was the *Medal of Honor.* Progress!

I glanced back. Still no one about – a flipping miracle! I clicked on the *Wikipedia* entry for *Medal of Honor* and scanned through the article with growing amazement.

It turned out the Medal of Honor was created during the American Civil War and was the highest military decoration presented by the United States government to a member of its armed forces. It said:

> *"The recipient must have distinguished themselves at the risk of their own life above and beyond the call of duty in action against an enemy of the United States."*

It was so rare that despite millions of Americans soldiers fighting in the armed forces in the last 150 years, the President had only award-ed 3,471 of these Medals, often only after the medal winner had died in action.

I sat back and took a deep breath. Frank wasn't just a war hero, he was a supremely brave man. A soldier that had *so* distinguished himself, the President of the United States had awarded him a medal.

I couldn't quite absorb it. It made absolutely no sense. What on earth was someone like that doing in an utter shithole like Rotney, performing illusions in run down pubs with a false beard and cheap wizard's hat?

Not only that, he was getting involved in scrapes and knife fights with the locals.

I stroked my chin, shaking my head and still thinking hard.

It was such an unusual award, I wondered if I could track down who Frank really was and what he'd done that was so impressive. I carried on reading.

The entry had photographs of the three versions of the Medal of Honor. The design differed depending on whether it was for the Army, Navy or Air Force. I studied the designs carefully. There was no doubt. Frank had the Army's version around his neck in the photograph. The post-1944 design.

As I scrolled down the article, it detailed the number of recipients for each conflict, together with dates. I estimated that Frank was in his late seventies or early eighties so he was born in the 1930s. This meant that he was too young to fight in the Second World War, which ended in 1945.

He was in his late teens or early twenties when he won the medal. So, the conflict had to have taken place in the early 1950s. It couldn't have been the Vietnam War because – according to *Wikipedia* – although it started in 1955, the Americans didn't really get involved until the early 1960s. Frank would have been in his thirties then.

So, his medal had to be for the Korean War which – said *Wikipedia* – ran from 1950 to 1953 and for which 137 Medals of Honor were awarded.

I might have known a very small amount about the wars against Germany but I didn't even know there had been wars in Vietnam and Korea. Obviously, America had been involved but I had no idea who had won or what had happened.

I looked at my watch. The lunch break ran from 12.10 to 13.30 and it was already 13.15. It had taken time locating a working computer and although I was reading quickly, it was a lengthy article. Not only that, I had to think and absorb its content. Even perform mathematical calculations!

It wasn't easy, especially in Rotney where using your brain wasn't an ability that was either valued or encouraged.

I thought about missing my next lesson. God knows when I'd be able to locate another working computer. But the problem was it was History, one of the few subjects I enjoyed. Not only that I quite fancied Mr. Shaw, the teacher.

If I allowed five minutes to get to History, I still had another ten minutes on *Wikipedia*. Hopefully enough time to discover some more about Frank. *Keep going.*

I clicked on the *Korean War Medal of Honor Recipients* link. This brought up a list of photos, names and dates together with details of service and action. I scrolled down quickly, hoping to spot Frank's photo. I hoped I'd recognize it immediately. I'd pressed the black and white image into my memory bank as firmly as possible.

But I couldn't see it anywhere. I reached the bottom of the list and frowned. Maybe I'd made a mistake and got the award or the conflict wrong. Maybe, both. I scrolled back up, slower, this time and – *oh my God - there it was!* How had I missed it? Well, it didn't matter, I felt elated. What a fantastic result!

I clicked onto the photo and there was the young Frank, as clear as anything. Except his name wasn't Frank, it was William Franklyn Truesdale.

I glanced at my watch again. *No,* only five minutes. I began reading. He was born on April 20, 1933 which made him 81. Place of birth, Charlotte, North Carolina - well, that explained the bunch of photos I'd found yesterday.

I skipped through the details of his military record. It stated he was a Master Sergeant of the 7th Infantry Regiment of the 3rd Infantry Division and had won a Purple Heart and Medal of Honor in the Korean War.

I scrolled down. The article gave details of how he'd won his Medal of Honor. He was a Corporal on the night of 6 September 1951 and the citation on his medal read:

> *Corporal Truesdale, distinguished himself by conspicuous gallantry and outstanding courage above and beyond the call of duty in action against the enemy. During the night, a numerically superior hostile force launched an assault against his platoon on Hill 284, overrunning friendly positions and swarming into the sector.*
>
> *Corporal Truesdale repeatedly exposed himself to deliver effective fire into the ranks of the assailants, inflicting numerous casualties.*
>
> *Observing 2 enemy soldiers endeavouring to capture a friendly machine gun, he charged and killed both with his*

bayonet, regaining control of the weapon. Returning to his position, now occupied by 4 of his wounded comrades, he continued his accurate fire into enemy troops surrounding his emplacement. When a hostile soldier hurled a grenade into the position, Corporal Truesdale immediately flung himself over the missile, absorbing the blast with his body and saving his comrades from death or severe injury. His aggressive actions had so inspired his comrades that a spirited counter-attack drove the enemy from the perimeter.

Corporal Truesdale's heroic devotion to duty, indomitable fighting spirit, and willingness to sacrifice himself to save his comrades reflect the highest credit upon himself, the infantry and the U.S. Army.

I gawped at the citation until my vision blurred. He jumped on a grenade to save his comrades! How can you measure that kind of astonishing bravery?

10

hen I noticed the little digital clock in the bottom right hand corner of the computer screen. 1.27.

Only three minutes to go!

I clicked out of *Wikipedia* and logged off the computer. Then I withdrew my login card, slipped it into my pocket, grabbed my bag and hurried down the hall. But I was still thinking about Frank, not focusing on where I was going.

It was a large school and – as I did, many times, in my few first days – I took a wrong turn somewhere and ended up in the wrong block. My watch said 1.33 and I didn't have my bearings. Panicking and heaving, I wheeled round and swung left. Then I veered right, then left again. I was looking for the sign that marked the direction to the science laboratory. I could find my way from there.

But as I bounded down the corridor, sweating like an armpit, I missed the sign and ended up near a pile of ruined lockers. I was about to turn around again when I detected the sound of something slamming into metal, then whimpering. Then thudding. Then again.

I recognized the sound immediately. Some poor little kid was being ripped apart. Probably at knifepoint. The bullies were shameless in this school, teachers rarely intervened.

I slowed down, then stalled completely, tilting my head and listening closer. There it was again. Coming from behind the lockers. Pitiful.

Yelp...yelp.... yelp.

I shook my head and swung left. Now I was directly behind the lockers. Ten short paces, then straight ahead. A large, white boy punching a tiny black victim in the stomach. No knife, this time, only brutal force. Deliberate, malicious, savage. Stone cold rage meeting utter terror.

Fear streaked down my spine. What was I doing? God...Frank hadn't guided me this time. Now I'd just blundered into a torture scene. And – let's face it - I hardly looked like the cavalry. Just a skinny girl you could knock down with a gust of wind.

But still - an *angry* skinny girl.

"Leave him alone," I said quietly to Mr. Bully. He wheeled slowly and performed a visible, double take.

"Who the *fuck* - are *you?*" He sneered furiously, dropping his prey onto the floor.

Then he approached. Large gold chain, fat metal ring, silver ring in his left ear, tattoo snaking along the right side of the neck. Scars on the right cheek, two of them. A right, nasty bastard.

Still I couldn't see a knife or knuckle-duster, or any kind of weapon. Then again maybe he was concealing a deadly object with the intent of rapidly gutting my insides. Getting closer, closer, then stopping, just inches away. Pungent and dripping from the thrill of the hunt. Staring.

"Well?"

I measured the distance to his face. Taller than Demi but no problem grabbing the cheek. Alternatively, one hard punch to the throat. I stood rigidly, lowering my head slightly and narrowing my eyes.

Then I glared back.

"I'm *Antonia.*"

Mr. Bully snorted out his nose. "I don't a give a fuck who you are. Just turn around and walk the fuck away – or you are dead. Do you understand me, you little cunt? *Dead.*"

I shook my head. "No. *You* turn around and walk away. Or I will inflict more pain on you than you've ever felt in the whole of your life. Make you scream for your mother before you pass out. But – then again – maybe I'm just bluffing. So…your move."

I kept glaring, my right hand forming the claw. Mr. Bully stared back, unwavering, then suddenly I felt his resolution draining away. He pursed his lips, slammed the wall with an upturned palm and turned around. Then he wandered off, like an enraged rhino, shaking his head and cursing.

I ran over to his victim. "You OK?"

He was trembling, mumbling. "Thanks, man, thanks man…. I'm good." He tried to gather himself but didn't really succeed. Then he looked at me with bewilderment, "*shi-i-it* - how you face that guy down?"

I shrugged my shoulders, "I don't know. He just annoyed me."

It turned out his name was Nathan and a Year 7. He was pretty shaken up and hadn't just been punched in the stomach. Mr. Bully had whacked him around the face too. But Nathan recovered his breath eventually and straightened up slowly.

Nathan told me the bully's name was *Donny* but didn't know why he'd been attacked. The bully wasn't after money - I think he just really enjoyed torturing small pupils.

After thanking me a few times, he drifted down the corridor towards lessons, or whatever Year 7s did on a Monday afternoon.

Meanwhile, I showed up at History class almost fifteen minutes late. Incredibly, I got away with my excuse that I was just back from a doctor's appointment. Fortunately, Mr. Shaw seemed in great spirits and I avoided a detention.

The afternoon passed without incident, although, after school, I was worried that Donny would ambush me with a bunch of cronies. There was no sign of him, though.

I walked home slowly, thinking about Frank again. He'd made my recent exploits look like a dreamy stroll through Purchester Park. I *seriously* wanted to talk to him about what I'd discovered but suspected he'd just try and change the subject, or something.

Unfortunately, there was another test of courage waiting. When I got home, I found Dr Huck settled comfortably on our battered couch, nursing a mug of tea. I could hear Mum humming in the kitchen.

The doctor nodded politely as I walked in but I just ignored him.

Our living room was so small that it was extremely difficult to keep my distance but I sat on the rickety table chair and looked down. What on earth was Mum doing with this man? He still wore the same cheap suit and I could see the dirty fingernails on his right hand as he gripped his tea mug. Vile human being.

Mum came out of the kitchen.

"Hi, Toni darling, how was your day?"

"OK."

"Get much done?"

"Not really." It seemed inappropriate mentioning that I'd just discovered my old friend was a Medal of Honor recipient. Or that I'd narrowly avoided a violent conflict with an insane, teenage sadist. Instead, I smiled briefly as she passed over my Hello Kitty Prairie mug.

I switched on the television and continued blanking our guest. There was a loud quiz show on ITV. The contestants were trying to outfox some know-all and win a load of money. Very tedious but I studied the screen as if the universe depended upon it. Meanwhile, I hoped I was radiating sufficient *get lost* vibes in Huck's direction.

Mum and Huck began chatting. It was some dull stuff about Huck's business and legal case. I stopped listening after a few seconds.

The quiz show wasn't a great distraction but I was too lazy to switch channels. I couldn't answer any of the questions and it was just another reminder of how ignorant I was.

After a few minutes, the show finished and I switched to a programme about people who wanted to buy a property in the country. The areas they were looking in were so beautiful compared to the sordid reality of Rotney that I could barely believe it was the same country. In fact, the second property they viewed looked a bit like our former house in Purchester – obviously, minus the large dent in the front door.

Then Mum excused herself and went to the loo. I was alone with Dr Huck. *Oh wonderful*, I thought. *Please* don't start talking to me.

"So how are you finding Rotney High, Antonia?"

Typical.

I shrugged, "OK…"

"Big, tough school, though. A lot of poverty there."

I shrugged again. Hurry up, Mum, *please*.

"Must be quite a shock after Purchester."

I shrugged again. What a terrific conversation.

"Just a stony silence…." remarked the doctor.

I ignored this and carried on watching the television. They were admiring a very floral bathroom. It looked about twice the size of our flat.

But Huck wasn't quite finished.

"Such a pity but there's no investment in education or in the area generally. Living in Rotney is hardly a magical experience."

I flinched. Was that a deliberate hint that he saw me at the magic show or was I being paranoid? Was he baiting me? I considered turning around but then I heard the toilet flush through our paper-thin walls.

Mum re-appeared seconds later. She immediately picked up her previous conversation with Huck and I reverted to the floral bathroom.

I continued ignoring them and Huck finally left about twenty minutes later.

I tried speaking to Mum about Huck before dinner. Got me nowhere.

She just said he was friend and kept changing the subject. Then, after serving a jacket potato and beans for dinner, Mum started complaining about her back. She stretched out on the couch with her bottles of pills and began snoring.

I left her a scribbled note and headed off to the pub down the road, hoping to find Frank. It was always a potluck thing because I could never call or text him.

Halfway towards the pub, I was struck by the alarming thought that perhaps he'd suffered a huge stroke like Granny Strictness and was either dead or parked up in Rotney's closest hospital, whimpering like a demented baboon.

But I was in luck. As soon I went through the pub doors, I saw him standing in front of the bar, watching the television bracketed in the corner. Without thinking, I ran up to him and hugged him tightly.

Frank hugged me back but seemed slightly embarrassed by the sudden attention. "Whoa! What's all this?"

I looked up at him and grinned. "Hero," I pronounced.

"Excuse me?"

"Hero," I repeated and hugged him tighter.

"I am?"

I glanced up again. He really was an old man, an 81-year-old man - I knew that now - but his body felt sturdy. It seemed unlikely he was going to suffer a debilitating stroke soon, thankfully.

"God, yeah! I mean…." Suddenly, I stalled. This was a problem I hadn't thought about. How could I tell him I'd discovered his military record? I didn't want him to know I'd been snooping around his things in the backroom. He might take real offence.

I released my grip.

"What?"

"I…" *Now what?* Where could I begin?

"Hey…" Frank sensed my discomfort. "I've got some new furry friends behind the bar. Fancy a look?"

I tipped my chin to the right. "Bears or monkeys?"

Frank laughed. "No, no – they're much smaller than that! Wanna see?"

I nodded happily.

"Well, come this way, young lady," he instructed with a flourish and led me into the bar's storage room.

It had changed - again. The box containing the assorted photos had been replaced by several cages accommodating rabbits and guinea pigs.

They were outrageously cute and Frank let me take them out their homes and stroke them. Maybe I was getting a bit too old to be so taken by furry animals but I didn't care. They were such a comfort.

One of the rabbits, a white boy with random black patches had a particularly wet nose and kept nuzzling my arm. I couldn't help laughing. It made such a change from all the tattoos, knives and aggression.

"That's Lincoln," advised Frank.

"Lincoln!" I held him even closer. "Oh, he's so *sweeeet!*"

Frank smiled. "By the way, I got your note. I'm surprised they let you in here without me but its fine. I'm back now, anyway."

I fondled Lincoln's silky ears. "Go anywhere exciting?"

"To visit my son for a few days. Actually, I did mention it to the landlord."

"Your son lives in this country?"

"Yeah, in Sidcup. Kent. His wife is English and they settled here."

"What does he do?"

"He's a graphic designer. Quite a good one. Works in what they call electronic media."

"So why don't you stay with him? Don't hang around here!"

Frank grinned. "No call for magicians in Sidcup."

"Really?"

"Really."

Frank shot me a subtle *back-off* glance so I went back to stroking Lincoln. Then I had an idea.

11

I figured if I could get him to show me some early photos, I could "accidentally" discover the photo in the silver frame. Then I could ask the obvious questions. The problem was – as I'd noticed, almost immediately - the box containing the photographs was nowhere in sight. This meant I couldn't politely enquire what was in that box.

Still, I had an opening.

"Where did all these cute animals come from? I'm sure the boxes were a bit different when I came in here a few days ago."

"It's not really my room," admitted Frank. "The pub lets me use it for some of my stuff, provided I move it along. The animals are for a couple of tricks I'm working on now."

I exhaled loudly and shook my head. "I'm sorry, I *just* don't understand."

"Understand, what?"

"Well, for a start. What are you even doing here? It's the biggest dump in the world, the only thing they appreciate here is violence, crime and drugs. I mean, you're, like, the most amazing magician I've ever seen and they don't appreciate it at all, they're just total idiots, I mean why perform to them anyway...?"

Oh God, I was babbling. I stopped mid-sentence and frowned.

Frank looked calm. "It's a long story, Antonia…but, well, I kind of wound up here."

"Why? Of all places! I'm only here because my life is a total disaster but I hate it. *Hate it!* If it wasn't for you, I'd either be insane or dead."

Frank nodded sadly but didn't say anything.

I tilted my head. "Frank?"

"Yes."

"Please tell me the truth. *Please.*"

Frank shrugged. "You wouldn't believe me, if I did. No one would."

"I would, I *swear* I would. I know stuff already."

I covered my mouth. I didn't mean to say that. Now I couldn't un-say it.

"What do you mean?"

I was silent, worrying.

"What do you mean?" he repeated but not in a hostile way.

"Nothing".

"Antonia?"

"Nothing, Frank, really."

"*Antonia?*"

I exhaled again. "Your real name is William Franklyn Truesdale. You're 81 years old and you won the Medal of Honor for valour for your actions in the Korean War in 1951."

Frank looked shocked. I mean, *really* shocked. His jaw dropped so much I thought it might hit the floor.

"Jesus!" he exclaimed. "How the hell did you know that, young lady?"

"I found the photo of you wearing the medal in one of the boxes when I came in here the other day. I'm so sorry, Frank. I didn't mean to peek. I just wanted to find out more about you. I couldn't understand what you were doing here and I was just looking for clues. That's all. The photo was in a heavy silver frame, face down. I turned it over and looked at it."

Frank sat down heavily, completely stunned.

I lowered my head sadly. "I'm sorry. I memorized the award you were wearing round your neck, it just looked so impressive. Then, this afternoon, I looked up the award on *Wikipedia* and found out it was the Medal of Honor. The army's version. Then I worked out what war you were in - you know, from your age - and I got all your details."

Frank kept gawping. Utterly speechless.

I kept my head down, then raised my eyebrows. "I said you were a hero."

Still, no response so I raised my head. "I'm sorry. Really. Was it a big secret?"

Frank closed his mouth. "A silver framed photo, you say?"

"Yes, tucked under some black and white photos of Charlotte. I think it was called Charlotte. In North Carolina."

"My hometown." He paused and shook his head. "So, you too?"

"What?"

No response.

"Frank – what? Me too – *what?*"

"Stay here."

He stood up and strolled out. I waited for a few minutes and stroked Lincoln who started rubbing his moist nostrils against my arm again. I felt uncomfortable, the conversation had veered off course. Still, at least it was out in the open, now. Hopefully, I could start getting some answers.

Then, suddenly, Frank was back, carrying the box of photos.

"I moved this crate back into my room this morning when the animals turned up. Needed more space. This *is* the crate you found, right?"

I nodded. "Certainly, looks like it."

Frank put the box on the coffee table and began removing the contents. He found the black and white photos soon enough and placed them on the table. "They're mostly photos I took back in the day. You see the one of Elvis?"

I nodded.

"I went to that concert, you know. 1956 was his breakthrough year. Amazing voice, terrific performer but the girls screamed so loudly you just couldn't hear him!"

"Wow." I knew my Dad was a fan of Elvis but didn't know anything more about him really. I wasn't even sure if he was still alive.

"Anyway, have a look in the box now and tell me what you see."

I glanced down and described the remaining objects inside. "Old records, magazines, combs, pamphlets, wooden things - I don't know what they are – drumsticks?"

"They *are* drumsticks. Very good."

"OK, thanks and – "

"And?"

I looked more closely.

"Em…that's it."

"That's it?"

"That's it."

"Where's the silver framed photo?"

"I don't know. Can't see it." Then I jerked my head up and my Rotney instincts kicked in. "I didn't take it!"

Frank broke into a wide smile. "I know. Hey, *relax*. You couldn't have taken it."

"Why?"

"Because it disappeared forty years ago."

Now it was my turn to look confused.

"*What?*"

"It disappeared in Borneo Island in 1972, if I recall correctly. My only framed photo. Heavy bastard, too. Got stolen with all my luggage."

"Oh, shut up! It was in the box a few days ago – definitely!"

Frank shook his head. "No, I lost it years ago and I've been through this box, many, many times. I may be an old man but I'm not senile. Well, not yet, anyway!"

I frowned. "That doesn't make sense. It didn't just *appear* out of nowhere. I'm not the magician here."

Frank studied me and then scratched his white hair. "You know, though, ironically, it does explain some things."

"Explain what? You're not making any sense. You *never* make any sense." I protested.

Frank stopped scratching his head and adopted a stern expression.

"OK, Antonia, I'll make you a deal."

"What kind of deal?"

"A big deal. I know you've got a lot of questions – and rightly so. Turns out I have some questions of my own now. But – as I said – I'm going to make a deal with you. I want you to meet me back in this room in twenty-four hours." He checked his watch, "so that's nineteen hundred hours or seven o'clock pm."

"That's your deal?"

"Not quite," said Frank. "When you come back, I'll answer all your questions truthfully, even though you'll have a tough time with some of the answers. In the meantime, I want you to do something else for me."

"What's that?"

He unbuttoned the top two buttons of his shirt and stretched the collar back.

I gasped. *Loudly.* He was wearing an extraordinary stone, hinged on a thin black cord around his neck. Frank unbuckled the cord from behind his neck and handed it over.

I examined the pendant with something approaching awe. It was the most exquisite gem. A very unusual, perfectly round, red stone.

"Whoa! That is *sick*!" I exclaimed.

I wasn't exactly a stranger to jewellery. When Dad was doing very well, he regularly bought Mum expensive bracelets, rings and earrings. But they were nothing comparing to the stupendous trinket on Frank's neck cord. I studied it further. "What is it?" It's not a ruby, is it? It's something else."

Frank shook his head. "Twenty-four hours, Antonia. You'll have all your answers, I promise you. In the meantime, I want you to wear this stone around your neck and give it back to me tomorrow evening."

Now I was shaking my head. "I can't do that. It's *yours*. Jesus, it must be worth an absolute fortune. I'll only lose it or get robbed. This is Rotney, you know? They mug babies for their dummies."

"Sure, you can! I trust you. Just wear it round your neck and keep it safe. You'll do fine."

"But why?"

"Well, I want you to observe everything very carefully. Just until you give the stone back. Let me know if anything unusual happens."

"*Unusual?* Like what?"

"Oh, anything. Maybe you'll see something, maybe you won't. All you have to do is keep your eyes open and report back tomorrow evening."

"Well, what kind of thing could happen? I mean, does this stone have mysterious powers? You're not making sense, Frank!"

He shrugged. "You'll just have to find out. And quit with the questions, will you? You'll get your answers soon enough."

I still didn't understand. He was being deliberately obtuse again but I had to admit that the prospect of something unusual happening over the next day was intriguing.

"Fine," I said, "I'll do it. Although I think you're very weird, even if you are an amazing war hero."

Frank reached over. "Here, let me put it on". He fastened the narrow cord around the back of my neck, then I adjusted it further. The stone nestled under my shirt.

"That's great" said Frank. "Now a just couple of ground rules and then you're good to go. But important stuff. OK?"

"OK."

"Right. Never talk about the stone and *never* show it to anyone. *Anyone.* Understood?"

"Understood – but why? Please don't get all weird on me."

"Just don't do it, OK? I'll answer your questions tomorrow."

"Whatever…Anything else?"

"No, that's it." He produced a fist and I punched it. "Twenty-four hours - now get going."

"Can I say goodbye to Lincoln?"

"Sure."

"Thanks."

I hugged and kissed the rabbit and put him back in the cage. Then I waved to Frank and set off home, observing everything carefully.

12

The problem was Frank had been so vague. What I was supposed to be looking out for?

I wondered if the stone possessed magical powers. Maybe I'd arrive home to discover Dad had been released from prison, Mum's back had permanently healed, Granny Strictness was discharged from hospital and we could all go back to Purchester and carry on as before.

But even as I walked home, I knew it was just a ridiculous pipe dream. Life just seemed to kick you in the teeth repeatedly. Then just when you thought you'd weathered the final kick, you got punched in the head.

Perhaps I'd made a little stand against that repulsive bully, Donny, this afternoon - but what did it really matter? I mean, overall? He'd probably try and get his revenge, soon enough, for being humiliated.

Rotney. It made you *think* like this. Maybe that's what brought on the violence and hatred, the lack of any hope or future. I really hoped Frank had a very good explanation, tomorrow evening, for what he was doing here. I was owed some answers.

When I got home, nothing had changed. Mum was still snoring on the couch, my scribbled note lying unread on the table. I sat on the armchair and switched on the television. There was a documentary on about the daily happenings in London Zoo and I watched the whole thing. Animals always fascinated me. Then, I clicked off the box, went into my bedroom and stretched out on the bed.

It was all very boring and predictable. I hadn't developed any superpowers; the stone hadn't directed me towards a trove of hidden treasure and I was still stuck in my awful flat.

I missed *Snapchat* and *Instagram* and *Twitter* and *WhatsApp* and *Facebook*. I missed my computer, my iPhone and my old friends. I missed *banter*. Mum and I hardly spoke these days. I missed my Dad, my old school, decent food, clean surroundings and luxuries. I missed being liked. I missed being happy. I missed being safe. Just being able to walk down the street without worrying about getting raped and mutilated.

Still, there was always astronomy. I sat up and grabbed my telescope from the bedside table. I went over to the window and squinted through the telescope lens, adjusting the tube to the right.

I was gradually getting better at recognizing the heavenly bodies, especially Orion. Orion was so easy. I wondered if the stone would suddenly teleport me to another planet or, better still, an alternative universe where Rotney didn't exist. But of course, nothing like that happened. All the same, I enjoyed looking through my antique hosepipe now, escaping to places where Donny and Demi didn't stalk the streets, beating up little kids.

Eventually, I folded up my telescope and put it back on the bedside table.

I sat on my bed and unclasped the black cord from behind my neck, then held the stone in my palm. It was flawless. Unique. Gorgeous. What was its history? I'd certainly ask Frank tomorrow evening.

I replaced the black cord around my neck and toyed thoughtfully with the pendant. Then, I undressed, brushed my teeth, switched off the bedroom lights and got into bed. But 1 couldn't fall asleep because my head was buzzing with all the events of the day and – as usual – I could hear every tiny nocturnal sound.

Well, that was another thing I missed. Double glazing and sound proof walls.

I listened to people talking and swearing outside the window and someone shouting from a house further down the street. Why did everyone yell so aggressively round here? Selfish, inconsiderate idiots.

⁂

Seven o'clock in the morning. News on Kiss FM. Exhaustion, utter exhaustion, waves of choking anxiety, rolling over me again and again.

I just didn't have the strength to get up and considered calling in ill. It was always so tempting. But I knew I couldn't. Today was different. Frank's little experiment.

I forced myself out of bed, showered quickly and dressed. Then I grabbed a packet of crisps in the kitchen and checked my school bag. Mum emerged in a pink nightdress, holding the right side of her back. She put the kettle on and then the doorbell rang loudly.

Oh no. Mum and I exchanged weary looks and shook our heads.

A car passed slowly outside the window, casting a fading shadow across the kitchen wall. I backed up against the corner, dropped my head and stared my feet. We waited…waited. Then the doorbell rang again. I jerked my head up and scowled.

Then I motioned with my head. *Better get it.*

Mum nodded sadly then turned slowly into the hall. I listened to her small, deliberate footsteps approaching the front door. Then she halted briefly before withdrawing the bolt back and turning the handle.

Harsh voices filled the corridor. Aggressive, raucous, Cockney tones. Mocking and heartless. Mum argued back, begging, almost crying. But it was useless. It always was.

Still it dragged on for several minutes. Then there was a bit of scuffling and swearing followed by heavy footsteps. Two enormous, sweaty men appeared in the living room. They ignored my glares, paced around the flat in their muddy boots, before nodding at the couch. Then they carted it down the hall and out the front door.

I watched through the window as they heaved the battered settee into a white van and drove off. Mum walked back down the hall, still shaking her head and rubbing her lower back.

If the police were the biggest villains in my book, the bailiffs ranked a close second.

I didn't really understand why we were still so heavily in debt as Mum's job paid quite well. Good legal secretaries were always in demand. But from what I could gather from the furtive conversations between my parents, in prison, the court's fine still hadn't been cleared and so the interest kept increasing.

Every time a payment was missed, the bullies arrived in their bullet proof vests and helped themselves to some more possessions. Not that there was anything left now. Just a toaster, two broken armchairs – and my telescope.

By the time, the bailiffs disappeared, I was *so* late for school. I hoped the bus was waiting at the bus station, otherwise, I'd have to run the whole way - and in only twenty minutes. If I missed assembly, it was a definite Room 18 detention.

I kissed Mum quickly and burst out of my house, sprinting towards the bus stop as fast as I could. But as I veered around the corner, the bus sailed past me and picked up speed.

No, I yelled aloud and kept running. I was going to maintain this pace for some time and my regular diet of crisps and jacket potatoes hadn't made me any fitter. In fact, after five minutes, I began slowing down and my breath became painful and searing.

Nevertheless, I pushed forward, fighting my way through horrible discomfort until I saw the sinister form of Rotney High. Then I slowed down slightly, perspiring profusely. Giddy and teetering with lack of oxygen, stumbling forward.

But something was awfully wrong and I couldn't work it out. I checked my watch. It was 8.27am – I had made it, just on time – three minutes to assembly. *But it was all wrong.* I wrestled with the difference, forcing myself to think. Then I grasped what it was.

Every morning, I was smacked by an immense avalanche of sound, a ghastly, terrifying roar. The belligerent *howl*. But now there was just an eerie silence. The contrast in volume was simply staggering. I slowed from stride to walk, then I caught my breath and looked around. The usual number of pupils were surrounding the school gates and school building - no change there, then – but they weren't talking, just gawking in my direction.

It was extremely unsettling. I returned their blank looks quizzically but it didn't spark off any additional reactions. Then I kept going, straight through the main gates and directly into the school. But it was even worse in there. Teachers, students, all utterly silent, just gawping directly at *me*.

I felt so intensely awkward that I glanced round, then immediately changed direction and headed towards the nearest toilets. These were located twenty metres to the left of the school entrance. There was a group of six pupils hovering in front of the toilet door but as I approached, they immediately parted. Same staring, vacant expressions.

I hurried into the loos – fortunately, empty – and locked myself in the first cubicle. I sat down quickly, closed my eyes and waited until I fully caught my breath. Then I checked myself. I was still very hot and wet from running so hard and my white school shirt stuck to my front. I was going to be late today but I didn't care now.

I glanced down and saw a distinct glow emerging from under my shirt. I ripped open my top shirt buttons and pulled out the stone. It was shining brightly. Not only that, it felt very warm.

I unclasped the black cord from behind my neck and placed the stone in the palm of my hand. I brought my palm just under my eyes and stared closely at the stone as it radiated and beamed liked an eternal star. I gasped audibly and raised my palm higher, still transfixed and mesmerized by the gem's beauty and power.

Then it faded back into its original state and lay cold within my palm.

I replaced the neck cord and buttoned my shirt up. I had no idea what was going on but as soon as the stone became lifeless again, I considered a few wacky explanations.

Maybe there was something within the stone that reacted to heat.

Perhaps when I started sweating, it set off some odd, chemical reaction that caused the stone to glow and produce a weird, supernatural effect. Maybe the staff and pupils consciously or unconsciously detected the glow and it stunned them into silence, or possibly the stone emitted some sort of vibration which interfered with their brain waves and shut them up.

However, when I finally came out of the cubicle and checked my reflection in the mirror, there seemed to be a much simpler reason for everyone's odd behaviour. I looked an absolute state. My hair was branched out in every direction and my face was still bright red from the effort of running so hard. *Well, that pretty much explained it.*

No doubt Frank would explain to me why the stone had lit up although I couldn't exactly see how that tied in with a Medal of Honor and spending your twilight years dressed in a fake beard and silly hat. In Rotney.

Then reality hit. I was late for assembly. It was the second consecutive time this week, meaning an inevitable detention. I would be stuck in school until around five this afternoon – but I could still easily make my evening appointment with Frank.

I smartened myself up quickly, then headed towards my first lesson, English. We were reading *Animal Farm* by George Orwell, which I was quite enjoying. As I walked towards the classroom, there was a sudden strident roar as pupils poured out of assembly. They bolted down the school corridor, jabbering excitedly and shoving me aside.

Whatever excitement or misunderstanding had occurred earlier was certainly over. Indeed, I was quickly intercepted by my form teacher, Miss Patel before reaching the English class. She slammed a Room 18 detention note into my hand, for persistent lateness and stormed off. I folded the note in two, stuffed it into the inside pocket of my blazer and turned towards my English class.

Later, when lessons finally finished, I headed towards Room 18 on the first floor. This was my second visit in five days. Last week, Mr. Sutton, the chemistry teacher sent me there because my shirt was hanging out the back of my skirt and apparently, I "exhibited dissent when cautioned".

What a joke. Because the teachers avoided the school's genuine offenders, I knew I'd only be sharing the detention class with people who had picked their nose during assembly or chewed their food with their mouth open.

This afternoon was no exception. My company were two skinny Year 7 girls and an acne-ridden Year 8 boy.

It was the usual punishment, copying out the School Rules. Irritatingly, The Rules were painfully long-winded. Not only that, you had to keep your work tidy or you could end up copying out The Rules twice.

I sat at a desk near the back and the supervising teacher – or Detention Tutor, to give him his official title – handed me a set of Rules for copying. I recognized the teacher as the Head of Year 10 but he'd never taught me and I couldn't recall what his chosen area was. Possibly, Geography.

His name was Mr. Reid. He was quite thin, stooped and grey with an outrageously large head. I imagined clawing his face for sport although my grip probably wasn't wide enough to get a good hold. Still, it would have been fun to have practised on him, pressing down on his cheek until he keeled over backwards and banged his massive skull on the floor.

I glanced at the clock above the tutor's desk – almost four o'clock. It felt like I was always checking the time these days, either because I was late for something, or because I was bored, or impatient.

I picked up the Rules and started scribbling as quickly as possible but keeping a careful watch on my handwriting and margins.

An orderly, morally sound, safe and clean School environment reflects a sense of self-respect and respect for others. It is also essential for positive learning. For these reasons:

- *Students should exercise self-discipline both in and out of the classroom; they should treat everyone with courtesy and consideration; they should never distract other students or use inappropriate language;*
- *Students should arrive punctually at lessons; if a student has been delayed by another teacher, s/he should ask for an explanatory note to give to the next teacher;*
- *Students will not wilfully damage/vandalize school property or use any of the School's equipment inappropriately.*

I glimpsed at the Year 7s a few metres ahead of me. They were a couple of skinny black girls who both looked like they badly needed a healthy meal. They looked harmless enough and were also scribbling away, no doubt also eager to get out of Room 18 as soon as they could.

I turned towards the classroom windows. It was beginning to drizzle outside and there were fewer departing pupils now. I closed my eyes tightly for a second, sensing Frank's stone resting under my school shirt.

There was no warmth there, now. Then I opened my eyes, yawned loudly and continued writing.

It took 45 minutes, keeping neat really slowed you down. I was also using a cheap biro and rushing too much could smudge my work. When I finally finished, I raised my hand, waving it in Mr. Reid's direction.

There was no reaction, though, because he was reading something intently. Probably a graphic thriller about a mild-mannered teacher changing into a serial killer. My arm kept dangling uselessly and eventually I started coughing. The huge head rotated upwards in my direction.

"What is it?"

"I finished, sir."

"Show me."

Obediently, I picked up my sheets and marched over. He examined them closely, really examining the handwriting and margins. After turning the sheets over, he looked up again and scratched his left eyebrow.

"What's your name?"

"Antonia Davidson, sir."

"And what are you here for?"

"Failing to be punctual, sir."

"Failing to be punctual, "he repeated, slowly, weighing the words. "You copied the school rules, so you will hopefully note that Rotney High will not tolerate tardiness. It demonstrates poor self-discipline, lack of personal organization and disrespect."

Whatever. I bet he wouldn't have given the same pompous speech to Demi. She would have hacked off his skull with a meat cleaver, scooped out the brains and fed them to her mother.

I looked back, sheepishly. "Very sorry, sir."

He glanced down at my work and started scratching his eyebrow again. *Come on.*

"I don't want you back in Room 18. If I find you before me before me again, there will be more serious repercussions. Do you understand?"

"Yes, sir."

"Do you?"

"Yes, sir."

The little sadist stared for a few more seconds, then frowned. "Well, I sincerely hope so. Now, get out."

"Yes, sir."

I departed immediately, whipping through the corridor, veering left, stomping down the stairs, sprinting along the ground corridor and shooting through the main exit.

It was just after five in the evening and nearly all the pupils had left the school grounds. A few students stayed for after school activities – the usual art and science clubs – but I was more concerned about the alternative minority that hung around near the school gates with the intention of snatching your purse and stabbing your face.

There was no shortage of alternative Demis in Rotney. Clawing her cheek had earned me a respite but it wouldn't last long.

And that was before even considering Donny the psychopath.

I approached the High Road, eyes flicking left, right, backwards, forward, behind, in front. Searching, searching. Still nothing. Just hurrying pedestrians and cars sweeping by.

The rain picked up slightly, dancing off the surfaces. Its fresh moisture tickling my nostrils and lips. I inhaled deeply.

Home. Just get home. And turn up to Frank's early. I picked up my pace, hitting a brisk stride, then I maintained speed evenly for a few hundred metres. Good going. Not long now, just a...*Ooooh!* Wow. There, *there.* Something not quite right. But what? *What?* Too indistinct.

I touched my throat. Was it my breathing? No, lower. I moved my fingers below my neck, then kept going. *Odd.* It felt warm. Hot, even. Then I noticed the eerie glow from beneath my school shirt.

The stone was heating up again.

13

I felt an obvious thrill, then a sudden expectancy.
Now what?
I swung into Rotney Way, which wasn't as busy as the High Road. Then I slowed into a steady walk, head swivelling in every direction. Tightly alert. Waiting.

A bird darted overhead and I watched its uneven path as it descended over the rooftops. Fat specks of rain smacked my hand, exploding into the air. Two cars swept by.

Anything else?

Well, physically, nothing much. I couldn't fly or stop time or teleport or crawl walls. I hadn't magically developed incredible agility or extra sensory perception. In fact, a bit disappointingly, none of that Hollywood stuff had happened. But still...

I felt an odd connection. Maybe *to* the stone or *through* it. It wasn't clear. I needed more information, more experiences. More evidence.

Meanwhile, the stone was getting much warmer now. Almost scathing. Any hotter and I'd have to remove the necklace somehow.

I crossed a side road and approached a small parade of shops. It wasn't my regular way home but I had taken this taken diversion a few times before so I knew the stores.

The parade consisted of a butcher, a kebab shop, a newsagent and a barber in that order. I reached the butcher and glanced through the window. It was empty, the man behind the counter just gazing wistfully ahead. Same with the kebab shop and newsagents, vacant and sad.

Ouch!! Like a *volcano* now. I stepped into the newsagents, hoping I could remove the necklace urgently and discreetly. Irritatingly, though, a bell clanged loudly overhead as I pushed the door forward.

"Stay where you are!" bellowed a nervous voice.

I stalled, unsettled and distracted.

"Don't move! Don't you *fucking* move!" screeched the voice again. I froze completely but my eyes instinctively darted toward the counter.

A wired, black guy, even thinner than Mr. Reid, was pointing what looked like a bayonet sword at an Indian lady behind the counter. He was wearing a white puffed up jacket of some sort and obviously totally high.

And two other things. The poor woman looked even more terrified than tiny Nathan and the bayonet appeared even older than my telescope. Maybe, the same army officer had used them while fighting in the Napoleonic wars, or something.

I remained motionless. Trapped between nightmares. I gawked uncomfortably at the huge blade hovering under its victim's throat. *Whoa, go easy with that thing!* Antique weapon or not, it was one menacing piece of steel.

The way-too-skinny black guy tensed and fidgeted furiously, calculating his next move. I had obviously blundered into his armed robbery and was now a witness to his crime. His druggy agitation continued for a few more moments before his eyes suddenly became transfixed. Then he began gawping like a hypnotized fish at the centre of my chest. I lowered my head slowly. The stone was gleaming in a perfect, burning circle under my shirt.

"What the fuck is *that*?" He nodded at the stone, then the nodding transformed into shaking. Then a violent shaking. Poor man. In different circumstances, I might have offered him a cup of tea.

"I don't know," I answered, truthfully.

More intense trembling, then a sudden flurry of action. The robber dropped his bayonet and shot out the shop's front door, trailing fear, desperation, drugs and God-knows what else. He bolted madly down Rotney Way, almost comically colliding with an old lady before disappearing around a corner.

Then the stone faded underneath my shirt. I felt the burning sensation decrease rapidly, bringing immediate physical relief. I instinctively exhaled slowly, then inhaled back.

I ventured further into the newsagents and retrieved the discarded bayonet. It really was a weighty, deadly weapon on closer inspection. I shook my head and placed it on the counter.

Oh dear. The poor lady behind the counter was also shaking vigorously, utterly confused. I ran forward and hugged her tightly. Eventually I let go and we both peered down at the blade and exchanged astonished looks.

The old lady sat slowly on a plastic chair behind the counter and composed herself. Then she asked why the man had been so startled. Maybe she hadn't seen the strange glow from where she was standing. Or perhaps she had but it just hadn't registered.

I shrugged. *Obviously off his head*, I explained knowingly.

I spent several minutes more comforting her, then I made some polite excuses and turned towards the shop exit. But the lady called after me, requesting my details for the police incident report. *Yeah, right.* If the blue boys got involved, I'd soon be arrested for intimidating an honest customer. They'd probably end up confiscating the stone and sending Frank bank to America, the dummies.

So, I just ignored the lady and kept going through the exit. Didn't turn around.

When I got home, Mum served tea and Marmite on toast. She didn't ask why I was home later than usual – just as well as I had no intention of telling her. Her back seemed marginally better and there was no sign of the dirty finger-nailed doctor.

We chatted about a few trivialities, munching our toast and watching television. I mentioned I was popping over to the library after dinner and she just nodded. The same old rubbish excuse just kept on working.

Empty space had replaced our rotten old couch. Pathetic, really. No one would pay more than a tenner in a car boot sale for that hunk of junk. The bailiffs clearly removed it out of spite and frustration. Losers.

We watched some tedious current affair show on the BBC and I checked my watch every few minutes. Finally, at six forty, I set off for Frank's pub, maintaining the library pretence by clutching my school bag.

Even though I walked slowly, I arrived at the pub fifteen minutes early. It wasn't particularly crowded and the sour girl behind the bar nodded as I came in.

"He'll be down in a minute."

"OK, thanks."

I sat on a barstool, waiting quietly. Some music I couldn't recognize resonated out of ceiling speakers. I could feel the stone resting inches under my neck, cold and still inexplicable.

There were some descending footsteps and I stood up as Frank appeared at the bottom of the stairs. He beamed at me and I shot over.

We hugged each other, for a few moments, then Frank grabbed a bottle of diet coke and we headed into the usual room behind the bar.

It had changed once again but not by a huge amount. There were no animals and a few more cartons and crates. We sat down in the usual seats and looked at each other.

Then I got straight to the point.

"So, Frank, *please, are* you going to give me some answers now?"

"Sure. The full nine yards."

"What does that mean?"

"You never heard that expression?"

I shook my head. "No."

"Yeah, I guess it's not an English thing. You know, it means the whole caboodle, the works – everything! So, I mean, I'll tell you everything I know, but I'm not sure it'll answer all your questions."

"Well, OK - thanks."

Frank adjusted his seat, then glanced up. "But Antonia…" a more serious tone. "Before I do that, can you tell me if anything unusual happened today?"

"You mean, with the stone?"

"Yeah."

I frowned.

"Anything? Big? Small?"

"I'm not too sure…". I told him about the two incidents involving the stone in the morning and, then again, as I was coming home from school. I described how the stone had heated up and illuminated and the peculiar reactions I'd received.

Frank listened very carefully without responding. Then he sat back in the saggy pub chair and closed his eyes. I wasn't quite sure whether he was thinking intensely or had just fallen asleep. But eventually he opened his eyes and smiled.

"Thanks, Antonia. All understood. Can I have the stone back, please?"

"Sure." I unclasped it from behind my neck and handed it over. He studied the stone wordlessly for a few moments, then fastened it around his neck.

I leaned forward. "What is it?"

"What's what?"

"The *stone*, Frank. What's the stone?"

He shook his head. "I don't know, Antonia. I genuinely don't. But it's surely one of the strangest things in this universe."

14

He stretched out his hands.

"I'm 81 years old," he said, slowly. "Well, you know that, don't you? Your little bit of detective work with the computer. Very impressive, young lady... but the truth is I'm just an old man.

"Since I was a young fella and for reasons I'll get to, I wasn't always too well. About 15 years ago, when I was in my late sixties, my health took a bad turn, then just kept on going south. I figured I was on my way out. My head and stomach started feeling like hell, it hurt when I peed and I started developing a *bad* shake. And that shake was the worst of it!

"Well, this all went on for quite a while. I went to a bunch of doctors and had a whole load of tests but they couldn't find all that much wrong. They checked me over for Parkinson's – you know, cos of the shake - but that was ruled out. Mind you, they say it's a difficult disease to detect.

"Anyhow, when I got to around 75, something *real* strange happened, Antonia. You might even say unprecedented."

I raised my eyebrows, "what?"

"Well, to put it bluntly, I started to get better – *a lot* better. The aches and the pains and the shakes started to go. Slowly, at first, then quicker. *Much* quicker. I began feeling pretty, darn good. Started doing stuff I couldn't even do 50 years ago. I mean jogging, lifting weights, jumping hurdles. Jesus, it was just *crazy*."

"How? Why?"

Frank smiled and waved a bony finger. "Ah, gee, well, that's the *64-million-dollar* question. Took a long while to get any answers – hell, even these days, I don't know the half of it. But I know some. See, I guess to answer that question – or *try* to answer that question - I need to go all the way back to the beginning."

I sipped my diet coke through a straw and motioned with my head. "Go for it."

"I was born in 1933 in the States. Place called Charlotte, in North Carolina. You've seen the old black and whites. Anyhow, the city was starting to expand when I was born. Matter of fact, it doubled in size after the First World War. Gets very hot there, you know, not like Rotney. Over 90 degrees Fahrenheit, for weeks sometimes. Tough on the old folks.

"And you're right, I was christened William Franklyn Truesdale. Technically the second, or Junior. My late father was William Truesdale, the first, or Senior. Died in 1970."

Frank rubbed his jaw, thoughtfully. "Well, growing up, I guess I was a fairly regular kid. I loved baseball. When I was your age my big hero was a fella called Jackie Robinson. You ever heard of him?"

I shook my head.

"Man, not only was he a great ball player and a real gentleman but he broke what they called the colour line."

"What was that?"

"He became the first black guy to play in Major League Baseball. Started on first base for the Brooklyn Dodgers. And no matter how much the white folk shouted abuse and insults, he never rose to it. He had the guts to turn the other cheek and play great baseball instead. Shut them up and earned their respect, eventually. I learnt how to conduct myself from Jackie Robinson. Now, he was a *real* hero."

I nodded appreciatively.

Frank sighed. "Anyway, everything changed after I joined the army. Entered service at a place called Forest City. I was only eighteen.

Still a boy. As you mentioned, there was a big war going on in Korea. Real nasty fight between the North and the South, went on for three long years. Ended in a stalemate in 1953. The North Koreans were the bad guys and they were supported by the Chinese and the Soviets, meanwhile the South Koreans were supported by the United Nations or the UN. From memory, the UN comprised 21 countries, including the British. But the United States contributed almost 90% of the soldiers.

"Anyway, like all wars, it was a pretty nasty one. About two and a half million people got killed or injured and in the end – as I said – nobody won and there are still big problems there today. It's run by a major asshole."

"Yeah, the fat bloke. Kim Yong-un or whatever his name is."

"Yeah, that's him." He nodded, thoughtfully. "So, the Korean War. The armies went backwards and forwards over the centre of the country - what was termed the 38th Parallel - and it kept being taken and retaken. There was a whole lot of action, at first, then it developed into what was called a war of attrition. That means one side just tried to grind the other one down. Bit like the First World War."

Frank shook his head, "ah hell, it was a bad business." He lapsed into silence.

I put my glass down. "But that's not the whole story, is it, Frank? As in - you won the *Medal of Honor!*"

He reddened. "Yeah, I did, although I don't really like talking about it. I helped attack the NK, inflicted some casualties and stopped a grenade from exploding. They gave me this big medal but I tell you, there were far braver guys in that war than me – and a lot of them didn't make it."

I shook my head. "I found the citation on *Wikipedia,* you did a lot more than that. It said you *repeatedly exposed yourself to hostile fire in the face of a numerically superior force* – I remember the wording! Then you fought off the other side, virtually single handled, captured an enemy machine gun and saved loads of lives by hurling yourself on a grenade. You're – like – the most incredibly brave man!"

Frank turned even redder. "No ma'am. I was just another soldier, I did my duty – and then the American Government made a whole big deal out of it."

I shook my head again, unconvinced. "Go on – please."

"Well, anyway, I became what's termed a *casualty of war.* The grenade tore me up pretty good and I lost consciousness for a long while. When I finally came to, I was in a field hospital with pretty nurses rushing around and cracking jokes. I'd been stitched up and given a load of medication and they were all treating me like a hot shot and saying I was going to get the Silver Star, or something. Then after a while, one of the nurses came up to me – a real nice girl, as I recall. Can't remember her name, though. Shame. She told me when I was stretchered in, my right fist was grasping something real hard.

"She said one of the surgeons tried to pry my fist open when they were operating but I wouldn't give up whatever I was holding. Eventually, he let it be, then another doctor tried opening my hand after the operation. Also got nowhere. Anyway, as this nurse is talking, I realize I'm *still gripping something.* I look down at my right fist and it's completely bunched up. So, I just let go - and it opens."

"Wow, what were you holding?" Then it hit me. "Oh my God, it was the *stone*. The stone I was just wearing! Right?"

Frank nodded, "the very same."

"Whoa that's *sick*! Was is part of the grenade? Where did it come from? Did it light up?"

Frank raised his hand. "Kid, there's a whole lot more. We're just getting started. You need to be a little more patient. I mean, you're going to find some of this *very* strange indeed..."

"OK, sorry. Please, carry on."

"Turned out, I was pretty badly injured. The grenade had ripped out a fair part of my guts. I was in the hospital for weeks, couldn't even eat solid foods for a time. Eventually, they sent me back home to an Army Medical Centre in Fort Bragg. Also in North Carolina. Now, Fort Bragg is a massive military installation, Antonia. Around 40,000 people live there now but during the wars there was almost four times that number.

"Anyway, I hung in there for a few months. They patched me up some more and in July 1952, a two-star General turned up at my bed. Advised me I was a Medal of Honor recipient and saluted me. *Saluted me.* A spotty, nineteen-year-old kid…

"Got a Purple Heart too because I sustained an injury. And then, at least until I got discharged, it was pretty damn crazy. Everywhere I went, people stood up and saluted me. Then, before long, it was off to the White House to meet Ike – that's President Eisenhower – and he shook my hand and hung the Medal round my neck. Then *he* saluted me too, t*he President of the United States…*I mean, *Jesus…*"

Frank paused and dropped his head. "Yeah, well…all seems a long time ago, now, kid. About fifty years before you were born."

I wiped away a tiny tear and sniffed. "That's amazing."

Frank shrugged, then looked down. "Few months after I got the award, I got discharged from the Army and had to find something to do with the rest of my life. I stayed on in North Carolina and settled in a town called Cornelius"

"Cornelius? So, is that where you got your name?"

Frank raised a finger. "Indeed, it is. Real pretty place, not too large. Adjoins the largest man-made lake in North Carolina, Lake Norman. You'd like it. It's a helluva lot nicer than Rotney, that's for sure!

"I was always pretty good at figures so I trained as a bookkeeper, got a National Association degree and then I worked for a couple of businesses. I did OK and no one was shooting at me. Got married, had a couple of boys – it was all good – but then in my early sixties, I just chucked in the job. I'd been going to bed every night, closing my eyes and all I could I see was columns and rows, columns and rows, going in and out, endlessly – and I thought hell, *there must be more to life than this*. I can't keep doing this awful crap until I die. So, I started looking around for something different."

"Sorry, Frank – "I interrupted, "where was the stone?"

"We'll get there, Antonia."

"Sorry, carry on."

"Well, after I ditched the bookkeeping, I pretty much found myself at a loose end and it was difficult to keep myself occupied. Occasionally, a local school or college wanted me to address their students, which I quite enjoyed. Besides that, I did a lot of reading, watched a whole bunch of videos, tended the garden, and just kept my eyes open. My boys were in college and most my friends were grandparents already. And I guess that's how I found my new lease of life."

"As a grandparent?"

"No, not exactly. One of my old army buddies – a guy called Sam Milton – invited me round to keep him company during his grandson's sixth birthday party. Not exactly my idea of a wonderful day out but I went anyway, I mean I didn't have a whole lot else to do. Besides, Sam was a real funny fella, always cracked me up.

"So, I turn up to this darned party, not expecting very much and Sam had laid on some big treats for the kids. First off, he'd hired a petting zoo with a couple of keepers. There were goats, rabbits, lambs, guineas pigs, ponies. Man, the whole works. And they were running riot in the front garden."

I smiled, "sounds amazing."

Frank smiled back. "Yeah, you'd have loved it. Anyway, it was all kind of crazy, with all these animals milling around, eating the begonias, shitting everywhere. But the kids loved it. Couldn't get enough. They were stroking the animals, feeding them little bottles. They were so contented, and delighted. Hell, Antonia, made quite an impression on me.

"And then it got *better.* Old Boy Sam had hired this real cheesy magician with a top hat and bow tie and magic wands. The kind with the black sticks and white tips. So, I'm watching this guy along with all the kids – and you know what? I thought he was *terrific.* And the kids loved him too.

"I don't think he did anything original – no levitating or sawing ladies in half – but he produced eggs from his mouth, rabbits from hats, a few card tricks. What else? You know - took nickels out from behind kids' ears, blew a few balloons into funny shapes. It was great..."

Frank paused for a second, beaming at the memory.

"So, it got me thinking, Antonia. I saw that animals and magic – or the illusion of magic – could give you a spontaneous thrill, a sensation of wonder. You could find yourself smiling and emotionally involved without even thinking. Maybe that sounds a little crude but I think when you've been a soldier and seen so much death and destruction and ugliness – you react stronger to those little rays of sunshine. And I felt I wanted to be a *part* of that sunshine, to add something positive and warm to this world. You know, this world which can be so brutal but so *beautiful* at the same time."

He paused again and exhaled. "I'm sorry, is this making any sense to you, or am I babbling?"

I smiled. "No, I totally understand. I really do. So, is this how you turned into *The Great Cornelius*?"

"I guess so. I suppose you could say it marked the beginning of the process."

15

"So, I'm now – what? Sixty, sixty-one and I suddenly decide to become a magician. And what's strange is that I'd never really thought about it before. See, most people that become magicians have felt they always wanted to perform, entertain or dazzle an audience. Like they were born with this mad craving in their blood. But not me. Saw a magician, one day and got sold on the idea!"

Frank shrugged. "But – you know – this was still a few years before the internet and you couldn't just google how to become a magician. I had no real idea how to begin. Just a mad desire.

"Well, I figured, the best place to start was in the library and – unlike Rotney – Cornelius had a pretty good one, book stores too.

"I started reading up on magic and bought this terrific book by a guy called Mark Wilson – written about 40 years ago but still really popular. It was called *Complete Course in Magic* and taught me some great stuff and ideas.

"So, I started doing all the stuff you're supposed to do. Practised all the time in front of the mirror, discussed tricks and tips with other guys in the magic trade. Learnt all the card tricks, even devised a few of my own – and gradually I started improving.

"But getting gigs was a problem. No one had heard of me, I had no track record – and I wasn't getting any younger. I put my name around a bit, even placed a notice in a couple of local papers but didn't get much interest. It was frustrating, that's for sure but I kept on going, kept persisting and eventually, I started doing the odd kid's party. One here, another one there. Then, maybe, a local function."

Frank frowned and tilted his head. "You know, it was *tough*, Antonia. I wasn't a natural performer. I couldn't joke or connect too well with an audience so I kind of emphasized my *mysterious* nature a bit more. But I guess I got better over time, more confident – and gradually I started getting more work and making a few more bucks. And you know what? I enjoyed it too! It was sure different to dodging bullets or balancing books. When I pulled off a good trick, it was great to see faces light up or give me the *"howdy do that?"* look."

"Did you call yourself *The Great Cornelius?*"

"No, not for a long time. I experimented with costumes. At first, I used to just wear a smart suit, although the pants had wider pockets! But then I got a bit more theatrical. You know – added a bow tie and a cloak. Finally, when I started gigging outside Cornelius, I kind of adopted the wizard beard and leather trousers. You could judge from an audience's reaction what they responded to and because I was an older guy, it seemed they preferred the Harry Potter look."

"Wizards don't wear leather trousers."

"Well, this one does. Helps with the tricks."

"I believe you."

"I'm glad you do. Anyway, I started building a reputation, even though – if truth be told – my tricks were unoriginal. I mean it was all rabbits from hats, parlour tricks, disappearing coins, that sort of thing. Nothing different. Then, as you know, ever since Korea, I had this slight trembling. Matter of fact, sometimes, it wasn't so slight.

"Became a problem. To be a good magician, you need a steady hand and flexible joints. You're supposed to practice coin manipulation all the time to keep your arms and fingers supple. Good for deceiving the audience, you know? Anyway, my shake got worse and it just got tougher and tougher to perform.

"Then - like I said - I got ill and that was it, really. No more magic. Or so I thought. The doctors gave me a whole load of pills and drugs and when I wasn't feeling too bad, I binged on movies and Ben & Jerry's. I figured I might as well enjoy myself before joining the big barracks in the sky."

Frank stopped. "Top up? Another bottle?"

I shook my head. "No, I'm fine, thanks. Please carry on."

Frank exhaled. "OK. Well, this is…. kind of where it starts to get weird. And I mean *weird*. Do you know what a cardinal rule is?"

I nodded. "A rule that can never be broken."

"Right. That's it, exactly. A rule that can never be broken. For magicians, the cardinal rule is never to give away your secrets. There's an exception to that rule, if you're writing a book for fellow magicians – but it holds true in all other circumstances. So, I'm about to break that rule and give away my biggest secret. I haven't told anyone what I'm about to tell you – but, then again, it turns out you're also a magician."

"I am? But I don't know anything about magic!"

"Well, actually, that's not quite true."

"I don't understand!"

"Don't worry, I'll explain as I go along. You *sure* you don't want another diet coke?"

"I'm fine, really."

Frank exhaled again. "Hmm, well here goes. You ever seen the original movie, *Superman*. The one with Christopher Reeve?"

"Yeah, they keep showing it on Channel 5."

"That's great!"

I smiled. "OK. Why?"

"Well, there's a scene in that movie that kind of shows what happened next?"

"Really? Did you see a helicopter falling off the top of a skyscraper and run into a phone booth to get changed?"

Frank laughed. "No, not that scene! No, this one was earlier in the movie."

He pulled his chair closer, his eyes animated.

"It's about 35 minutes in. Clark Kent wakes up in the middle of the night. His wireless radio is still clicking and he turns it off. He gets out of his bed and looks through the window to the barn next door."

Frank paused very slightly, obviously recalling the episode.

"He goes into the barn, opens the remains of his ship and discovers a glowing green crystal. Remember?"

I nodded my head. "Yeah…"

Then, suddenly, I realized he was talking about the stone again. I jerked forward. "Is that what happened to you?"

Frank grimaced slightly. "Kind of. Not exactly. I'd just turned 75 and my body was falling apart. I needed a stick just to get to the john and my hands were shaking like crazy. Few months earlier, I'd had to sign some papers to admit my wife into a care home because she needed all round attention and I couldn't provide that any more. So, I was living alone, although I had a daily nurse to help with my chores.

"Anyway, I woke up in the middle of the night and I remember my television was still on low – like the movie. I switched it off with the remote and was about to turn over and get back to sleep but – "

"But?"

"But, I don't know, Antonia, it's difficult to explain. I felt something *inexplicable* was compelling me to get up and resolve something. Well, usually, at my age, that means a bathroom call – but not this time!"

"Could you hear anything different?"

"No, not at first. Well, maybe on a higher level or something. I honestly don't know. But I sure *felt* something different."

"Wow."

"I remember putting on my slippers and gown, fumbling for my stick, turning on the sidelight and edging out of the bedroom. I walked down the corridor and checked all the rooms. Everything was dandy, nothing out of place. So, I went downstairs – which I didn't like doing much, anyway, especially in the middle of the night. Checked all the rooms on the ground floor. Again, all fine. Nothing strange. And then – then I heard it."

"Heard what?"

"I don't know, like – like…" Frank shook his head and ran his fingers through his white hair. "Like a really, high whistling, very intense I couldn't place where it was coming from. I kept looking around but because I was old and tired, it all took a long time. Not exactly Clark Kent, I'm afraid.

"Well, anyway, it turned out it was coming from the basement where I kept all my old junk. There was a stairway that led down into it. I flicked on the light, climbed down the stairs like a geriatric sloth and tried to find out what was causing the damned whistling."

"Could have been the boiler. Ours makes some very strange noises, especially at night."

Frank laughed. "Hell, no, this was no boiler. It was coming from a box of stuff that I hadn't opened in years. Stuff from when I fought in Korea, my uniform, bits of equipment, photos, memories, you know? Anyway, I open up this box and the whole basement just lights up as if it's on fire."

"The *stone*." I whispered.

"That's right. I'd kept it all those years in the box, forgot all about it. But now, it was like the green crystal in the *Superman* movie. Glowing, vibrating, buzzing, and whistling. Man, it was so strange. Well, I tried to pick it up but it was way too hot. And I'm thinking *what the hell?*

"I got an old rag lying next to the box and used it to pick up the stone. Then I held it in my palm, you know, still wrapped in the rag so I wouldn't get burnt and then – "

Frank looked at me.

"Then?"

"My trembling stopped."

I stared at him, "sorry?"

"My hand stopped shaking and then…then I started feeling like a million dollars. Like a *billion* dollars! I felt strong, mighty, powerful, potent, like I could take on the whole NK army again, like I could run a marathon, swim a channel, and pitch for the Dodgers. Like the clock had turned me back 50 years."

I kept staring at Frank. Was he joking? The stone had certainly displayed strange qualities when I wore it but he was talking about some magical Harry Potter device. Or something out of an old Disney film.

But on the other hand, maybe it wasn't so outlandish. Granny Strictness believed in healing crystals. She said they could contain energies, although they hadn't done her much good in the end.

"So, the stone made you better?"

"Not quite, it was more complicated than that. In fact, the whole thing is complicated, kid. The stone stopped glowing after a few minutes and my hand started trembling soon afterwards. But not as badly as before. Same with my walking, it had also kind of improved.

"Pretty soon after that, I glued a little ring onto the top of the stone, ran a thin cord through the ring and started wearing the stone round my neck. I had no idea at all why it had lit up that night but I figured that if it had power or qualities or whatever, I wanted to be near it."

"Makes sense. So, what happened? Was that the end of it?"

"Hell, no! It was just the beginning. Turned out I hadn't seen anything yet. Nothing at all."

16

H e leaned in.

"Well, I tell you, I started noticing that with this crazy stone hanging round my neck, I really was getting better. I mean, physically. Not suddenly, this time but slowly and gradually. Bit by bit. Piece by piece. First off, I didn't notice it too much, like the shaking and walking was just a little better but I just kept on improving until the trembling pretty much stopped and I didn't need to use my stick any more. I stopped having problems going to the bathroom, my stomach healed up, then I found I could even start jogging and swimming.

"And then I *kept* improving, Antonia. Found I could do ten, twenty, fifty, a *hundred* push-ups. Then, the jogging became sprinting and in the pool, it was the same story. No more leisurely breast strokes - I could power crawl through fifty lengths, no problem!

"I stopped feeling tired all the damned time. Instead, I felt alive and *bursting* with energy. Then I noticed other stuff too. I stopped forgetting things, got sharper all round. Everything changed and moved forward. Everything, that is, except one thing."

I frowned. "What was that?"

"The stone. It didn't light up again but I still felt like it was imparting its energy. I know that sounds like some new-age bullshit but that's how it felt."

I pressed my fingers together and rested my head on them.

"Unbelievable! Did you go to the doctor? Find out what was happening?"

"Did I? Yeah, that's kind of complicated too. But hang in there."

"Sorry, go on. In your own time."

"Antonia..." Frank shook his head. "The truth is I didn't want to tell anyone about the stone. Not even my family. I thought they'd think I lost my mind. I even went so far as downplaying all the stuff that was happening. Carried on pretending I was still a frail old guy..."

He paused, staring ahead. "You know because the whole thing seemed so damned *crazy*. I don't even know how I got the stone in the first place. Made no sense. Somehow it got into my fist in between the grenade exploding in Korea and arriving at the field hospital. How did that work? Darned if I know."

He exhaled. "But since you ask I did have to go my doctor for regular check-ups and he was... *astonished*. Ah hell, astonished doesn't even begin to cover it..."

Frank grinned and shook his head. Then he chortled.

"Yeah, I went to see my doc after a few months of wearing the stone. He doc examined me with his stethoscope, looked in my ears and my mouth and checked my hands and reflexes and all that baloney. Then he said something like "Goddam if that isn't the *strangest* thing I've ever seen. It's a complete remission.""

"What does that mean?"

"Remission is like a temporary halt to an incurable disease. But that wasn't really a very accurate medical opinion because I'd actually improved so much – and he couldn't explain that at all."

"But didn't you want to find out what the stone was? What it was doing to you? Maybe, it could have helped other people?"

"Antonia, please!"

"Sorry. Please go on."

"And no, at that stage, I just thought they'd send for the white coats and put me in a strait jacket. But anyway, I did eventually start considering what the stone was – but I'm getting ahead of myself. I'll get there. OK?"

I nodded.

"OK, then. So…as I was starting to feel a whole lot better, I started practicing my old magic routines again. Boy, I was rusty after years of sitting on my ass but I started picking it up again. Not only that because I'd developed this additional speed and flexibility, I could do a whole load of stuff faster and better. I felt so much more alert, you know? I kept practicing over and over – in front of the mirror again, like the old days – and pretty soon, I was good enough to start advertising again, looking for new gigs."

He grimaced slightly and rubbed his forehead.

"What?"

"Antonia. Around about this time, weirder stuff started happening. Stuff, I still can't explain. And you're just going to have to take a leap of faith for a while. Can you do that?"

I nodded again. "I'll try. I've worn the stone too, you know."

"I know. That's partly why I asked you to wear it, although we'll come to that too."

He didn't say anything and had a bit of a weird expression on his face.

"Frank?"

"Yeah."

"Go on."

He closed his eyes for a few seconds, then opened them again. "You remember that silver photo frame you found of me with the Medal?"

"Yes."

"I lost it, like I said, many years ago. That's a definite. It got stolen in 1972 in Borneo Island when I was on holiday there. But after a few months of wearing the stone, this damned frame kept appearing and disappearing."

A shiver, quite literally, ran down my spine. "What do you mean?"

"I kept finding it in unexpected places and then losing it again. Initially, I thought it was my mind playing tricks or the onset of dementia or something like that. But it wasn't. *It kept happening again and again.* Like a weird practical joke."

"Like, how?"

"First time, I was in my doc's waiting room. I needed the bathroom and there were a couple of people ahead of me. I went into the little bathroom, sat down on the john and noticed there was a pile of magazines on the left. I started leafing through them and after about the fourth magazine down, I found the framed photo."

"What?"

"I took it out the pile and stared at it. I turned it over, it was the same object I'd placed my official photo in, many years ago. Same heavy silver frame with the same, identical little dents on the back."

"Same as the one I saw..."

"Exactly – but what the hell was it doing in my doc's john?"

"Maybe he found it, somehow and took it home, forgot about it and it ended up in his toilet?"

Frank cocked his head. "Sure, I mean, of course. The doctor I'd seen for the previous 22 years entirely forgot he'd discovered and retained a heavy, silver framed photo of me wearing the Medal of Honor in his john? Does that sound likely?"

"No, not really." I shrugged my shoulders.

"Thing is, I took the photo out of the john, wrapped it in my coat and put the coat on the chair next to me. I remember that very clearly. Very clearly indeed. I planned to take it into the consulting room and right at the end, just after my doc had completed his usual examination and told me I was a walking miracle of nature, I'd produce this photo and ask him what the hell it was doing in his john."

"Sounds like a plan."

"Yeah, well it didn't work."

"Why?"

"Because by the time they called my name that photo – silver frame and all – had totally vanished."

"What?"

"Into thin air. I told you I thought I was going crazy – and I certainly wasn't going to start asking my doctor questions about it. Like I said, I didn't fancy the white coats coming around."

I stared at him. "No trace at all?"

Frank shook his head. "Zip. None. And then a few days later, it happened again."

"What do you mean?"

"Well, this time, I was invited to say a few words to a school. You know because I won *that medal*. I don't mind, I like to meet young people and – it's an honour, you know. Old fart like me."

"You're not an old fart!"

Frank smiled. "So, anyway, if it wasn't the strangest darn thing – and this is coming from a magician! When I arrived at this school, they made a big fuss of me, called me the big hero and all that crap. Then the principal's secretary asked me to wait in the reception room. Made me a cup of coffee and said the principal would be back in a couple of minutes.

"So, I sat in the Reception room, me, the big war hero, scratching my ass. Then I saw there was a bunch of magazines on the coffee table, just in front of me. I leaned forward, leafed through the pile and there it was again!"

"You're *lying*! The photo, in the silver frame?"

"The very same. Dents on the back, no mistaking it."

I gawped. "Well…someone was obviously having a laugh. Teasing you! That's absolutely – "

"No!" Frank raised his hand. "You're wrong. Like I said, Antonia, it was just the beginning. It kept happening again and again, all over the place. That was just the second time. I tell you, that damned photo frame kept appearing and disappearing. Sometimes, in the most unlikely places. But… "

He paused, looking up.

"But?"

"The first time, somebody *else* discovered it - was you. I take it that it wasn't you *having a laugh,* was it?"

Now I was dumbstruck. "No, it was in the middle of your box of old photos."

"Exactly."

"So…so…. - I don't know what to say."

"Don't say anything. Sip your coke!"

"Right."

And I did.

"Anyway, then a whole load of even *weirder* stuff started happening. About nine months after the stone lit up, I was practicing an old magic trick. One of the oldest, in fact. My friend, George, who only lived down the road, kept a bunch of pets and farmyard animals. Proved handy for me. Every now and again I used to go over there and borrow a rabbit. Not to cook, you understand? No, to produce from a hat, or, in my case, from a rectangular box with a false bottom. But that's a trade secret, OK?"

He winked at me. I winked back and kept on sipping.

Frank gazed upwards. "Ah, *Jesus*, how to describe this, without sounding like I've lost my mind?" He shook his head and continued.

"I was practicing with this damned box repeatedly and suddenly I swear I heard my father calling me. I could hear it as clearly as if he was in the room next door. *William! William! William!* Oh, boy…I should have been scared. Confused, at least. First, I'm seeing things and now I'm *hearing* them. But I wasn't. I was - I don't know - *comforted*. I thought, this is it, soldier. Time's up. You've done the best you can, made some good friends, raised a decent family, helped a few people along the path, stood up when it counted - but now your Daddy's calling you to the grave.

"Anyway, so I'm hearing my father's voice and having this profoundly spiritual moment – and I let go of the rabbit. Now the little fella didn't care if I'm hearing my Daddy's voice, or God, or Morgan Freeman, or whoever. No sir! He just takes off and scampers out my magic room about hundred miles an hour.

"Now I got myself a situation. One moment, I'm having a holy encounter and the next second, I'm chasing this damned rabbit out the room and down the stairs. Hell, he shoots into the ground lobby – but he's much too fast for me. Even with my new-found abilities and all, we're talking no contest. This is a wild rabbit George has reared, making its bid for freedom!

"So, then there's a whole load of scampering downstairs and finally I manage to corner the little fella in the utility room. I could see he was real scared so I chucked a blanket over him. And that did the trick. Rabbit fidgeted for a little while, then settled down under the blanket and kept still. For a few seconds, I could see the outline of this animal under the blanket. Then – *shazam* - the blanket crumbled onto the ground and when I pulled it back, the rabbit had disappeared. Gone."

"Well, it crept out from under the blanket, obviously."

"Well, no, in the first instance, I would have seen that. Easily. The rabbit had vanished. That's a definite, Antonia. Then in the second instance, I climbed back up the stairs, holding this blanket and shaking my head. Then as I approached the magic room, I could hear something different from inside the room like a scratching and a chattering. By the way, I call it my magic room but – you know – it's just a spare bedroom where I keep all my magic stuff. I don't want you to think it's, like, an *actual* magic room."

"No, no, I get it. So, what happened?"

"Well, yeah, I went inside, trying to locate the source of these strange noises. Then I realized pretty, quickly they were coming from the false bottom of the box I'm supposed to produce the rabbit from. So, I opened the box and – "

"And?"

"There was a monkey in there."

17

"A what?"

"A monkey."

"What kind of monkey?"

"Ah, hell, I don't know. What kind of monkey? Maybe a spider monkey."

"How did it get in the box?"

"Beats me."

"You're joking!"

"No, I'm quite serious."

"So, you changed a rabbit into a monkey?"

"Apparently so."

I nodded appreciatively. "Sick!"

Then I thought about this for a few seconds. "But you've no idea how you did it?"

"Well, no, not at the time."

"*Not at the time?* So, you know how to do it now?"

"Hmm…that's kind of a leading question."

"Sorry?"

I gawped at Frank. He noticed my expression and raised a palm. "Just let me continue, kid…where was I?"

"Monkey."

"Right, monkey" He paused and frowned. "Well, so I went into my bedroom and had to take a moment. *Obviously.* I mean I couldn't really understand what was going on. Still thought I was losing my mind. But I guess my primary concern was the fact that I'd lost George's rabbit. I mean what was I going to say? Sorry, bud, I lost the rabbit but how about a woolly monkey instead?"

"I thought you said it was a spider monkey?"

"Yeah, it was either a spider monkey or woolly monkey. Actually, it probably was a spider monkey."

"Fine, a spider monkey. So, what happened?"

"From memory, I left the monkey in the magic room with the door closed because I was worried about it crapping in the rest of the house. Then when I went to check on it about ten minutes later, it had also vanished."

"Oh no!" I brushed my hair back over my face. "I'm losing track of what's coming and going now. Did you find the rabbit?"

"No. George was pretty pissed at that."

I closed my eyes. My head was hurting. "I don't understand...I don't get it, Frank. Please. *Explain!*"

"Hey, you think you're confused?" Frank shook his head. "Antonia, I told you, I thought I was losing my mind. Hell, I even went back to the doc for another check-up but all he said was I was in great shape! And then – then it happened again..."

"What happened again? You found another photo frame? You turned a rabbit into a dragon? You turned your wife into a zebra? A spider monkey appeared in a photo wearing the Medal of Honor?"

Frank burst into laughter at this and I joined him. It was a welcome respite.

"So, what happened?"

"Well, basically, I discovered that every time I was trying to do a trick with an animal it plain vanished and another type of animal appeared in its place. If I started the trick with one animal, I could trigger an endless disappearing/appearing sequence."

"Like you do in the pubs?"

"Yup."

"But that makes no sense at all, Frank! How can you do that? Magic?"

He didn't reply.

"Frank?"

"See," said Frank, "it's the stone. It has powers. I know that, for sure. Within the first year of it glowing, I started hearing voices, things disappeared and other things reappeared. I mean real, crazy, shit. Inexplicable stuff. But - you know - for a long time it seemed entirely random, like there was no logic or pattern to it."

"But?"

"But it turned out there *was* a pattern. Something I could apply when I performed. I don't know what it meant, I *still* don't know what it means but I can *use* it now."

"Use what? You're still not making sense!"

Frank paused, thinking. "You ever seen a film called *The Prestige?*"

"No."

"Shame, it's actually a good movie – it's a film about magic, about two Victorian magicians who compete with each other. They keep trying to outdo each other – and both end up getting killed in the process – but there's a marvellous speech at the end of the film which kind of helped me understand what the stone was doing. Or, rather, not doing.

"It's given by a character culled Cutter – and Cutter is a stage engineer but kind of a father figure and teacher to the magicians too. He explains that every great magic trick comprises of three parts. The first part is called *The Pledge* where the magician shows you something ordinary like a deck of cards, a bird or a man. You can inspect whatever it is and check it's real. The second part is called *The Turn* where you do something extraordinary to the ordinary, like make it disappear. That's a difficult bit – but the hardest part is the third act where you make the ordinary thing come back. That's called *The Prestige*. Hence, the title of the movie."

I nodded.

"Well, here's the thing. What I found was that, with a lot of practice and provided I was wearing the stone round my neck and maintained a semblance of performance, I could perform the first two parts but never the third."

"Meaning?"

"I could take an animal, any animal and the stone would allow me to change it into another animal, or animals but I could never bring the original animal back. George's bunny disappeared, never returned. The monkey disappeared too, eventually. Probably went back to wherever it came from. See, I could never perform the third part - *The Prestige* – and make them re-appear."

I tensed. "But how? *How* was this happening? That's my question. It doesn't make any sense. Even if you couldn't bring the animal back, how were you changing it anyway? Or how was the stone doing that? How can you change a rabbit into a monkey? That's *insane*."

Frank held a hand up. "These are tough questions, Antonia – and I have plenty more to tell. I don't pretend to have the answers - I'm still looking for them. And I repeat I don't know how the stone can do it - I only have a theory."

"What's that?"

"You ever hear of a guy called Nicolas Flamel?"

"Who?"

"Nicolas Flamel."

I winced. "Rings a bell. Wasn't he in a *Harry Potter* film?"

Frank grinned. "Kind of. In real life, Nicolas Flamel was a scribe who lived in Paris about six hundred years ago. He was supposed to have invented the first Philosopher's Stone and achieved immortality, although there's no proper evidence he had anything to do with pharmacy or alchemy. In the first *Harry Potter* film, he's a wizard who invented the Philosopher's Stone that contains the secret to the elixir of life, rejuvenation and all that crap. It's the same stone that Lord Voldemort tries to get hold of."

"I read the first book. The stone can turn metal into gold, can't it?"

"Yeah, alchemy – but it's also a symbol of heavenly bliss, enlightenment, perfection, you name it. Philosophers, scientists and pharmacists have searched for it for centuries. Sir Isaac Newton virtually became obsessed with it."

"But Frank, hold on," I said. Then I started to laugh. "You turned a rabbit into a monkey, not metal into gold. I don't think Lord Voldemort would've been very interested in that." I paused, thinking about this. "Hey, you're not suggesting you have a philosopher's stone, are you? In *Rotney?*"

Frank raised a palm. "Whoa! No. I'm not suggesting that at all. But this stone does have properties. There's no doubt about it. For a start, I feel rejuvenated. I'm 81 years old but I can run a mile in 5 minutes. I could probably run a marathon too if I trained. You saw me a few days back. When I punch a guy, they sure as hell know about it. My stomach has cleared up, my shakes have stopped and no more bathroom difficulties, thank you."

"That's amazing."

"Then, I'm telling you, I can spontaneously produce and change animals provided I meet certain conditions. You've already seen it twice."

"Can't you do it now?

"No."

"Why?"

"Because I don't have an animal to hand. I need one, like Brian, to start the sequence. And the initial animal disappears which doesn't make me too popular with owners."

"All right. I understand"

"Good. Now, where was I?

"*Harry Potter.*"

Frank stood up, slightly agitated. "It's not *Harry Potter.* And it's not straight forward. This stone…it's not a Philosopher's Stone, a Sorcerer's Stone – or whatever you want to call it. It's not a magic stone that makes you invisible, or fly, or immortal, or teleport, or any movie crap like that. It's different, completely different – and I still can't work it out. Or why it came to me.

"But last year, just after my eightieth birthday, I got a further clue – and would you believe it? - it was my pal, *Superman* that prompted it again."

"What?"

"Yes. Well, *Superman 2*. They were showing it on cable. Have you seen the movie?"

I nodded. "Another one they always show on Channel 5."

"Great. Anyway, I'm watching *Superman 2* and I get my break-through. Superman has revealed his secret identity to Lois Lane and he takes her back to his home cave in the North Pole. He shows her the green crystal – the same one that glows in the first movie and he says, *"This is kind of difficult to explain but this crystal called out to me and led me here."* That's the quote. Not a famous or memorable one but it sure got me thinking.

"See, I figured, in five years, my stone had never glowed again. Not when I was doing magic tricks or studying it or admiring it. Most of the time, I'd be wearing it round my neck, even once in the shower – but it never lit up. Not once."

Frank tapped his forehead. "And now I'm thinking *real* hard, Antonia. And I think back to the first movie. What happened in that movie, exactly? Clark Kent wakes up in the middle of the night and the green crystal starts to glow and calls out to him. Then – and this what we learn in the second movie – the crystal directs him to the North Pole where it builds a cave and allows him to communicate with his parents. Even though they've been dead for thousands of years, by now."

"How does that help?"

"Well, I figured, maybe the stone wants to communicate too, maybe even direct me somewhere. You know, perhaps the stone also has a message, or even a mission for me. Maybe the stuff with the magic tricks and the silver photo frame is just a red herring, or maybe it's connected to a deeper purpose."

"Right… but how could you communicate with the stone?"

"Well, this is it. I needed to work out how to make it glow again. What exactly could trigger it?"

I sipped my diet coke and thought about this too. The stone had lit up twice today alone – but again I had no idea why.

"So, what did you do?"

"Well, it wasn't like a corny kid's movie or TV series. You couldn't utter magic words and get it to light up. In fact, I did try speaking to it, tried a few times. But it had no effect and you feel kind of dumb talking to a piece of rock."

I smiled at this. "So, what happened?"

"Well, I went back to the movie and took it in stages. The first stage was the stone directed Clark Kent to the North Pole. Now, we never learn how the crystal does that. It's funny, I've always loved movies, ever since I was a kid. But I never really liked cartoons. I far preferred books and papers. All the same, I got a couple of books on Superman and did some research and found out that his cave is called the Fortress of Solitude and contains memory crystals derived from Krypton. But there's no real clue as to how the crystal directs him to the North Pole. It's a plot hole, frankly and I think we've got to infer that the crystal communicated the information psychically.

"So, it looked like I'd hit a dead end. But I kept thinking about it, mulling it over – and then…I got this *crazy idea.*"

I straightened. "Go on…"

"I reckoned if I could find a massive atlas and run the stone over it, it would light up at my point of destination. Kind of like the Clark Kent thing, it could show me if I was needed somewhere else.

"But as usual when you think you've got a great notion; I didn't quite know how to achieve it. I mean, there was a large globe in the town library but I figured I'd get some strange looks if I started waving a rock at it. I thought about maybe using Google Earth on my desktop but that also struck me as…. I don't know, inappropriate. So, in the end I bought the biggest world atlas I could find in the book store and took it home.

"I opened up the book and right at the beginning I found the map showing the entire world. So, I unhooked my neck chain and ran the stone over the map. No joy. Kept opening different pages and different maps, running the stone over everything, but same result. Zip. Complete waste of time. Well, boy, did I feel deflated! I put my neck chain back on and went off for lunch.

"Anyway, a couple of days later, I was at a bit of a loose end, so I started leafing through the atlas again. Then, when I got to the centre of the book, I found, folded up real tight, there was a detachable world atlas poster. So, I pulled it out, opened it up and it was enormous, I mean *huge.* I tacked it on to the main wall of my magic room and just stared at it. Like a kid. I looked at the States, South America, Europe, Asia – Korea – Australia, the oceans. Seemed I'd seen so little of this world and life in general. Guess I was just a simple North Carolina boy, after all.

"Well, I don't know, I just stood there for ages looking at this damned world atlas, almost entranced you might say. And after a long while, I felt like the midpoint of my chest was beginning to heat up. Didn't notice it at first but it just got warmer and warmer, until it was practically burning."

"The stone. That's what it does!"

"Right. The stone. As soon I figured it out, I ripped the chain off my neck and held the stone out in front of me, facing the atlas and it acted like a laser, shining directly at the map. It shot this narrow beam of light straight at the atlas. And here's the amazing thing, it didn't matter how much I swung the stone or moved it around, it kept shining *at the same place.*"

"You're joking!"

"God's truth. Hell, you've seen it! You know the stone lights up. OK, maybe haven't you seen it act like a laser beam but you've felt it glow and burn! Haven't you?"

"Yes."

"Right."

"But that's just *insane.* Where was it pointing?"

"Where do you think?"

I stared at him, really stared. I knew the answer immediately.

"London," I whispered.

"Excuse me?"

"London!"

Frank nodded slowly, "yeah – that's it. London."

"But London's a big place," I protested. "Why're you in Rotney and not staying with your son? I don't understand."

Frank's lowered his voice. "Well, now, this is the really weird thing. The stone's laser pointed directly at London but it was a world atlas. The scale was too large for the beam to indicate exactly where in London. So, I went back to the book and thumbed through it, until I found a detailed map of the South East of England, including London. It was a double page spread but I ripped it out the atlas and tacked it on to another wall of the magic room. Funny, I remember my heart was thumping away. You know, I was *so* excited. My idea was working!

"I directed the stone towards the new map and– *zing*! Beams straight onto another location. And then…. same thing. Didn't matter how much I swung the stone or shifted it around, the laser just kept hitting the same location. And then – *it burnt a hole in the map!* Right where it was aiming so there was no mistaking it."

"Whoa. So where was it pointing?"

I looked at Frank but he just returned my gaze. Then my brain clicked.

"Oh no!" I blurted out. "You're not *serious*, are you?"

"Never more so, Antonia."

I shook my head in complete disbelief. Maybe transforming a rabbit into a monkey pushed my boundaries of belief a fair distance – but this was just plain ridiculous.

"*Really?*"

"Yeah."

"*Rotney?*"

"The same."

I stared at Frank. "*Rotney?*"

"Yeah."

I was going to say "*Rotney?*" again but I didn't think it would achieve anything useful so instead I just carried on gawking at Frank like an intoxicated horse.

Frank returned my gaze. He didn't seem particularly troubled by my flabbergasted response and there were a few moments of complete silence. Finally, I broke it.

"*Rotney?*"

"Yeah."

"Well, some insane sadist is having you on, then! No one in their right mind would come here! I mean – "

What did I mean? I slammed my glass down.

"Why would the stone send you to such a scumbag area?"

Frank raised his palms. "Yeah, look I agree with you. All things considered, I think I prefer North Korea."

I lapsed into silence.

Frank pulled his chair closer. "But maybe, you're missing the point, Antonia. Maybe *we're* missing the point."

"What do you mean?"

"I mean, maybe, that's why the stone wanted me to go to Rotney – because it's such a bad area"

"Why? To do what? Burn it down? Suffer? *Die?*"

"I don't know."

"Sorry?"

"I don't know."

I exhaled. More silence. I raised my glass, sipped my coke slowly and considered the position again.

"I mean it, Frank. Do you think maybe someone's just playing games with you? Mucking you around."

"Not at all. This is well beyond an elaborate hoax. The stone has real properties, powers if you will and it sent me to Rotney."

"But why?"

"We've just had this conversation. I have no idea."

I thought about this. "How long have you been here?"

"Em...coming up for two months."

"Two months! God, no wonder you need a magic stone to keep you alive!"

Frank laughed at this. Then, I sort of did too. It didn't help, though. I was so confused.

"What have you been doing here, anyway? Working out the best way to commit suicide?"

Frank shrugged.

"You know - I should get awarded a medal just for staying alive in this place." I sneered into my coke glass, squeezing it. "Either that or get committed for *trying* to stay alive."

Frank put a comforting hand on my arm. "I'm sorry. You're obviously very unhappy."

"You think?"

Frank exhaled slowly, then withdrew his hand. "Look, I'm telling the truth, Antonia, I really don't know why the stone directed me here. I'm looking all the time – the magic shows and all that? It's just to gain attention. I'm hoping the reason will eventually reveal itself, *somehow* – but right about now, I only have a couple of clues."

"Clues? What clues?"

"Well, work backwards. Think about our pal, Clark Kent, again."

"But that's also ridiculous – no offence, Frank."

"How so?"

"Well, from what I remember Clark Kent was from a different planet and eighteen years old when the crystal called him. You were – what, seventy-five? I mean, look...you're an amazing man. The bravest, most incredible, fascinating man I've ever met – but you're not *Superman*. He's just a stupid comic book character that flies around, battling Lex Luthor and - I don't know - wearing a *cape*. And pants on the outside. You can't compare your story to *Superman*. That's *mad!*"

Frank raised his palm again. "No, I'm not at all Antonia. Don't be silly. There are just certain interesting parallels I'm examining. For

God's sake, I couldn't even go the bathroom properly until recently, I'm hardly the *Man of Steel!*"

I threw up my hands. "OK, sorry. Go on. I won't interrupt."

"Thank you."

He leaned back. "Well, *Superman* - Clark Kent, actually, because this is before he made the transition to *Superman* – received his psychic call to go to the North Pole and build his home there. But once he did that, he found out what his *purpose* was because the crystal allowed him to communicate with his father. His father took him away, educated him for twelve Earth years, taught him about his latent powers and by the time he returned to Earth he knew not only what he could do but what he *had* to do."

I considered this, slowly and stroked my lips. "So...?"

Frank sat back slightly. "See, this is what I'm saying to you, Antonia. I'm still in the dark. I don't really know what the stone is capable of, I don't why I've got it, I don't even know *how* I got it. For crying out loud, I don't know if someone gave it to me, *who* gave it to me, *why* they gave it to me. Why it did nothing for over 50 years. Why it's sent me to Rotney, of all places. What I'm supposed to do or find here? Ugh!"

"But you said you had two clues."

"Correct."

"So, what they are they?"

"Well, the first one's obvious, isn't it?"

"Is it?"

"Isn't it?"

"Is it?"

"Of course, it is. The first clue is I found you."

18

I flinched. "Sorry?"

"I found you."

Three simple words but shot from left-field. "I don't understand…what have I got to do with any of this?"

"Not sure yet but you have to be my first clue, Antonia – for all sorts of reasons. I don't even know where to begin with you. I figured that if I started performing my magic tricks for all the local fools, something would happen sooner or later. Hopefully *sooner* so I could get the hell out of this place!

"But when you start producing exotic beasts out of thin air and there are no illusions involved, you would reasonably expect a measure of interest. Hey, maybe a round of applause, now and again. But all I got was dumb silence and aggression, like they just didn't get it. And when they didn't get it, it drove them mad."

"Frank," I said quietly, "they'll use any excuse to start a fight round here."

"Yeah but it happened *every time*, Antonia. Did you know that? See, you only saw a couple of shows. Fact is I performed several times round here before you arrived. Always the same reaction. *Every time.* At best - *at best* - a bit of muffled clapping but nearly always silence, confusion, then belligerence. I honestly never expected that reaction

– even from the kids. You'd think they'd like to pet the animals or something."

I nodded, "yeah, well they're worse than their parents. You're lucky they didn't set the animals on fire – and you with it!"

"Oh, I think, the way things were going, they would have sooner or later. But – you know – the only person that seemed to behave reasonably was you. I could see, straight away, you were bowled over by the magic – and then afterwards you tried to find me. So, in the first instance, you were the only one who could see – and I don't use this expression lightly – that I was performing *miracles*."

"I frowned. You can't read too much into it, though. Most of your punters are out of their heads, Frank. They wouldn't recognize a miracle if it bit them on the bum and belched on them."

Frank shook his head, sagely. "No. It was something deeper. That's a definite." He lowered his tone slightly. "Then, in the second instance, you had a grave issue with that girl. Demi. Gave me a great chance to help you out."

"Thank you *so* much. You probably saved my life. Seriously."

"My genuine pleasure - but it was *interesting* that I was given the opportunity, you know? And then came the *real* indicator. The stone's calling card. When you found the photo frame, I knew you had to be linked to all this. Became a certainty."

I closed my eyes and ran my fingers through my hair. "Frank..."
"Antonia."

"Why did you make me wear the stone today?"

"Looking for more clues as to your role, really. I had no idea what the stone would do, none. And twenty-four hours later, I have no idea why it did what it did. But these are all indicators. Hints. See, in my case, it took over fifty years for the stone to light up – and then another five years for it to light up again! Yet, it only took one day for the stone to light up for you. And not just once. *Twice*. So why? What's the significance of that?"

"I don't know," I mumbled lamely.

"I don't know either," echoed Frank. "I actually have no idea how you're bound up in all of this. Are you here to help me? Am I here to help you? Why has the stone chosen either of us, anyway? Is it something we've done, or going to do or can do? Are we here to start some something, or to stop it?"

I shook my head slowly.

"And this stone…" Frank removed his neck chain and held the stone out in his palm. "Where's it from, exactly? Another world? Heaven? Hell? Can we use it to communicate with angels? Or daemons? Or aliens? Or zombies? What's it really capable of?"

I kept shaking my head. "I don't know, Frank. I really don't. I mean…you've told me so much in the last couple of hours, I can't really take it all in…and I've got Geography in the morning."

Frank chuckled. "You know, it's funny. In the superhero films, they get to find out what they can do quickly. But this stone took almost 55 years to start calling. Jeez, I'm 81 years old now. What the hell can I do? OK, sure, I'm in decent shape now – but I could drop dead with an ailment tomorrow. I'm lucky to have got this far, as it is!"

"Please don't talk like that, "I said. "You'll easily live a hundred years at the rate you're going – and besides which, the stone clearly has a plan for you. Maybe you just have to wait a bit longer to find out what it is."

"Maybe. But the first time it started glowing, I didn't do anything, it came to me – as it were. But, since then, I've been proactive. Looking for answers and clues. Paying attention. And what have I found? Just more questions, really."

"But didn't you say there was a second clue?"

"Quite right. I did."

"Well, what's that?"

Frank's eyes scanned the room and then he leaned in.

"I'm being followed."

I flinched again. Harder. "*What*? By who?"

"A strange looking guy. At first, I thought it was a coincidence. He turned up to a couple of my shows. Then I noticed he always seemed to be parked around a corner, or looking preoccupied with something else. You know? But it was only when I spotted him, across the road, after visiting my son, I realized he was trailing me. Very low key, of course, but definitely keeping me in his field of vision."

"You think he's police?"

Frank shook his head. "Nah! They wouldn't be interested in an old guy like me, jumping around in a wizard's costume."

"So, who is it? Have you confronted him?"

"Nah! Wouldn't get me anywhere. He'd deny it. Right about now, I'm more interested in watching him watching me. Might lead to some answers."

"So why do you think he's following you?"

Frank furrowed his brow. "Well, apart from you, I haven't told anyone about the stone and its...*unusual* properties. Except, that's not entirely accurate. A few days after I arrived in Rotney, I visited the University of London's Earth Sciences' Department, in Gower Street. I showed them the rock and asked for their professional opinion.

"Of course, I didn't say that it was making me hear voices, directing me to an East London slum and producing apparitions. Didn't think that would fly too well. But I mentioned it glowed sometimes for no obvious reason and I'd obtained it, many years ago, in Korea."

"Wow, what did they say?"

"Well, they were very interested. Turned it over about a hundred times, placed it under a microscope and then asked me if they could keep it for a few days so they could run more tests. Said it was an unusual garnet."

"A garnet? But that's just a red gemstone. My Mum had some. Didn't look anything like yours, though!"

Frank shrugged his shoulders. "Don't know. To be honest, the only thing I know about garnets was what I could find on *Wikipedia*. They come in a bunch of types and varieties. Apparently, it's also the state gemstone of Idaho."

"Oh, well, that's useful, then. So, what happened? Did you let them keep the stone?"

"Well, I was really in two minds. I guess on the one hand, I wanted to know if they could work out what the stone was. More precisely, I mean. But on the other hand, I felt that a scientific response wouldn't help me at all – because I was maybe dealing with something *beyond* science. And then - I don't know - I felt that the stone was physically protecting me, *sustaining* me. Plus, it wasn't really mine to give away."

"But you gave it to me?"

"Yeah, I know. But that was only for a day – and besides, that felt completely right. You were obviously part of the mystery. I knew the stone would protect you too. That's why, when you walked into that shop being robbed, the stone did its thing to make sure you weren't in danger."

I beamed spontaneously, "I get it. That's sick!" Frank winked and I nodded back in appreciation, "so go on – what did you do?"

"I let them have the stone but then after a couple of days, I started regretting it. Found I couldn't perform any tricks without the stone round my neck and then my shake started up again. Stomach too."

"Oh no!"

"Oh yeah! Third day, I caught a cab back to Gower Street and asked for my stone back but they said it was at the lab and couldn't be returned immediately. So, I kicked up a big old stink, threatened them with the American Embassy, made a few speeches…and eventually I got it back. Took a few hours."

"Idiots."

"Nah, they were just doing their job – and I'd originally given them permission to retain the stone – so actually I was the unreasonable one. But I had no idea that my health could fold so quickly without the stone. Scared me, to be honest. I felt really fragile for the first time in months."

"Obviously."

"But when I got the stone back, I recovered pretty quickly. The lab hadn't really come up with anything further so I felt the whole episode was a waste of time. But, you know…"

Frank glanced around the room again.

"Maybe I'm just a paranoid old man but I think those scientists may have been holding out on me. I think they'd spotted something about the stone. They were perfectly polite and all and it's just a hunch. But a few after getting the stone back, the creepy guy started following me."

Creepy guy. That rang a bell.

"Can you describe him a bit more? Was he at the last show – sat right at the back, towards the left of the bar?"

"Yeah, but there were quite a few people sitting at – "

"Suit! Gappy teeth! Large, sticky out ears. Greasy hair? Dirty fingernails?"

Frank nodded, "can't say I've noticed his fingernails but the description sounds about right. Why? You don't know this guy, do you?"

I held my head in my hands. This really was way too much for one evening!

"You might say we're acquainted."

Now it was Frank's turn to look amazed.

"How the hell do you know him?"

"His name's Huck – Dr Neil Huck. He's a *friend* of Mum's. To be honest, I know very little about him. All I know is he's some type of scientist and he's instructed Mum's law firm on some big case. But I don't even know how they got *friendly*. I haven't asked many questions – and she never talks about him. I mean, it's all very uncomfortable with Dad not being around."

Frank listened carefully, "understood."

"He's been round to my house a couple of times, talks to Mum for a bit and then goes. That's it, really." I shrugged.

Frank frowned. "I wonder why's he involved your Mum? Seems very strange. Has he said or done anything unusual? Anything to go on?"

"No not really. He's just been a bit of an idiot." I thought for a second.

"Mind you, come to think of it he did made an odd comment a few days ago." I paused, stroking my lip. "What did he say again? Mum was in the loo and..."

"Go on. Could be important."

I frowned, memory straining. "Huck was sitting opposite me. Basically, I was completely ignoring him - or trying to - and he made some sort of remark about me not talking. Said I was giving him a *stony silence,* or something. Didn't really think anything of it, other than I just wished he'd get out the house – or, better still, drop dead. But that's what he said, though. *Stony silence.* Do you think it was just a coincidence?"

"Maybe. Maybe not. I'm not sure I believe in coincidences, anymore."

"Right."

"Let me think about this. Give me a moment. Another drink?"

"No, I need the loo now, anyway."

"You know where it is."

"Uh-huh, I'll give you a bit of thinking time."

Frank nodded.

I stood up, feeling quite stiff and made my way to the pub's toilet. It was much busier now and as I sat on the toilet, I checked my watch. We'd been talking for almost an hour, although it felt longer. I couldn't stay out all night. What if Mum's painkillers hadn't knocked her out and she started worrying?

I clutched my head. How could I absorb all this information? It was flipping excessive. I needed more concrete proof about the stone's properties. The notion that it could produce animals from thin air? That really was quite an outrageous claim. And then all the stuff about the stone directing Frank towards Rotney. That was *insane,* right?

I finished in the toilet and went back into Frank's room, closing the door quietly. Then I sat down and began talking.

"Frank, no offence again but I've been thinking – "

Frank held up a hand. "I did tell you I have a theory, Antonia and the more I think about it, the more I think the information you just gave me supports it. Obviously, I don't have any proof at this stage but I think I may be onto something."

I tilted my head. "OK. Go on…"

"Well, I think this is what may have happened – and somehow I need to find out if I'm right. You might have to help me."

I shrugged, "OK…"

"I think the geology boys had a fair idea of what the stone was, maybe an accurate idea – who knows? But they wanted to examine it further. Who knows why? Maybe they wanted to identify it better, or understand a certain feature. Maybe something unusual caught their eye or couldn't be explained. I don't know.

"But I think that during their further investigations, the stone did something unusual, inexplicable. Maybe not the kind of thing you and I have seen already. Or maybe it was. I don't know. Perhaps, it just lit up, or caused something to disappear, or appear. Or indicated Rotney on a map. Who knows? But I think it did something *supernatural*. Something those science guys couldn't analyse and interpret and write a paper on.

"So, they're scratching their heads and suddenly, I come back earlier than agreed, demanding the stone's return, behaving indignantly and threatening with this and that. It got their attention and they decided to keep tabs on me. Just as I originally went to them to get answers, now they're looking to me for an explanation. So, they dispatch this guy Huck – or whatever his name is – to keep an eye on me. Who knows what he is? Maybe he's a scientist with a fancy doctorate or maybe he's a PI. "

"A what?

"Private Investigator. Hired detective."

"Oh right."

"And this cheapskate guy follows me around and tries to figure out what I'm up to. He notices I'm getting friendly with you so in turn he gets acquainted with your Mum. All the time probing, hinting and looking for clues. Hey, you know, maybe I'm being paranoid and this guy's only trying to figure out whether to hire me for his daughter's birthday party. But then maybe I'm onto something."

"Possibly. Doesn't it seem a bit of a drastic move to get friendly with my Mum, though? Just to get closer you."

"Yeah, maybe, maybe not. I'd sure appreciate you finding out how he got so chummy with her."

I grimaced, "I have tried – a few times - but she just ignores me, or changes the subject. It's a complete waste of time. And I hate talking about him, anyway…" I tutted loudly and brushed my hair back. "Look, I'm telling you, asking questions doesn't work – it just irritates her - but if she mentions anything else about him, anything interesting, I'll definitely let you know, OK?

Frank nodded, "no problem."

I smiled sweetly. "But can you do something for me?"

"What's that?"

"Walk me home, tonight, please. This place gives me the creeps."

Frank grinned. "Sure."

Then we chatted some more.

19

I was watching a pigeon through the window. Quite a pretty pigeon.

It was two storeys below me, walking towards the entrance of the school. After striding quite purposefully for several metres, it ruffled its feathers and flew upwards

Pigeons really were so lucky, if you thought about it. They could fly, they didn't have to go to school and I suppose they got plenty of fresh air and exercise without worrying about being mugged and lynched by other pigeons

The English teacher was talking. That much was obvious. I could see her lips move and her hands were demonstrating. But I wasn't listening, though. I was thinking about my stomach, which hadn't been fed this morning. Mum had left earlier than usual and I discovered that the fridge was completely empty. The kitchen cupboard, too. Not even a small chocolate bar lurking at the back.

I was small and thin so I didn't need a huge amount of food but skipping breakfast didn't help my mood or concentration. I kept looking through the window hoping for something more exciting than a few pigeons, maybe a panther or polar bear, or perhaps a tank. That would be great, wouldn't it? A tank smashing through the school gates and firing at the staff room. Pupils and teachers fleeing for their lives. *Wicked.*

I glanced up. Observing the teacher's mouth, then staring through her.

I was just fifteen years old. Only a stupid, dumb kid – but now I knew that not only was life unjust and unpredictable – it also contained major, in-your-face elements that just couldn't be explained by someone in a suit, or television celebrity. This teacher - the English teacher, ahead - may have been twenty or thirty years older but she was probably as dumb and ignorant as anyone else, however, much she tried to impart her knowledge. Whatever that was.

Moaning stomach, walking pigeon, droning voice. Titters to the right. Yawn. More titters. Another slow yawn.

"Wake up, Antonia! I asked you a question."

I jolted up. Heart pounding. "Sorry, Miss. Would you mind repeating the question?"

The teacher rolled her eyes. "I asked how you'd characterize Boxer."

I exhaled slowly and thought about this. The teacher's name was Miss Karia and I didn't like her. She was abrupt, sarcastic and obviously deeply frustrated that her teaching career was in the toilet.

Over the last two weeks, I'd become slightly more philosophical about Rotney High. It seemed that the school wasn't completely uncaring about its pupils and their welfare, just simply too overwhelmed by its countless problems. All the same, I remained convinced that, in the absence of a nuclear bomb, or even a couple of tanks, the school's best way forward was a spectacular self-detonation.

I wondered how many pupils in my class understood the word "characterize". My classmates were a bit friendlier these days but I was still largely ignored. An oddity with a middle-class accent. A freak, an outsider, a peculiarity. Plenty of girls in my class wore scarves and even more gabbled in languages I couldn't comprehend. I didn't even know where half of them were from, for God's sake.

Concentrate, Antonia. I checked my watch. It wasn't even eleven o'clock and yet I was so hungry. Just a packet of crisps, salt and vinegar and it would all go away. Well, for several minutes, at least.

"Antonia?"

I studied Miss Karia. She was wearing faded jeans and a shapeless brown cardigan. Quite a pretty, Indian lady but she behaved like a half a tree was lodged up her backside.

A pigeon. I could be a pigeon, fluttering my feathery wings and leaving Rotney far behind.

"Antonia, I'm not going to ask you again! You're looking at a Room 18 detention. Is that what you want?"

"No, Miss."

"Then, are you going to answer my question?"

"Yes, Miss."

"Thank you. And?"

"And – I would say Boxer served as an allegory for the Russian working-class who helped to oust the Tsar Nicholas and establish the Soviet Union, but were eventually betrayed by the Stalinists."

The class burst into laughter at this and someone to my right shouted, "yeah"

Miss Karia took a step backwards, perplexed.

Tyrese Thorn, a mixed-race kid, sitting on my left, smiled at me and I could feel myself blushing. He was quite good looking.

The class kept laughing and Miss Karia looked furious.

"Hey!" she shouted. "*Hey!*"

Then class quietened slightly and she turned to me. "Antonia! Pick up your bag and get out of the classroom. Wait for me outside and I'll talk to you at the end of the lesson."

"Why, Miss? I was just answering the question."

"Go on! Get out!" yelled Miss Karia, "Don't even think about challenging me. Go on!"

I picked up my bag and walked quickly out the classroom, closing the door behind me.

Once outside, I peered through the small pane of glass in the door and watched Miss Karia continue the class. Then I soon lost interest and wandered down the hall hunting for a chair, or better still, a discarded biscuit.

I located a wooden chair quite quickly. Surprising really because most abandoned chairs in Rotney High ended up smashed into pieces or halfway through someone's forehead. I brought the chair back outside the classroom, sat down and checked my watch.

Just over ten minutes remaining. Not too bad, really.

I couldn't believe I'd been chucked out the classroom. It was a bit unfair because I was only answering her question by quoting from the introduction. What was weird, though, was that I remembered the line word-for-word. I'd never been able to do that before, especially when I was hungry.

I shook my head. Why was I here? In Rotney?

It was the usual one-word answer: Dad.

He was appealing his conviction now but Mum said it a was slow, painful process. And very expensive too.

Then I started thinking about Tyrese. Yeah, he was fit but like half the pupils in my year, he fancied himself as a budding gangster. Funnily enough, the one thing we probably had in common was a hatred of the police. I found that out at assembly this morning.

A police offer had addressed the whole school and I thought he gave a pathetic show.

What had brought the unwelcome sight of the officer was an incident that been widely covered by the tabloids. I don't know why the gutter press picked up on this incident - far worse things happened in Rotney all the time. I suppose it was because it was this year's trendy crime.

Last week, a girl in Year 10 had been cyber-bullied by several pupils in Rotney High and ended up hanging herself. She made a cyber-suicide note on *You Tube*, saying goodbye to her family, friends and puppy. Then the video went viral before *You Tube* took it down. I never saw it because I don't have a computer but I know it caused the usual mass indignation.

Hence the blue boy in assembly, this morning. He droned on about how the police would exercise *zero tolerance* in dealing with cyber bullying and any infringements would be punished severely, including by lengthy imprisonment. It didn't go down too well. The sense of hostility in assembly was *so* palpable that even he must have sensed it.

All so far away from Purchester.... I closed my eyes and began daydreaming about my former life.

Then a few minutes later, the pupils in my class streamed out of the door, chatting loudly and laughing. No one glanced in my direction.

BEHAVIOR AND DISCIPLINE
CORE PRINCIPLES
The Governing Body believes that to enable effective teaching and learning to take place good behaviour in all aspects of school life is necessary. It seeks to create a caring and learning environment in the school which:

- *Encourages, acknowledges and rewards, good behaviour and discipline;*
- *Promotes self-esteem by encouraging students to value and respect themselves and others;*
- *Provides a safe environment free from disruption, violence, bullying and any form of harassment;*
- *Promotes early intervention to address behaviour and/or bullying issues;*
- *Ensures a consistency of response to both positive and negative behaviour;*
- *Encourages students to take responsibility for their behaviour.*

Room 18. Again.

Miss Karia said that I had displayed *insolent behaviour* and created *disruption of a calm and purposeful environment*. All for answering her question properly!

In the afternoon, I had to report to my form teacher, Miss Patel. She was also scathing and I was issued a detention note and warned that *continued infringements* would result in an internal exclusion.

I'm not entirely sure what internal exclusion is but I think you're required to sit in a room by yourself for a day while the rest of the school laughs at you through the window. If you get enough internal exclusions, you get a proper exclusion – which sounds much more like a reward than a punishment.

As usual Room 18 was dull. There was nothing much better going on at home, or elsewhere, so I was relatively philosophical. But I also worried about getting ambushed on my way back.

I wrote out the school rules as quickly as possible and literally kept my head down. The room was more crowded than last time with social deviants and examples of humanity gone horribly wrong. The fat pupil directly in front of my desk amused himself by farting loudly and protesting that his neighbour – an equally vile Year 10 student – was responsible. Meanwhile, the nauseating smell wafted directly up my nostrils.

It took only 35 minutes to complete the copying - a personal record. Then Mrs. Sanders - replacing Big Skull Reid, for the evening - just let me go! I belted down the two flights of stairs and through the school corridor towards the main school exit. Then, just as I approached the doors, I heard my name called.

I swung round. It was Tyrese and I stalled abruptly, blinking in surprise.

"Hey…" I managed.

"You OK?"

"Yes, thanks."

"Room 18?"

I nodded.

"Sucks, right?"

I nodded again and brushed my hair back. "How come you're still here?"

"Football practice but I twisted my ankle – so I came off early."

I glanced down at his trainers, then back up. "Oh, does it hurt?"

He shrugged. "A bit...not really."

I think, at this point, I had equalled my record for the longest polite conversation I'd ever had with another kid at Rotney High. The equation *shy girl* plus *hostile, cliquey school* equals *not a lot of talking*.

I shifted awkwardly, thinking of a suitable response. But Tyrese took the lead. He motioned towards the exit with his head. "Are you walking down the High Street?"

I nodded a third time.

"Can I join you?"

My God, a *friendly gesture*. I started smiling, then bit my lip. Hard. What if it was a cunning plot or something? A trap. Maybe he was really Demi's first cousin or nephew or close relative – not that he looked like Demi.

But then maybe I was just being paranoid? Maybe he was just being good natured. Ah, *whatever.*

"Sure."

"Great." He drew level and we walked through the exit doors, past the school blocks and towards the main street.

I felt quite cool. Tyrese was handsome, athletic and very tall. Shame he was a Rotney High pupil. It was kind of like giving your romantic hero terrible body odour and missing teeth.

Suddenly he stopped. "Sorry." He knelt and rubbed his right ankle, wincing.

"You OK?"

"Yeah, just a bit sore."

"Oh."

I glanced around warily. No signs of an ambush, just a stretching, overweight tabby on the other side of the road.

Tyrese stood up. "OK…let's go".

We carried on walking.

"So where do you live?" he asked eventually.

"Opposite St Saviour's Church, just round there."

Tyrese nodded. "Oh, OK. That's not too far. Past the parade, right?"

"Yeah…you?"

"Shit Row."

"Me too."

He stopped walking again and cocked his head. "Why?"

"Why what?"

"Why you in Shit Row?"

I shrugged. "I don't know."

Tyrese considered this profound exchange for a few seconds, then carried on walking.

We approached the shops in silence. Then, unusually, I took the initiative.

"So how did you twist your ankle? Did you get fouled?"

"Yeah. Year 10 slide tackled me from behind. Dirty bastard."

"Sorry. Try putting ice on it. It might help with the – "

"I got him back."

"What?"

"I got him back. Just before I went off. The wanker was on the ground and I stamped on his knee. Ref didn't see. Got my studs right in there."

I nodded. It was the Rotney Way.

"Sounds like he deserved it…"

"Too fucking right. Prick!"

There was another pause, then he changed the subject

"What kind of music you like?"

I thought about this, struggling with the answer. I couldn't stream music on *Spotify* anymore, hadn't watched *YouTube* videos for weeks, and only really used the old clock radio for falling asleep and waking. I needed a cool response but was what that exactly?

"Em…I don't know…. I quite like rap?"

"Rap, yeah – like who?"

"Em…Nicki Minaj…. Lil Wayne…Drake…he's quite good…"

Tyrese nodded. "Yeah, they're solid. Nicki Minaj – she's good… yeah, definitely."

I half grinned again.

"You ever listened to Old Skool Rap? Check out the influences?"

"Em…such as?"

"KRS, Naz, Rakim, Snoop, Notorious B.I.G., Mos Def...?"

"Em.... not really."

"You should check that stuff out if you like rap. I mean we're talking *hard core* hip hop. Those guys kept it real, you know. Easy E, 2 Pac, early Dre, KRS again...I mean these are motherfuckers with attitude, very cool shit. You know? You'd like it."

I shook my head at these foreign names. "It's difficult..."

"Difficult? Why?"

I paused. I couldn't really explain. Not at this point, anyway. I'm sure he also thought, like everyone else, that because I had a white face and comparatively posh accent, I had money. Not an empty fridge, rat-ridden hovel and jailbird father. So, I just shrugged and lapsed into silence. Fortunately, Tyrese left the question dangling and we soon drew level with the newsagents.

"Hey, Antonia? Mind if I pop in here? I'm fucking *starving.*"

"No problem."

"You want anything?"

I blushed. "I haven't got any money."

"That's OK, it's on me."

"Really."

"No sweat, girl."

"Oh, thanks! I wouldn't mind some crisps."

He flashed a grin. "Flavour?"

"Salt and vinegar, please."

"Sure." He opened the newsagents' door and I followed him in. It wasn't the same shop that I'd surprised the armed robber in a few days ago.

That was a few hundred yards away.

Tyrese strode towards the counter while I hung around at the back of the shop, riffling through the newspapers. I vaguely wondered whether there was any more media coverage of the cyber-bullying suicide, perhaps a mention of the police visiting the school in the local rag.

located the *Rotney Times*. There was nothing on the front page. That was all about how someone had set a sleeping tramp on fire, then posted a selfie on *Instagram*. Maybe there was something else further inside? I picked up the top copy, intending to look through it. But I never got that far because as soon as I removed the paper, I was immediately greeted by a familiar, eerie sight.

I dropped the rag and stared ahead as a gigantic shiver rolled up my spine. Then my whole body shuddered as I stumbled backwards.

I retreated through the newsagent's door and collapsed on the floor, hugging myself. Then I bit my lip so I didn't cry and waited quietly. A couple of minutes later, there was some movement from behind and a packet of salt and vinegar crisps dropped into my lap.

"There you go."

I nodded very slightly but didn't move. Instead, I just gazed ahead.

Tyrese closed in. "Hey, I thought you wanted some crisps!"

I glanced in his direction, then turned away.

Tyrese waited patiently for my response, then seated himself to my left when he realized he wasn't getting one.

"What's up?"

I shook my head.

"What?" he repeated.

"You wouldn't understand…." I began.

"Understand what?"

I didn't reply.

"Hey, Antonia…" a softer tone, "what is it? Trouble at home? It's all right…"

I still didn't respond and we sat quietly for a couple of minutes, possibly more. Then I turned in his direction. "Can you do me a favour? Please."

"Sure. You want cheese and onion flavour instead?"

I grinned slightly, then shook my head. "No, it's not that."

"OK. What is it?"

"Can you go back inside the newsagents? Please. On the first shelf, on the left, you'll see a pile of local papers. The *Rotney Times*." I sniffed and looked directly at him. "I want you to tell me if you see anything on top of that pile."

"Like what?"

"Please just tell me, OK?"

"Yeah, all right..." he furrowed his brow and stood up. Then, limping slightly, he went back into the newsagents.

After a few seconds, he came back out, shaking his head.

"There's just papers in there. Nothing else."

Oh God, now he was going think I was crazy. But I wasn't. I knew exactly what I'd seen.

"You sure?"

"Absolutely."

"OK."

"Well, what did you see?"

"Nothing, don't worry about it." I covered my eyes with my right hand and shook my head. Then, embarrassingly, I started to cry softly.

I couldn't help it. I was just so confused.

I thought Tyrese would think I was seriously unhinged at this point and walk off in disgust. But I was wrong. He sat down again and held my left hand. Not in a flirtatious way or anything, just a little act of solidarity. Without even thinking, I lay my head on his shoulder.

We stayed like this for a little while before I finally collected myself and tried taking control of what had turned into an awkward situation.

"I'm so sorry," I said. "Obviously a stupid mistake. I'm so sorry."

I stood up and let go of Tyrese's hand. "I'm so sorry," I said again.

"Long day, obviously. You don't have to stay."

Tyrese stood up too. "Hey," he protested, "at least tell me what you *thought* you saw."

"No, really, I can't, I'm sorry," I said. "It was nothing, anyway. Just a silly mistake."

"Nah, it wasn't," replied Tyrese, firmly. "I'm not that dumb. You saw something. Tell me. Please."

I didn't say anything.

"Come on...I got you some crisps."

I half-smiled but then shook my head. He would never understand. Maybe I should just lie. I tried to think of something remotely convincing.

"I know what you're doing, Antonia," said Tyrese. "Please. Don't do that. Tell me the truth. Even if it sounds crazy."

Still, I couldn't.

"Please."

"It wouldn't mean anything to you. Really. Can we just leave it?"

"I just want to know. That's all. Tell you what, you tell me the truth, I give you my word not to ask you any questions about it. You just tell me the rest when you're ready."

I thought about this offer. It seemed reasonable. But he still wouldn't understand.

Tyrese clenched his fist and beat his heart. "Tell me."

"No questions, all right? Not for now, anyway."

"Deal."

I exhaled.

"Promise? No questions."

"Absolutely."

"OK...I found a photo of an old mate. In a silver frame."

20

Of course, Tyrese was bewildered and didn't understand the significance of what I'd seen. But – to be fair – he kept his word and didn't ask any more questions.

I ate my crisps outside the newsagents, then we shuffled down the High Street, separating a few minutes later.

The flat was empty when I got home. Although I'd just eaten, I ransacked our tiny kitchen again for more food but all I could find was a battered tea bag behind the toaster.

I popped it into my Hello Kitty mug and switched the kettle on. Then I brewed a cup of tea, without milk and sugar and went into my bedroom. I sat on my bed, sipped from my mug and stared directly ahead.

Then I heard footsteps outside and a key in the lock.

"Toni, I've got a couple of bags. Can you give me a hand, please? My back's really killing me."

I jumped up, helped Mum through the front door, and grabbed the plastic shopping bags.

"Sit down, Mum. I'll put the stuff away in the kitchen."

"Thanks, darling."

She sat in the armchair, whilst I emptied the bags and found homes for the contents. There wasn't much, to be honest. A box of eggs, some jam, bread, butter, milk, sugar, coffee, tea bags, a few assorted tins and a packet of sausages.

In Purchester, we had a large American fridge-freezer which was always packed full of stuff. My friends and I were always raiding the fridge but it never seemed to get any emptier. These days, we could run out of food in just a few minutes.

Still, it was good to have something in the kitchen, although it had obviously hurt Mum to go shopping. She was grimacing in pain so I fetched her medicine box and a glass of water. She swallowed half a dozen pills, then grabbed her side,

"Do you want to lie down, Mum? That chair's no good for your back."

"I think I'll have to. Sorry, Toni."

I helped her into the bedroom, lowering her onto the bed, then tucking her under the moldy blankets.

"Thanks, honey. I'll feel better when the painkillers kick in."

"Was work OK?"

"Not too bad. How was your day?"

"Yeah, fine. Fancy an omelette or something?"

"Ah, that would be marvellous. Would you?"

"Sure."

I went back into the kitchen and began preparing dinner. I moved quickly. Mum's medication was so powerful; it would knock her out for hours very shortly. I decided that as soon as she was snoring, I'd head off, looking for Frank.

Five days since I'd last seen him. Five days since our *big conversation*.

After an hour, Mum was sound asleep and I'd also eaten. I didn't even bother telling her I was popping out. Instead, I just left a note on her bedside table, saying I'd be back in a few minutes. Then I walked down the road, ignoring the usual menacing hoodies and arriving at the pub just before seven o'clock.

I spotted Frank immediately. He was sitting at the bar, sipping from a white, chipped mug, and gazing vaguely ahead. I pulled alongside, pecked him on the cheek and plonked down beside him.

"Hey, hero."

"Hey, stranger, where you been?"

"Oh, you know, Rome, Paris, New York…the usual."

Frank nodded. "How are you keeping?"

"All right. You?"

"Just terrific."

I turned to him and lowered my voice. "Listen, something very weird happened this afternoon. I need to talk you about it."

Frank poked his mug forward, then tilted his head in my direction. "Really? But I've got the stone back so nothing should…. oh!"

"What?"

He didn't reply, standing up instead.

"Just remembered. We can't go behind the bar this evening. They've put a load of stuff in there."

"Can't we just talk here?"

"No. It'll fill up in a few minutes. We can go upstairs. Plus, there's something you need to see."

"Really – what's it this time? Another rabbit? Guinea pig? Monkey? Lion cub? Dinosaur?"

"Yeah, yeah – I get it. No, it's not an animal this time. But something you should check out."

I raised my eyebrows. "OK…"

Frank stood up and led me up the rickety stairs. Then he turned left and unlocked the first door in the narrow hall. We entered a pokey room containing a metal bed, saggy armchairs, lopsided cupboard and chest of drawers.

"Welcome to the Ritz. Have a seat."

I sat on an armchair while Frank walked towards the curtained window.

"So anyway," I began, "something really weird – "

He immediately held up a palm, then placed the tip of his finger over his pursed lips.

I stopped mid-sentence – *what?*

He pulled the curtain back slowly, beckoning silently with his fingers. I stood up, shuffled obediently behind and peeked through the narrow gap in the curtain.

I couldn't see anything, just a dark street and a few parked cars.

I shrugged, "what?"

"Keep looking, fifth car down."

I shifted my gaze, focusing intently on the stationary cars. I counted them slowly - one…two…three…four…*five*. What? It was too dark, or was it? I squinted, adjusting my position. Yes, there it was. A small, red car. Possibly a Vauxhall Astra. But so, what? I stared harder, *harder*. Then I saw it.

"Oh, God!"

My head jerked towards Frank who just raised his eyebrows and nodded slowly.

"How long's he been there?" I whispered.

"At least an hour – at least."

"How did you spot him?"

"Practice."

"*Practice?* What do you mean? Has this been happening every night?"

"Maybe. Can't say. He's been busy, though."

I peered through the window again. It was Huck, all right. Just sitting there, motionless.

"What's he doing? What's he waiting for?"

"I don't know. Come away from the window, now. Just in case." He released the curtain which swung back over the glass and I settled back in the armchair, shaking my head.

Then I shot up, again. "Come on, Frank. Let's go and talk to him. What a total weirdo! Seriously, let's go and speak to him."

"No."

"At least, report him! He's…he's harassing a ninety-one-year-old man, we can get him on that."

"*Eighty*-one years old."

"Whatever. He's *stalking* you, Frank."

Frank sat on the edge of the bed, looking completely calm. "Sit down, kid."

I just stood there, glaring.

"Antonia?" More firmly.

"Yes?"

"Will you have a seat, please."

I sat down again, still scowling. "Frank, you got to *say* something. *Do* something."

"Why? He's not bothering me."

"Well, he bothers me. His *face* bothers me." I crossed my arms, frowning even more.

Frank grinned. "Hey, stop sulking."

"Not *sulking.* Just want to whack you round the head."

"Oh, listen to you!" He raised his eyebrows. "Maybe I should report you instead."

I exhaled, in disgust. "Go right ahead. They won't listen to you. They never do."

"Well, there you go, maybe that's why I won't report your pal, Dr Huck."

"*Pal!*" I spluttered, then I saw he was joking so I lapsed into silence. Plus, he was right, of course. I was sulking.

Frank stretched his arms, slowly. "Cup of tea? Diet coke?"

I shook my head, then tutted. Then, I exhaled again. "What are you doing here, Frank? In this *horrible* room – and even more *horrible* place?"

"I told you that last time."

I shook my head. "And where's your wife, Frank? You never talk about her. Where is she?"

"She died – just over four years ago."

"Oh...I'm sorry." I shook my head and blushed, "I'm sorry, that was out of order. It's just I don't really understand anything. I mean, for the *hundredth* time, what is Huck doing out there?"

"Not very much, last time I looked – and it's OK about my wife. She was very sick?"

"Cancer? – I mean, if you don't mind me asking..."

Frank nodded, *yes.*

"I'm sorry. Really."

"It's OK."

There was a slight pause.

"Look," said Frank, "Antonia, I don't know what he's doing or why he's trailing me but that's OK, for now, because - like I said, before - I'm also watching him, trying to figure out his game. Sooner or later, one of us will get the answer he's looking for."

"So, you're not going to say anything to him?"

"No point."

I shrugged in resignation, "whatever…"

I sat back in the armchair and raised my head, studying the cracks in the ceiling. I could hear the music thumping from downstairs. Then I closed my eyes.

The bed creaked opposite. "Hey, Antonia?"

My eyes blinked open and I lowered my head. "Frank?"

"You said you wanted to talk…What's up?"

"Oh, yeah…" I told him about finding the silver photo frame in the newsagents. He reacted with surprise and triumph.

"Hey, I didn't put it there? I mean - how could I, anyway?" Then he raised his palms, "how much more convincing do you need, kid? Like it or not, you're involved with this whole crazy thing. Right?"

I nodded. "But, why? Really – I've got my own problems, Frank - I don't need any of this. I just went to see your first magic show because I thought I was going mad and needed to get out of the house."

Frank shrugged. "Beats me – but…hang on a moment…" He stood up, walked back to the window, pushed back the curtain and glanced out. "I think I've worked out a way forward."

"You have?"

"Yeah." He sat back down on the bed and smiled.

"Well?" I prompted.

"We have to find out what this stone is - I mean, what it really is. What it's capable of. Whether it has a purpose."

"OK – how?"

"Same way it directed me here. Either we get the stone to tell us itself what it is, or get it to point towards someone who can. And I don't mean a geologist, or a jeweller or Inspector Clouseau sitting outside."

"But *how?*"

"I don't know."

"Great. What a terrific idea."

I shook my head, in exasperation. Then we sat in complete silence for a few seconds. Finally, I burst into laughter. "This is hysterical. We're *so* hopeless. We haven't got a Scooby what we're doing."

"Scooby?"

"Scooby Doo. Clue."

Frank looked confused.

"Cockney rhyming slang. Oh, don't worry about it."

"I won't."

I kept on laughing but Frank didn't join in. He creased his brow, looked down, then suddenly straightened.

"Hey! We do the same thing as the atlas. Give the stone a selection of likely areas, likely names – whatever – and let it direct us. It's worked before."

I stopped laughing and considered this. "Again, *how?* How would you do that? Get a telephone directory and keep skimming through it until the stone lights up?"

"No, that would never work." He shook his head. "But we've got to be proactive, keep trying – until we get lucky. See, the thing is, I feel like the stone *wants* to help us but we have to help *it*– if you see what I mean?"

"Yeah, I do. Really. But I still don't know how. Keep thinking, though. I'm sure you'll come up with something."

Frank nodded back. Then I looked round his room again and changed the subject.

"What do you all day, Frank? You can't just visit your son and prepare for magic shows? And how long you staying? Don't you have to go back to Florida?"

"North Carolina – not Florida!"

"Sorry. You know what I mean."

"Yeah, I guess so…Well, they're all good questions."

"Thank you. So, can I have some answers, please?"

"OK, well…I can't stay in England for longer than six months without a visa. I'm just here looking for clues, hints, answers. When I'm not doing the magic stuff, I just go around town, wearing the stone, hoping it will light up and give me a – what did you say – Yogi?"

"Scooby."

"Yeah, give me a Scooby."

I raised my eyebrows, wearily. "So, you've just been wandering around London, hoping to get lucky?"

Frank shrugged, "pretty much."

"But that doesn't make sense, the clue's in Rotney."

"*A* clue."

"No, *the* clue."

Frank shook his. head. "No. *You're* the clue, you're the Rotney clue - I'm fairly sure of that - but it's only one piece of the jigsaw. A main piece, certainly, but not the whole picture."

I straightened up, slowly. "And has the silver photo frame appeared anywhere else? I mean, apart from when I looked in your box of photos. And today. Obviously."

"No."

"OK…" I nodded. "And how long are you going to stay? Six months?"

Frank chuckled. "Well, actually, I'm very much hoping it won't take that long. London's very nice and all – but not Rotney."

"But you don't need to stay in Rotney," I protested. "Certainly, not now you've got your *Rotney clue*. Why can't you go and stay in a decent hotel? Or with your son?"

"Maybe."

I swept my hair back and glanced around the shabby room. "You said you had some more ideas what the stone could be?"

"Yeah, I've given it some thought. To be honest, it's pretty much all I think about these days."

"So, what are your theories?"

"Well, the way I see it, the stone is either terrestrial or extra-terrestrial."

"Meaning?"

"Terrestrial means derived from this planet, extra-terrestrial means of alien origin, created outside or beyond the planet."

"So, it could be a meteor or something?"

"Maybe."

I tilted my head and looked at him accusingly. "Frank, are we talking about *kryptonite?*"

He chuckled again. "No, not at all. Forget about *Superman*, now. I'm being serious, kid. The stone is either from earth or from *beyond* earth."

"How would we know?" We were both a bit unnerved it seemed.

"Very difficult but either way if it's been around for a long time, there may be references to it in ancient literature or drawings."

I jolted forward. "So, somewhere in France, there could be like a cave painting of someone turning a rat into a leopard."

"Maybe. Or accounts or paintings of a stone glowing." His eyes flicked towards the window, then back in my direction. "Or maybe it didn't glow or transform objects, maybe it did something else."

"Like what?"

"I don't know. We don't know. But every kind of gut feeling I have is screaming out that this stone is capable of something else. We haven't tapped into what it truly is, or does."

We. I thought about this. Hating to ask, but I did. Thinking of the car down below. "But it does sound a bit mad, doesn't it? I mean it could just be a stone that lights up for no particular reason – and then you and I scrabble around trying to find a deeper meaning, when, in fact, the whole thing is totally random."

"But it doesn't just light up, does it, Antonia? It has properties."

"Yes," I admitted, "it does." There was another reflective silence. I was beginning to hate those.

"Have you looked online or anywhere else?"

"Yeah, a lot - and I've done a fair bit of research. I also went to the British Library in Kings Cross and a bunch of second hand bookstores in the West End."

"Wow. I'm impressed." My days were spent looking after Mum, and being stuck in school. "Did you discover anything?"

"Not really. This is the problem. I found a ton of stuff about magic stones, enchanted gems and suchlike but nothing that matched the description of our stone."

I frowned. "Nothing at all?"

"No. The closest I could find are so called magic stones where no one really knows what they look like. So theoretically they could be something to do with our stone. But even that's a long shot."

Oh, great, more riddles. "Such as?"

"Well, one of the most famous stones is Lucifer's stone which is supposedly the stone that fell from the Prince of Darkness's crown. It's believed to be source of his power and possibly even the Holy Grail. There's a whole load of history behind it. All very interesting but..."

"But?"

"But everything I read said it was probably an emerald. No one really knows, though."

I shook my head. "Doesn't sound like our stone, does it?"

"No, ma'am, it doesn't. See, I figure that when I get a clue, it'll fairly jump out and smack me across my big mouth. I'll *know* it when I *see* it, that's for sure."

"So, what you going to do?"

"Just keep looking, keep thinking, I don't know. Something will turn up. You'll see."

"I hope so. Good luck, I guess." I checked my watch. "I better get back, actually."

"Already?"

"Yeah, long day. Sorry." I stood up slowly, my back tweaking slightly from the old armchair's lack of support

Frank exhaled and got up. "I understand."

I turned towards the door, then wheeled round. "Can I look at it?"

"The stone?"

I nodded.

Frank opened the top of his shirt, unclasped the neck chain and handed it over. I held it in the palm of my hand and gazed at it.

Red, round. Mesmeric.

I kept studying it. "You strange thing. What's your secret?"

There was no response.

I lifted it by a few inches. *"Why Frank?"*

Nothing.

"Why, me? *Why Antonia?"*

Nothing.

"Come on. *Please.* Why are you here? What do you want? How can we help you? How can you help us?"

Still nothing. I handed the stone back to Frank and watched him place it around his neck again.

"It's true," I mumbled, eventually. "You do feel pretty dumb talking to a piece of a rock."

Frank grinned. "Ah, don't worry about it. I've also done my fair share of asking it questions. Especially, after its light show. Come on – I'll walk you back."

"Thanks." I smiled widely. "But won't Huck see us leaving together, though? Realize we're a team or something."

Another chuckle. "I'm sure he knows anyway."

"Fine," I shrugged.

Frank grabbed a jacket from a hook on the bedroom door and we descended the pub's stairs together. There were more people on the ground floor now, unknown music thumping through the ceiling speakers. We dodged through several tattooed arms and shaved heads, then out through the main exit.

Frank paused for a moment, peered down the street, then started walking.

"Still there," he whispered.

"Hmm. So, weird."

We kept going and I could see my miserable block of flats getting closer all the time. Suddenly, I stopped and looked at Frank.

"The clue is the silver frame, isn't it? It *must* be. It's the photo." I took a deep breath. "I mean, why that photo? It's not just a random object, or a random picture. It's a message, Frank. To you. And to me. I'm sure of it. It's the key that unlocks the whole thing. It has to be."

Frank nodded slowly. "Yeah...but I can't work out why. You know, I never liked that photo much. I was pretty glad to lose the original all those years ago."

"That's a shame. I think it's stunning."

We looked at each other, paused in thought. Then I noticed two hooded figures shuffling quickly towards us. I nudged Frank gently and he glanced up.

The two hoodies slowed down slightly and closed in on Frank.

Not the usual grubby ones that circled my flat. These two were dressed more fashionably and clean-shaven. I estimated they were in their late teens, early twenties. Both tall, pale, gaunt and sporting assorted rings, studs and finger tattoos. The taller one wore white Adidas trainers and his shorter mate wore blue Nike sneakers.

The taller one opened proceedings. "Hello, mate. Nice evening."

"Yes, quite pleasant," agreed Frank. "How can I be of assistance?"

"Oh, cool accent. Where you from?"

"North Carolina born and bred."

"Where's that - America?"

Frank nodded. "That's an affirmative."

"All right!" The hoodies exchanged approving glances.

"'Oi mate," called the second hoodie, "you been to Hollywood?"

Frank wrinkled his nose. "Yeah, a few years back."

"Wicked. So, do you know that bloke? Fuck me, what's his name? Oh, you know, he was in..." He tapped his forehead. "Ah, *fucking hell*...can't remember now..."

"Gents," interrupted Frank, "this is all very interesting but I need to escort this young lady home so if you don't mind..."

He attempted to walk on but the first hoodie blocked his path. "Steady, mate…steady…" He pushed Frank back slightly. "Just wanted to ask you another question, that's all."

Hoodie two scratched his chin and grinned.

Frank frowned. "I'll let that go but not the next time. What's your question?"

"My question?" repeated hoodie one. "My question is what's in your fucking wallet? That's my question, grandpa."

"Don't carry one, sorry. But there's an ATM around the corner."

"A what?"

"An ATM. Automated Teller Machine. I believe the English call it a *cashpoint*. So, if you require funds, I suggest you pay it a visit – and take your pal with you."

The first hoodie laughed and was quickly joined by the second hoodie.

Then hoodie one reached into his trouser pocket and snapped open a large flick knife.

He leaned in towards Frank, his mirth suddenly transforming into a psychotic glare. The knife dangling from his right fist.

"Wrong fucking answer, my ancient *cunt.* SO be a good *cunt* and hand over your wallet, otherwise I'm going to cut your girlfriend's face open and slash your fucking windpipe. And my mate, here, will piss in your mouth as you lie dying. How would you like that, you dirty piece of shit?"

Hoodie two grinned and blew me a wet kiss.

Frank raised his eyebrows. "Well, seeing as you put it like that, maybe I do have a wallet after all." He fumbled inside his jacket, "now where is it…. hey, here it is!"

His right fist shot out so fast, I didn't even see it. Neither did hoodie one as it smashed into his face. He reeled backwards, collapsing onto the pavement. Then Frank stepped forward and kicked him viciously in the crotch, forcing him to scream in agony.

Hoodie two immediately darted in but Frank side kicked his extended knee so powerfully, it snapped his leg, leaving the lower half jutting at a grotesque angle. The hoodie teetered backwards in complete shock, blood gushing through his right trouser leg and seeping downwards.

"That's a compound fracture, pal, "advised Frank, coldly. "Three months in hospital, I'd say. Maybe more. They can get complicated."

But Hoodie two wasn't listening now, he was screeching. Wailing like a demented dog before tumbling awkwardly on top of his mate. Then both drifted into silence as they blacked out.

Frank turned back, "you OK, kid?"

I stared at the small obscene pile of bodies and shuddered. Frank gripped my arm gently. "Antonia?"

I looked up into his eyes, shaking even more.

"Hey…it's OK, kid…. it's OK." He pulled me closer until my trembling eased, then let go gradually. "Come on, now. It's all over. Let me take you home."

21

The next morning at Rotney High was tedious. Tyrese smiled at me but we didn't talk, then we had double Science.

I kept running last night's conversation and events through my mind but couldn't reach any dazzling new conclusions. When I closed my eyes, I could see Hoodie two's distorted leg. I imagined him regaining consciousness, maybe writhing on the ground, moaning, screaming, and passing out again. Horrible.

And his charming buddy was in even worse shape. Slammed by the meanest, fastest punch I had ever seen, including in the movies. Then the old man had crushed his balls. Charming.

Still they both deserved it.

Half seriously, I started looking out for the silver photo frame again. Wondering where it would turn up next.

But two hours later, I was hurled back to reality. As I was leaving the lunch hall, I spotted a familiar, unwelcome figure in the queue. She wasn't stabbing another pupil in the face, or ripping out their heart. Just standing still, gawping ahead.

Demi.

Where had she been, anyway? I hadn't seen her since our little incident and hoped she'd either been excluded, or banged up. Sadly, not.

Tremendous.

She didn't see me and as I headed down the Hall to the West Block I began thinking, quickly. There was only another three hours of school left. I just had to keep out of her way, then head over to Frank's for a refresher course in beating her up.

I sincerely doubted whether she'd learnt any kind of lesson. She was too dumb for that. I'd humiliated and punished her - she'd *certainly* be out for revenge, sooner or later. Probably, sooner. Maybe she'd replaced her flick knife for a samurai sword or machine gun.

Oddly, I didn't feel frightened. She was just a repulsive bully - but I didn't want the aggravation of another encounter. If only Frank could use his stone to make her disappear, or at least transform her into an insect. Then I could stamp on her.

I hurried down the hall, checking my timetable, Single History, then Child Development. Not too bad. Could have been much worse – double Maths, for example.

I arrived at the classroom a few minutes early and sat quietly at the back.

We'd moved on a few centuries from the Gunpowder Plot and were learning about the causes of the First World War.

The History teacher, Mr. Shaw, was a much better teacher than Miss Karia. He even had a sense of humour!

The truth was I quite liked History. It was a guilty secret. I also found big wars fascinating. It demonstrated what happened when human beings couldn't sort out their differences and behave like "grown-ups".

In the case of the First World War, they blew each other into smithereens and killed off a whole generation. Then, twenty-one years later, they killed each other all over again, except on an even bigger scale.

I closed my eyes. There was Hoodie two's leg again, smashed and distorted. The coward's reward for calculating an old man and young girl were easy pickings. I tried changing the mental image but it was impossible. You just can't visualize peaceful summer meadows in Rotney. Only blades and broken limbs.

Kids started filing in to the classroom. An ugly lot – apart from Tyrese. Losers in life's nasty lottery - like me.

What had they done to end up in Rotney? Possibly something seriously evil in a former life. And it was karma. Or maybe they hadn't done anything. Maybe they were just the victims of a bored, sadistic Being. Who knew?

All these teachers, policemen, prison officers, journalists and politicians couldn't explain why life was so totally unfair and despicable, could they? Silly, pompous idiots – all of them. Full of empty air and rubbish.

I sighed and opened my eyes as Mr. Shaw walked into the classroom.

After fifteen minutes of the lesson, it all went wrong.

What happened was – predictably, I suppose – Mr. Shaw asked me a question.

There are two basic types of teachers. Type one – and vastly preferable – is the type that poses a question to the class. Some show-off usually replies and gets a few brownie points, even if their answer's wrong. Type two, picks on you – then behaves sarcastically if they sense you don't know anything about the subject.

Miss Karia was a type two, the dismal cow. However, Mr. Shaw was a type one but with type two *tendencies*. This meant that most of the time he would ask open questions but occasionally threw out a specific one.

Today, the Battle of Tannenberg.

Mr. Shaw asked me to list the factors for why the Germans had destroyed the Russian Second Army. Not a hard question and I knew the answer. The required response was:

> *"Sir, it was the German's rapid rail movements and the Russian's failure to encode their radio messages."*

Job done. Move on.

But - I don't know. Maybe I was riled by seeing Demi again. Maybe I'm just an idiot. Or maybe I just saw an opportunity to be clever.

You see, Mr. Shaw didn't specify which Battle of Tannenberg. Last week, I stumbled on an empty computer bay and read around the subject, on *Wikipedia*. I now knew there had been an earlier battle of that name in 1410.

Mr. Shaw was obviously talking about the second Battle of Tannenberg, which was fought in August 1914 but he didn't say that. In the second Battle, the Germans had destroyed the Russians but in the first battle, the Polish-Lithuanians had thumped the Germans, or more accurately the Teutonic knights. So, this is how it played out.

Mr. Shaw: "Now - Antonia – what factors led to the Germans destroying the Russians at the Battle of Tannenberg?"

Antonia: "Excuse me?"

Mr. Shaw: "Try paying attention, please. I asked what factors led to the Germans destroying the Russians at the Battle of Tannenberg?"

Antonia: "Battle of Tannenberg, sir?"

Mr. Shaw: "Yes, the Battle of Tannenberg, Antonia."

Antonia: "Sir, I think you're confused."

Mr. Shaw: How so?

Antonia: "Well, sir, the Germans were defeated at the Battle of Tannenberg.

Mr. Shaw: Antonia, the Germans wiped out the Russian Second Army at Tannenberg and the Russian commander ended up killing himself."

Antonia: "No sir, at the Battle of Tannenberg the Teutonic Knights were defeated. And it wasn't the Russians. It was the Polish-Lithuanians."

(Thoughtful frown, dramatic pause, then sharp glare.)

Mr. Shaw: "Room 18 – and get out the class."

Antonia: "But it's true, sir! The Teutonic Knights were defeated at – "

Mr. Shaw: "Get out! You know perfectly well what I'm talking about. And I'll be talking to Miss Patel about your disruptive behaviour! Out!"

So, I got out. The class watched in complete silence, even Tyrese. I'm sure not even one of them knew what I was talking about. But once I was back in the school corridor. I cursed my stupidity. I had proved nothing, amused nobody – and now recklessly placed myself in danger. Leaving an hour after school was dangerous, especially with Demi back.

I banged my head slowly and deliberately against the wall. Stupid idiot.

This would never have happened at Mount High. Thanks Dad. You've ruined my life. He was the one requiring parental and child development lessons, not me.

Lesson number one, Mr. Daddy Davidson. Don't break the law and get sent to prison.

Lesson two, don't get your name splattered all over the tabloids and lose all your earthly possessions. Lesson three, don't let your poor, innocent family, especially your precious daughter, wind up in a tiny, rat-infested, flat in Rotney.

Got it? Three simple lessons, Mr. *Ex*-Compliance Partner.

I checked my watch and looked around. Twenty-five minutes to go, this time. Probably not a big deal, unless Demi and Nose Ring appeared around the corner.

I walked slowly through the corridor, searching for a chair. After a few moments, I passed a classroom and peered through the small pane of glass in the door. It was full so I kept going. However, the next class-room down was empty. I bounded inside and grabbed the nearest chair.

As I turned around, I heard an object drop loudly inside the cupboard, to the left of the teacher's desk. Most classrooms had the same layout and furniture and there was nothing unusual about this one.

I wondered if Demi was hiding in the cupboard, she was so sneaky. Possibly another ambush. Then I dismissed the thought, headed back towards the hall, then changed my mind and turned around. I walked towards the cupboard and opened the door. There was nothing very exciting on the cupboard's shelves, a few textbooks and mugs but I could see what had fallen on the floor.

I recognized the dents in the back.

I didn't freak out this time. It was almost a welcome distraction, like discovering an old friend. I picked the silver frame off the floor, turned it over and wiped the dust away from Frank's familiar mournful expression with my sleeve. Then, still holding a chair, I walked out of the classroom, closing the door behind me.

I planted the chair outside Mr. Shaw's classroom, then sat down and stared intently at the photograph, grasping the frame with both hands.

Why had it shown up, again? In my school, in a classroom, in a *cupboard*?

What had Frank said again about the photo frame - *it started to keep appearing and vanishing all over the place.* And yet... in the few examples he'd given – the toilet, the waiting room and the study – the frame appeared when he was alone. Then what? It somehow vanished when other people came along. Was that a connection?

Come on Antonia, think! The first time I discovered the frame was behind the pub, just me. The second time was in the newsagents. Again, just me. Tyrese didn't see the frame and then it disappeared. Now, the third time - again, *just me.* No one else around.

So, there *was* an obvious pattern. What would happen when other people appeared, when someone walked through the corridor, or when Mr. Shaw's history lesson finished? Would the frame vanish, or become visible to others?

I smiled. This was the breakthrough. I checked my watch. Seven minutes to go. *Not long.*

Maybe I just should just burst into the history class, waving the silver fame. That would solve the problem all right. I didn't care about the Battle of Tannenberg, or Room 18, or exclusions anymore. I just cared about the silver frame.

The minute hand clicked again. I heard it. Six minutes. I wondered if Mr. Shaw was finishing off now. I edged towards the classroom door and peered discreetly through the pane of glass. No one was putting their textbooks away so I paced up and down the corridor for another couple of minutes, then looked through the pane again.

Great. Pupils were placing their belongings in their bags and standing up. *At last.* The lesson was clearly over. I pressed my head against the pane, watching closely, then suddenly an enormous object slammed into the centre of my head and threw me backwards. The world unwound and thudded to a halt, descending into blackness.

When I came to, I was sitting on a chair in an empty classroom.

Most doors open inwards. If you're going into a building or a room, you push the door away. Then when you leave that building or room, you bring the door towards you.

But there are exceptions and I'd just encountered one. Literally.

A few months ago, a group of Year 11 pupils set part of the West Bock on fire. I don't know the specific details but apparently, the fire damage destroyed all the structural frames and hinges. When the classroom doors were reinstalled, they all opened externally.

The meant that people strolling through the Block's corridor occasionally got badly smacked, or even knocked out, if they strayed too near a classroom door

Pressing your head *right against* an externally opening West Block door – especially when a class was concluding - wasn't very intelligent behaviour. So, when I regained consciousness, my first thought was – *my head really hurts.* Then I just felt unbelievably stupid.

Mr. Shaw's head appeared on my left. "Oh, hello, you back with us?"

For a moment, I considered responding in French and insisting I was Joan of Arc but dismissed the thought. For a start, I couldn't speak French and secondly, I was more concerned about puking.

"Shouldn't stand too close to that door." A younger voice, from behind. Tyrese.

"You think?" I groaned.

Mr. Shaw half smiled. ""How do you feel, now?"

"Terrific, Mr. Shaw, thank you."

In fact, I felt like a large pack of hyenas had used my head as a toilet. Then an elephant had turned up and stomped on my brains.

"All right, Antonia, just sit there for a little while," instructed my teacher, "until you feel better."

"Thanks, sir. I wasn't planning on going anywhere."

I closed my eyes and took some deep breaths. Then I *remembered*. "Sir…"

"Yes."

My eyes flicked open." Did I drop anything on the floor? Apart from my bag?

Mr. Shaw frowned. "Like what?"

"Like… "

I almost blurted *a silver photo frame*, when I realized it would freak Tyrese out. He'd think I gone completely insane. Blubbering about the same stupid thing again.

"Like…anything?" I added, lamely.

"No. Why? Do you think you dropped something?"

"Just a Cartier necklace, sir. Doesn't matter. I've got plenty more at home."

Mr. Shaw shook his head. "Always, joking, aren't you, Antonia? You're a pain in the neck. Do you know what happened to men with a sense of humour in the First World War?"

"Yes, sir. They ordered thousands of men to walk very slowly at firing machine guns."

Mr. Shaw thought about this. "Tyrese, can you go and get Antonia a glass of water, please? Thank you."

Movement from behind, then it faded.

"I think he cares about you," whispered Mr. Shaw. "Insisted on hanging around until you were OK."

I shrugged. "He probably just wanted an excuse to miss the beginning of

Child Development."

"No. I think he cares about you."

I just shrugged again.

Mr. Shaw leaned slightly closer. "I'm not your form teacher, Antonia, as you know. That's Miss Patel. I spoke to her recently about you because...well, I was quite concerned about you."

"Are we going to have a heavy talk, sir? Only I think I'm going to chuck up."

"I think you'll be OK. Unfortunately, you're not the first person to have been hit by that door. And we're only chatting."

"Yes, sir."

Mr. Shaw paused for a few seconds. "You know, Antonia, we're not completely unsympathetic. We know you've had a torrid time because of what happened to your father. We know you're obviously angry, probably frightened too. Let's be honest, Rotney isn't the greatest neighbourhood. And this a tough school. *Very* tough. No doubt about it.

"But the way you're going...you're going to get excluded. And you might think that would be a wonderful thing but it wouldn't be, I promise you. You'd end up somewhere even worse and then somewhere even worse after that – and the tragedy of it is you could achieve so much if you wanted to. If only you had a better attitude."

Whatever. My head was pulsating like a metronome on steroids.

Tyrese reappeared, carrying a plastic cup of water. I accepted it with a little smile.

"OK, thanks, Tyrese," said Mr. Shaw. "Go to your next lesson now, I can handle this."

Tyrese shuffled uneasily and glanced in my direction. "Are you feeling a bit better?"

I nodded. "Thanks for the water."

Tyrese nodded back but didn't move.

"Tyrese," said Mr. Shaw again, "I got this."

"Yes sir." He winked at me and set off for Child Development.

I sipped from the plastic cup and adjusted my position. I was feeling slightly less woozy but my forehead still hurt like hell.

I wanted to go home but Mr. Shaw hadn't finished. He sat down opposite me and pinched the bridge of his nose.

"Look, Antonia, as I just said, you've had a tough time, a really tough time – no doubt about it – but it could still be an awful lot worse for you. You need to try and count your blessings and be grateful for what you have right now."

"Right now, I have a massive headache, sir."

"You know I'm not talking about that, Antonia, in the same way that you knew perfectly well which Battle of Tannenberg I was asking about. But you couldn't resist getting your little joke in, could you?"

I didn't respond.

Mr. Shaw straightened up, slightly. "You know, my grandfather was killed in August 1916, at the Battle of the Somme?"

I glanced down. "I'm sorry, sir. I lost family too."

"Really. Who?"

"My great-great-uncle, sir. He was gassed at the Battle of Loos. I think he was trying to gas the Germans and the wind blew it back into the British trenches. His gas mask didn't protect him and he was blinded. For a bit. He survived, though, but then he got his legs blown off at Passchendaele, two years later."

Mr. Shaw shook his head sadly. "Poor man - a brave man, though. So many of them were. I think it makes a difference when history actually affects you personally."

"Yes, sir."

"But do you remember what I just asked you?"

"About Tannenberg, sir?"

"No, about men with a sense of humour in the First World War."

"Yes, sir, I thought I gave you an answer."

"No, I think you gave me a critique of Douglas Haig."

"Sir?"

"He was called the Butcher of the Somme because of his military tactics which – as you mentioned – involved a lot of men walking slowly towards firing machine guns. But, in fact, Haig was fairly instrumental in the Allied victory of 1918 and quite a maligned figure."

I nodded sympathetically. I felt like someone approaching a machine gun blasting golf balls at my forehead, with devastating accuracy.

"But I digress, Antonia. The men with the sense of humour in the trenches were particularly valued because they kept the others going. Kept their spirits up despite all the horror, violence and death surrounding them. A sense of humour is the most valuable, attractive commodity but it must be used appropriately or it can become a weapon. Do you understand?"

"Yes, sir."

Mr. Shaw tilted his head.

"Your father was a Cambridge scholar, wasn't he?"

I frowned. "No, he went to Cambridge but he didn't get a scholarship. The tabloids just lied about that. And he didn't get a first either. Another lie. He got a second from Trinity Hall."

"Well, a degree from Trinity Hall is still very impressive. You obviously come from a clever family."

"Yeah – but it all went wrong with me, sir, I'm so stupid it hurts." I rubbed my head to demonstrate this.

"Nonsense, you're a very bright girl. And I absolutely shouldn't say this but you're a bloody Einstein, compared to some of the kids in this school."

"But so are the living dead, sir."

"What?"

"The living dead, sir. Zombies. Undead walkers. They're also Einstein compared to half the kids in this school."

Mr. Shaw laughed at this. "No comment." Then he leaned forward again. "You know who one of the greatest wits of our time was?"

I thought about this. "Hitler?"

Mr. Shaw rolled his eyes. "No, not Hitler! I'd hardly describe him as a stand-up comic."

"Yeah but he had a funny moustache, sir. Made me laugh. What about the Pope? He wears a funny hat and gown."

Mr. Shaw shook his head. "Obviously that door hit you harder than I thought. No, not the Pope. I'm talking about *wit*, Antonia. Verbal comic ability. Something you seem to have no shortage of."

I thought about this some more. "The Queen. I love her Christmas broadcasts."

"No, now you're just being silly."

"I'm not, sir! I *do* love her Christmas broadcasts."

Mr. Shaw exhaled. Yes, I'm sure you do, Antonia. I was talking about Winston Churchill. In fact, not just a brilliant wit but also a great leader. Certainly, saved our bacon in the Second World War, and arguably the civilized world."

"Yes, sir. Are you comparing me to Churchill? I mean, don't worry, it's easily done."

"No, I'm not, as you well know. But what I'm saying is that you can take humour, intelligence, wit and talent and shape it in any direction you choose. Look, I think everyone can achieve greatness – but I think you have more resources than most to work from, Antonia. As I just said, if you apply yourself, there's no limit to what you can achieve."

"Isn't that a film quote, sir?"

"Possibly. Probably. It's hardly an original concept but that doesn't make it any less valid. Here's another quote. *There are no limits. There are plateaus, but you mustn't stay there, you must go beyond them.*"

"Churchill?"

"No. Bruce Lee."

I beamed. Bruce Lee again! "That's cool, sir. I like that."

Another flickering half-smile. "After the First World War, we'll study Churchill and the Second World War – but Churchill featured heavily in the First World War, as well. He learnt and adapted from his mistakes and adverse circumstances. The Gallipoli campaign in 1915 was his baby but it went terribly wrong and he spent the next 20 years defending his actions. But Churchill came back from his adversity and wilderness years to play a vital role in facing and defeating the greatest evil of our time."

Mr. Shaw paused for a few seconds, then leaned closer.

"Look, Antonia," he said. "I know you probably think I'm a bit of a jerk. A conceited, know-nothing teacher, but there's a fundamental difference between teachers and journalists. Journalists are interested in bringing a person down. That's why they gleefully repeated the fact that your father was a Cambridge scholar and had a big house. Crushing him made good copy and fed the dark, envious side of the masses. But teachers are interested in raising a person up, inspiring them, trying to get them to achieve their potential. And believe me, you've got potential, Antonia. You really have."

Suddenly I lost my desire to maintain the wisecracks. For a second, I thought I might even cry – but that was unforgivable in front of a teacher. Instead, I breathed in and composed myself.

"Thank you, sir. My Dad's a good man, despite what those idiots wrote. But as of now, the only thing I can really concentrate on is just keeping it together and not drowning."

Mr. Shaw nodded, slowly. "I know. And it can't be easy. But maybe this is your trial and by going through this, you'll learn how to gain strength and resilience. And once you've overcome it – and you *will* overcome it, believe me – you can refuse to accept the way things are and help make the world a better place."

"How can I do that?"

"By tapping into your passion and through one positive act at a time. I'm not saying anything new here but you learn through *doing*, not just reading and hearing. You should *internalize* the message and act on it. But you must never give up, you must keep going forward. As the German philosopher Nietzsche is supposed to have said, *"Whatever doesn't kill you, makes you stronger."*

I nodded. "Yeah, I think I've heard that one before. It's a quite a famous saying, isn't it?"

Mr. Shaw nodded back. "Yes, it is. And worth paying attention to."

We lapsed into silence, then I leaned forward. "Sir?"

"Antonia?"

"Can we make a deal, sir?"

He raised his eyebrows. "A *deal*? What kind of deal?"

I coughed, nervously. "Well, sir, I was thinking. If you could let me home early as I have a truly terrible headache and let me off Room 18 – and stop asking me direct questions in class – you know, let me volunteer answers instead – I'll be a good girl and stop annoying you. Not only that, I absolutely promise to make the world a better place."

Mr. Shaw laughed. "That's your deal?"

I maintained a straight face. "Yes sir."

Mr. Shaw studied my expression, carefully. "All right. Tell you what, go home now and I'll think about it."

"Yes, sir. Thank you, sir."

I winced slightly as I stood up. Then I grabbed my bag and bolted out of the door before he changed his mind.

22

I t's funny but when I got out of the classroom, I couldn't quite
tell if I was elated because I'd got out of Room 18 and could go
home early, or just lightheaded from being concussed. Probably,
a combination of both.

After leaving the classroom, I quickly scanned the hall but there
was no sign of the silver photo frame. Maybe this was the real reason
I was feeling high. I knew I'd had my first breakthrough.

It seemed clear that only Frank and I could see the silver frame.
But *how?* And *why?*

I bolted down the flight of stairs on the first floor – probably a
bit too quickly as I still felt distinctly strange – and strode along the
ground floor leading to the main school gates. Then I emerged into
the fresh air, a chilly wind piercing through my nose and ears.

I breathed in deeply, threw my head back and flung my arms open
wide. *Freedom!* I didn't care that loads of other pupils could probably
see me out their classroom windows. This was my moment. Antonia's
special time.

I gathered myself slightly and walked, almost skipping, out the
school grounds, turning right into the High Street. Then I froze.

Demi was standing about twenty metres away, in the middle of
the pavement, talking to three huge black boys. I recognized one of
them, he was in Year 11 but didn't exactly look like a pupil. More like

a fully-fledged gangster. The other two, looked older, in their late teens and were heavily adorned in bling.

I think my heart stopped. I really do. That's not just an expression. My breathing ceased entirely and I became incapable of movement. Then I tried thinking – but I couldn't. I was paralyzed.

Instead, I gawped at the small, menacing group from the edge of the street corner. Five seconds…. ten seconds…. fifteen seconds. *Do something.* Come on, or they'll see you. Turn around? *No.* Walk past them? *You're joking.* OK, so what? *Cross the road discreetly and hope for the best.*

The four of them seemed pretty absorbed in their conversation so, without thinking any more, I wandered ever-so-casually across the road. I didn't turn around but my body was pulsating with agitation again. I imagined every stride was a step nearer safety but I resisted the increasing temptation to burst into a sprint.

I reached the other side, turned right and kept going. A few seconds later, I was parallel with the posse. *Just a few more paces,* I thought, *then break loose and run like hell.* Slowly, slowly, I began pulling away.

Then I heard it. A brutal, tribal yell.

"OI!"

Demi.

Instinctively, my head jerked back in the direction of the disturbance but then my legs overrode all bodily functions and I burst into a frenzied dash. I accelerated faster than a rocket, driven by pure, burning fear.

Trees, houses, pedestrians, parked cars and shops flew by as I tore down the centre of street, panting heavily, my forehead thumping with pain. Then suddenly a wave of acute nausea flooded the back of my head and seeped forward.

Oh, God. I began gagging and tumbling, legs crumbling below. *No, no.* The High Street began darkening. *I was losing consciousness!* I kept forcing my way forward, just a few more metres, just a few more…

Then a hellish concoction of sickness, terror and resignation slammed my gut with everything it had and I hit the pavement. I rolled around groping and choking, still fighting uselessly. But what was the point? This was the end. A sad, pathetic death in the centre of Rotney High Street.

Maybe even a small paragraph on page 11 of *The Rotney Times.*

I'd got it all wrong. Finding the frame wasn't a positive thing, quite the opposite. It was a ghastly omen. And now Demi would be my judge, jury and executioner.

I kept battling as everything continued dimming. Clinging on desperately. Breathing slower, deeper, steadier but Rotney kept fading away and I finally let go.

"You all right, love?"

I opened my eyes. *Groggy.* Then I glanced down slowly. All my limbs appeared present, no sign of any meat cleavers.

My brain started rebooting and I tilted my head upwards.

"Can you hear me?"

A blurred, hovering image, pulling into focus. Two peering observers, strangers. The first, a middle-aged lady, worn jeans, rings, white jacket, no tattoos, respectable. The second, an older man, duffle coat, brown trousers, blue, button down shirt, also respectable.

I was lying on the ground. *God…how long had I been out?*

"You all right, love?"

Same question - again. Just being kind, I suppose, but *all right people* don't exactly pass out in the middle of the High Street. Not before pubs close, anyway.

I nodded slowly, then I remembered.

Demi? Where was she?

I tried sitting up so I could survey my surroundings better but felt so nauseous I fell back.

"Whoa! Easy, love!" exclaimed the lady.

I ignored her. *Priorities, Antonia.* My eyes darted around crazily but my line of vision was so compromised, I could only make out moving legs and car wheels.

"I shouldn't have missed Child Development," I groaned.

The lady looked confused. "What, dear?"

"Nothing. I'm sorry, I need to get out of here. Can you help me up, please?"

"Don't you need an ambulance?" asked the older man. "I can call one. You should always get yourself checked out at A & E if you pass out."

"No, really," I insisted, "I'm OK, just overdid it a bit after running into a door earlier."

I tried sitting up again, slower this time. More deliberately. Nausea struck again but I struggled through.

From my raised position, I examined the street again. There was still no sign of Demi, or her band of villainous brothers. In fact, I'd covered *a lot* more ground than I thought. The school was at least half a mile down the road. I must have been really spooked!

But the situation was still dangerous, obviously. Demi was so devious.

I exhaled. "Honestly, I'm fine, really…. but I need to get out of here."

The lady remained concerned. "You in trouble, hon? Someone attack you?"

"No, no, really," I mumbled. She was very sweet but this was just embarrassing. "I have to go…I'm sorry. Thank you. Thank you, again."

I pulled myself up and began walking shakily down the street. My brain debated the merits of blacking out again but finally injected my body with renewed energy.

I picked up pace again, still madly surveying my environment. I didn't fancy being savagely ambushed or bundled into a waiting car.

By the time I got home, I felt terribly sore, thirsty and tired but mightily relieved. I was early, of course. Mum wouldn't be back for a couple of hours. I went into the kitchen and made a cheese sandwich. I wolfed it down, then checked the cupboard. No silver photo frame, this time, but two tins of baked beans. Once I located the tin opener, I scooped up the beans with a metal fork and finished off my little feast with a cup of tea.

At least there was food in the kitchen today. Well done, Mum.

I headed into my bedroom, whipped off my jacket and shoes and sunk onto the bed. God, it was absolute bliss. I stared up at the dented ceiling, counting the familiar cracks. Then I closed my eyes, ignored the thumping pain in the back of my head, breathed ever so deeply then fell into a beautiful slumber...

PIIIIING! The doorbell. A jarring, intrusive whine.

I ignored it, cursing silently. Then it rang again. And again. I checked my watch. Just after five in the evening. I'd been asleep for over an hour.

Maybe Mum had forgotten her key? I rolled carefully off the bed but as soon as I sat up, I felt raw. Then another thought. *What if it's Demi?* Maybe the psychopath had followed me home?

I rubbed my forehead with my palm, frowning. Then I stood up slowly.

Boy, I felt *terrible.* I hated being woken up from a deep sleep. It was so disorientating.

I stumbled down the hall, swearing at the persistent ringing. Even at my sleepy, awkward pace, it was a very short journey. Then I halted at the front door, bewildered. There was no spyhole, or anything like that, so I did the next obvious thing.

"Who is it?" I yelled.

"Antonia! Thank God. Where've you been? Open up!"

Frank. Of course. He knew where I lived but I'd never invited him in. It was too embarrassing – plus, Huck might show.

I opened the front door quickly, hoping there wasn't a problem. But there clearly wasn't. In fact, the old man was virtually dancing on the spot, beaming with excitement and clenching his white fists.

I smiled, despite myself. "What's up with you?"

He bounded forward and hugged me. Then he spun me around, grinning insanely. Eventually, I broke free.

"You're crazy! What is it?"

Frank shook his head. "Massive breakthrough. *Massive!*"

I stepped back. He was clearly serious. "Really? *What?*"

"Not here - and not my place either. And by the way, I'm pretty sure I know what our pal, Huck, was up to."

"You do?"

"Uh-huh."

"What?"

"No, not here."

"Oh, OK…sorry, what are we doing?"

"I know somewhere." He glanced at my socks. "Come on. Put some shoes on."

I exhaled loudly. "I'm actually half asleep. And I might pass out on the way - if you can handle that?"

"No, you won't. You'll be just fine. Put your shoes on."

"Whatever."

I turned towards my bedroom, then turned back.

"Hey, how do you know I was in and not still at school?"

"I didn't. Well – I had a hunch."

"A *hunch?*" I shook my head. "What does that mean?"

He grinned. "Hurry up."

"All right…. Stay there, I'll get ready."

I slipped back into my bedroom and pulled on my shoes and jacket. Then I popped into the bathroom and soaked my face in cool water. Feeling more alert, I grabbed my keys from the kitchen, strode down the hall and joined the old man outside. I locked the door and faced him.

"Let's go."

Frank set off immediately, surging forward at an outrageous pace. I accelerated into a fast jog just keeping up, my shoes clattering rapidly along Rotney's seedy pavements.

"Whoa, easy! *Easy!*" I gasped. "Where we going? And why can't we go back to your place? At least it's got a couch."

"You don't have a couch?"

"No, the bailiffs took it. "

"Bailiffs?"

"Yeah, bailiffs. The guys who take things away if you don't keep up payments."

"Oh – repo men?"

"Yeah, *repo men*. My couch got repossessed."

"I'm sorry to hear that. Those guys are obnoxious."

"Yup." I swear he was getting faster! "So, are you going to tell me where we're going?"

"Little quiet coffee place. About hundred yards away."

"What? No such thing in Rotney!"

"Yeah, there is. Discovered it by chance. It's quite pleasant, actually - so no one goes in there."

"Impossible, it would have been burnt down by now."

"Yeah, you'd think!"

He was moving so furiously we covered the distance in a few more seconds, then Frank turned sharply right into a small café. In fact, it was *tiny* which probably explained why I'd never seen it before."

It was entirely empty apart from a Mediterranean-looking guy standing behind a counter. He nodded at us amiably as we entered. There were only a couple of tables, both surrounded by four chairs with a small vase, containing a few dry flowers. Strong, homely aromas of bacon, toast and coffee beans wafted through the air, tickling my nostrils. All very un-Rotney-like.

We sat down at the first table. I was panting slightly but Frank was perfectly collected, as always.

"What do you fancy, kid?"

"Three weeks in Florida."

"To drink, smart-ass."

"Cup of tea, guvnor."

Frank nodded and mouthed *two teas* to the chap behind the counter. Then he stretched back in his chair.

"We had a guy in our Company called The Governor," he recalled.

"Really? What happened to him?"

"Run over by a Soviet T-34."

I frowned. "What was that? A tank?"

Frank nodded. "Yeah. Horrible war, a lot of good men died."

"I'm sorry. Do you want to talk about it?"

"No, not now."

I nodded. "OK...So?"

"So?"

"So?" I raised a palm. "What's the great breakthrough? Do you know what the stone is?"

Frank just raised his eyebrows quizzically.

"OK, let me guess," I said. "It's an alien turd. Deposited on earth by a wandering extra-terrestrial after a bad meal."

Frank smiled. "Hey, wouldn't that be something?"

"It certainly would."

"Hmm." He stopped smiling. "Anyway, in answer to your question. I still don't know what the stone is but I now know a man who does."

I frowned. "How, exactly?"

Frank shook his head and started raising his eyebrows all over again.

"Well, I tell you, it was the most God-damned thing, Antonia."

"What was?"

"How I found out."

"And how was that?"

But Frank didn't respond. Instead, he stared into a space, just above my head. I didn't say anything and after a few more seconds the counter guy brought our teas, together with packets of sugar and spoons.

"Frank?" I said eventually.

"Yeah."

"Do you mind if I go back to sleep? I've got a hell of migraine and if we're not going to do this now, I wouldn't mind going home. Sorry for being ratty but you know – tough day at the office and all that."

Frank raised a white palm. "You ever read Marvel comics?"

"Are we talking about Superman again?"

"No that's DC Comics. Marvel is Iron Man, Captain America, Spiderman, Guardians of Galaxy…"

"I haven't read the comics, I've seen some of the films."

"OK, well a couple of days back, I was still thinking about mythical stones and I remembered that Marvel Comics have this thing called the Infinity Stone."

"Yeah, I think I remember from the films. They're all powerful or something."

"Correct, they are six of them with distinct characteristics, all mystical and – like you say – all powerful - and if you can combine all six stones, you can boss the whole universe."

"OK. So, you think this is an infinity stone?"

"No, I don't – but what I remembered was an Infinity Stone can be used as a weapon, after all it's a source of huge power. And I began thinking what if our stone is actually a kind of weapon?"

"A weapon?"

"Yeah, a weapon."

"What kind of weapon?"

"Well, either an offensive weapon – like a sword – or a defensive weapon – like a shield."

"OK, so what if it's a weapon?"

"Then I'd have to establish what type of weapon it was and how to deploy it."

"I see."

Frank didn't say anything.

"Is that it? That's your breakthrough?"

"No."

"*No?*"

"No."

I raised my hands. "So, what was the breakthrough?"

Frank stared at me. He seemed dazzled.

"Frank…. you OK?"

But he wasn't listening. "So, this morning, I took off the stone and lay it next to the laptop. I figured what I'd do is stroll through different online images of weapons and conflicts and locations and eras and maybe, just maybe, I'd get lucky and it would start to glow or something."

"OK. Sounds like a plan. What happened?"

"Well, I scrolled through hundreds of images, probably thousands, in fact."

"And?"

"Nothing."

"Oh," I frowned, "but I thought you said – "

He raised his hand.

"Few hours later, I gave up and switched off the laptop. But – it was weird, – I sensed something was going to happen. Like in a movie, you know? Something always happens, just when you think you're plain out of luck."

"Go on."

"So, I've got this little TV in my room, as you know. It's pretty crap but it's wired to the pub's satellite dish or something – and I get the cable channels. Or the satellite channels - whatever they're called in this country."

"I know what you mean. Go on."

"Anyway, when I'm not watching movies, I like watching the *Discovery Channel*. I mean, there's some great content on that channel. So, I switch on the TV and there's this documentary on about the Arab Spring. You know what the Arab Spring was?"

"Sure. The demonstrations and uprisings in the Arabic world a few years ago."

"Correct. Anyway, listen, the Arab Spring began in December 2010 in Tunisia and it quickly spread to Algeria, Jordan and Oman."

"OK."

"Then it hit Egypt and ended up overthrowing two governments. Now, these protests and demonstrations centred on a location called Tahrir Square. But unfortunately, something else is located on Tahrir

Square, the Egyptian Museum in Cairo. An incredible museum with all their cultural treasures.

"So, if I recall correctly, in January 2011, this museum was hit by over a thousand looters and protestors. They raided jewellery, smashed display cases and stole exhibits. The heads of two mummies were broken up and the looters tried to remove them from the fire exits."

"Yeah, I remember something about this," I added "My parents talked about it. They visited the museum, years ago, and said it was, like, the most amazing museum they'd ever seen."

Frank nodded slowly, then titled his head. "Never been. Sadly."

"Well, me neither."

His eyes misted over, concentration slipping.

"Go on, Frank," I prompted. "What happened?"

The eyes focused suddenly. "Well, as the programme started discussing the Egyptian Museum, the stone began glowing."

I jerked forward. "What?"

"The stone started glowing."

My mouth gaped and I knocked my mug over in surprise. The tea swam over the table, dripped down the legs and spooled in a messy puddle on the floor. But I hardly moved. Then the counter man sprang forward with a cloth and mop.

"So sorry…." I began.

"Hey, no problem – just an accident." Foreign accent. Greek? Spanish? Arabic?

Seconds later, he'd cleaned up and replenished my mug. I watched him shuffle back to his original position, then I whipped round. Voice shaking.

"I can't believe it! What did you do?"

Frank clenched his right fist, raising it. "Right, so I saw this and started paying very serious attention to what was playing on the screen. I grabbed the stone and held it in front of the TV and then…"

"Then?"

"Then came the breakthrough."

23

I straightened up. "What happened?"

"Well, the programme moved away from the Arab Spring theme and began concentrating more on the Cairo Museum and the all the amazing stuff in there. Then a bunch of talking heads started going on about the importance of its cultural heritage and the like."

He grasped his tea mug, "so…from memory…they featured a director of the museum, an archaeological digs guy, a historian and then a Professor of theology. You know what theology is, right?"

"Study of religion?"

"Pretty much. Technically the study of the concept of God and religious truths." He winked. "*Wikipedia*. Looked it up this afternoon."

"OK – so?"

"So, this Professor of theology was talking to the camera about Ancient Egyptian polytheistic beliefs or something and – Zap! Bang! – a beam of light shot out the stone and hit his face."

"What? You serious?" My jaw dropped so much it almost sent my tea flying again.

Frank burst into a huge grin. "Never more so!"

"You are joking! Right?"

Frank nodded broadly, "hell no."

And then we high-fived.

"Holy crap" I said, slowly.

"Well, that's an appropriate expression. I mean, in the circumstances."

"Holy crap," I said again, not really hearing Frank's earlier comment. Then the questions smacked me like a classroom door. "So, who's the Professor? And what does it mean? Is the stone Egyptian? What was it doing in Korea then? Doesn't make sense!"

Frank raised his palm, again. "Whoa! Go easy, marine."

"What does it mean?"

"OK. I've been busy. *Real busy*. The guy's name is Professor Harold Gibson. There's a fair bit about him on the net. He's a former Professor of Divinity at Cambridge University and a Trustee at Princeton. He's written a bunch of books on Theology and the Old and New Testaments and now he's part of some World Economic Forum for World Dialogue or something. He's an academic hotshot, basically."

"But…" I thought about this but my head was hurting again, "…is the stone to do with Egypt, you think?"

"Maybe. Not sure. He specializes in religions more than Egyptology. I don't know."

I sipped my tea and considered this, "religions…"

"Well, technically, religious thought."

"Right so maybe the stone is important to a particular religion – or religions."

"Maybe. Possibly. Anyway, the great news is we'll find out whatever it is because I've arranged to see him next Tuesday evening."

I slammed my mug down. "No *way!*"

"Straight up. He's in Honk Kong this week but I spoke to his secretary about an hour an ago and she's arranged an appointment for us to see him."

Frank explained that he'd told Professor Gibson's secretary he'd made an exceptional discovery and needed the Professor's urgent appraisal. He'd managed to deal with her subsequent questions easily, without giving away too much information about the stone. The Professor had an office in the Barbican, near the Museum of London.

We discussed the upcoming appointment for a bit longer and then I told Frank about finding the silver photo frame and my latest theory.

He considered it, carefully. "Yeah, come to think of it, there is a pattern. The frame only appeared when I was alone. Interesting. Because the stone does its thing when other people are around. Must be some significance there, you'd think. But I don't know what…"

He shrugged, then I narrated the second part of the story, concerning Demi and the incident on the High Street. But his response was different. He frowned and shook his old head slowly.

"Wrong move, kid. I mean – look, don't get me wrong – most times, the best of course of action when threatened with grave danger is to run like hell. Most so-called heroes wind up dead, you know? There's a real thin line between courage and dumb stupidity. But sometimes you got to step up. Take a stand, yeah? Otherwise you encourage the bad guys."

He gazed into his mug, wistfully. "You shouldn't have run when she started hollering. OK, maybe you should have just turned back into the school when you saw her hanging out with those guys. Avoided a confrontation. But when you crossed the road and she yelled out, you should have just kept on walking, ignored her."

I frowned. "Hey, easier said than done, Frank. When someone yells 'OI' at you - you know, *aggressively*? I'm telling you, you don't think like that. You just run for it."

"Maybe. Point is you've sent her the wrong message now. You stood up to her before – big time – and she would have been real wary of you. Now she thinks you've turned chicken again."

"*No…*you don't understand, if she was *real wary*, she wouldn't have yelled at me like that."

Frank shrugged. "Just a bit of show-boating, probably to impress the fellas she was with. Matter of fact, if you'd have ignored her, she'd have looked even more stupid. Think about it."

I frowned. "*Think about it?* Frank! When a psycho, surrounded by the meanest, biggest boys ever seen yells 'OI', you bloody well run. I just you told you that! What planet are you on?"

A tear ran down my eye. "You know we're not all like you. I'm just a kid, all right? Trying to get through every day without being stabbed or killed or cut up into a million pieces! I'm *so* sorry I haven't won the Legion of Honor and jumped on a grenade but – "

Frank touched my arm gently and smiled. "Medal."

I winced. "What?"

"Medal."

"Medal *what?*"

"Medal of Honor. The Legion of Honor is French."

I turned sideways. "Whatever…"

"No matter – and by the way that's all baloney. You've got balls – big balls. You stood up to that piece of trash before and you can sure as hell do it again."

I shrugged. "Yeah, well, maybe if it was just her – or even her and her stupid girlie gang – but she was surrounded by these massive black guys – they could have broken my back with their little fingers."

Frank shook his head, dismissively. "Nah! You don't know who those guys were. They could have been threatening her for all you know. Maybe they were undercover cops. My point is you have no idea."

I snorted. "They weren't cops; I know *that* much." Then I tilted my head further away, glaring outwards.

Frank exhaled slowly. "Antonia?"

"*What?*"

"Look at me," Gentle but firm. I tilted back.

Frank blinked slowly. "Kid, I'm sorry…look…it's OK to be frightened. Hell, I'm supposed to be the big war hero but I'm scared of my dentist."

He breathed out again and shook his head. "Fear's a tough thing. Powerful, overpowering, *compelling*. But it's your friend too, your survival instinct. It's what's getting us going and protecting us. And - like I said - most times, in the face of real danger, your best option is to just beat it. But sometimes that's not OK. Sometimes you can't take the easy option because other things are at stake. I'm not talking about personal honour and pride. That's all bullshit. I'm talking about making a stand for the things that really count."

"Like what?"

"Like your family, your companions, your friends, your country. Decency, justice, equality and sticking it to the bad guys. Those are the things worth fighting for, demonstrating a bit of bravery. You know what John Wayne said?"

"Who?"

"Before your time, kid. Big movie star, made a lot of Westerns. Used to play the all-American hero."

I shrugged, "what did he say?"

"He said "courage is being scared to death…and saddling up anyway.""

I smiled. "I like that. Second good quote I've heard today."

"Really, what was the first?"

"From your old mate, Bruce Lee. Something about not accepting plateaus, pushing yourself beyond them."

Frank nodded. "Yeah, sounds like Bruce."

I raised my eyebrows and sipped my tea. "Anyway, so right now my priority is staying alive for next Tuesday evening. And as I'm not exactly Bruce Lee, I need your help."

"Well, look, kid, I'll make a deal with you." Frank undid his top shirt buttons, unbuckled the stone, placed it on the table and pushed it in my direction. "You hang on to the stone until we see the Professor. In the meantime, avoid Demi *discreetly*. But if confrontation becomes inevitable, you keep calm and kick her ass."

"How do I do that? Can you teach me some more moves?"

"You don't need them and don't even worry about it. The stone's got your back and I have a feeling you'll know what to do when the time comes. Don't get cocky, don't start anything and keep out her way – but if you get cornered, take her out."

I put my mug down. "Where to, Frank? The cinema?"

He didn't respond, just nodded towards the stone. "Put it on."

I looked down.

"No. You need it."

"I'm giving it to you, Antonia. Pick up the stone and put it on – *please.*"

I turned away. "No, Frank. It's yours – and you need it. You said yourself you get ill without it. I'll be all right. Please – just take it back. I don't want it."

Frank folded his arms. "No dice. I'll be just dandy. Now pick up the stone *right now* and put it on, otherwise I'm getting up and walking away. Oh - and I'll see the Professor myself."

I rotated my head slowly in the stone's direction. Frank was right, of course. I did need its protection and I could always return it if his health deteriorated. Besides, I had no intention of missing next week's appointment in the Barbican.

I grabbed the stone and held it in my palm, then I glanced at Frank. He was smiling.

"Numpty," I mumbled.

24

Maybe it was purely psychological but I swear, after putting on the stone, my headache improved almost straight away.

The journey home was much more comfortable and by the time I arrived back, Mum was cooking dinner. But as soon as I saw her, I recalled Frank mentioning he thought he knew what Huck was up to. Irritatingly, I hadn't followed it up.

Of course, I didn't have a mobile phone, and there was no point asking Mum. It would just have to wait until next time. Then I noticed Mum was humming!

I raised my eyebrows. "What's up with you? Last time I looked, we were still living in Rotney."

"I was in Holborn this afternoon."

I leaned against a kitchen counter. "Back specialist?"

"No, that's a bit better today."

"I'm glad." I sniffed the air. "What're you making?"

"Well, someone ate all the beans – probably the rats – so I'm making chicken nuggets."

I scowled. "Great."

I noticed Mum was still wearing the same simple dress outfit that she wore yesterday – and last week. She really had sold almost everything. I looked up at the kitchen ceiling, cracked and grotesque. Broken.

"Toni?"

I kept studying the ceiling. "Yes, Mummy?"

"Aren't you going to ask what I was doing in Holborn?"

It was a fair question. I lowered my head and shrugged.

"What were you doing in Holborn, Mummy?"

"I had a meeting with Daddy's legal team. The barrister and solicitor who are doing his appeal."

I sighed. "And how much is that costing?"

"I wouldn't worry about that. It's covered."

"Who by? Granny Strictness? Doesn't she need the funds for her care?"

Mum frowned slightly. "I said it's covered."

I tilted my head. "Auntie Grim?"

"It's *covered*."

"And how much do we still owe on this fine? Are you ever going to tell me?"

Mum didn't reply.

I raised a palm. "It's all right. Write the figure on a piece of paper, put it in an envelope and give it to me on my 21st birthday. I'm sure it can keep."

Mum shook her head. "Toni, don't be like this. I wanted to tell you – "

"And are you ever going to get your back looked at by someone who knows what they're doing? I mean, for God's sake, Mummy – "

"*Toni!*"

"What?"

"Can we please not talk about my health, or finances, right now? I want to tell you about the meeting in Holborn."

I shrugged. "Fine, whatever..."

Mum smiled. "Thank you. Well, look, it's good news, basically. They're optimistic."

"About what?"

"About Daddy's chances on appeal."

I squinted. "Why? What's changed?"

"Well, they think your father did make some quite serious mistakes – but nothing deliberate. I mean Daddy was just exhausted all the time, his partners were imposing ridiculous billing targets, they kept telling him the firm was struggling, never gave him any proper support and – basically – he couldn't keep up with all the necessary compliance. And…what they're also saying is Daddy wasn't the real villain."

"What do you mean?"

"They think his mistakes were seriously exaggerated by the police and the CPS. They were obviously desperate for a higher profile arrest and conviction."

I folded my arms and glared. "You mean they *stitched* him up?"

Mum exhaled slowly. "Look, Daddy wasn't Snow White. Basically, dodgy funds entered the firm's client account, on his watch. For whatever reason, he didn't spot it, report it or do whatever he was supposed to do. But the police and the CPS and the bastards at the Solicitors Regulatory Authority took a load of liberties and presented a convincing case that he engineered the whole thing and was some sort of master criminal."

I nodded. "I get it. Dad was an idiot and then got stitched up by some headline seekers. I hate the police, you heard what they kept saying to Dad? *Ooooh!* You've done very well for a Cambridge scholar. We can't all be as intelligent as you, sir. They teach you that at Cambridge, sir? And that's before they smashed up half the furniture and china."

Mum stood very still and bowed her head. She didn't say anything for a few seconds, then spoke in a quiet voice. "You know, I'm angry too about the way they behaved. Of course, I heard what they said. They said some horrible things to me too, you know. Including threatening to take you away. But you just have to get on with it and that's why I think what happened today is so important."

I also stayed still, for a little while, then I stood up and marched into my bedroom. Then I slammed the door shut, collapsed on the bed and glared upwards.

I needed the toilet much later in the night. As always, freaky, eerie sounds echoed through our wafer-thin walls. Maybe hungry foxes, or dying murder victims.

I hadn't removed Frank's stone. It felt cold and unresponsive around my neck but oddly protective. Was it working its mystical power already? My headache had certainly vanished and I felt unusually alert.

After finishing in the bathroom, I padded towards my bedroom window and peered through the filthy pane. There were a few parked cars outside but thankfully no sign of Huck. I shifted my gaze upwards and studied the Orion constellation. Twinkling bright specks formed eons ago.

My senses sparkled. I could feel the scratchy, threadbare rug under my feet and hear Mum's disjointed snoring in the other bedroom.

I suppose I felt vaguely excited about the possibility of Dad returning home but assumed the police and Crown Prosecution Service would break every rule maintaining their reputation. They were just a more sophisticated version of Rotney hoodies, basically.

Meanwhile, what could I do? Nothing. I was just a stupid, helpless kid that smacked into classroom doors and made inappropriate comments.

I tried falling asleep again a few minutes later, but it was hopeless.

The next two days were oddly uneventful.

There was no sign of Demi at school again and the teachers left me alone in class. Miss Patel even smiled at me after morning assembly.

I got another wink too! A sneaky one from Mr. Shaw after I volunteered a correct answer in History. At lunchtime on the second day, I even sat with Tyrese and a couple of classmates, laughing at their crude comments about *Love Island.*

The silver photo frame didn't materialize in odd places, although I half expected its sudden appearance. Meanwhile, I wore the stone under my school shirt but it didn't start glowing, or anything like that. Nothing peculiar happened, although at the end of the second day, I ran the entire length of the High Street and was barely out of breath when I got home.

I must admit I felt more confident wearing the stone, although, again, maybe I was just imagining it.

I popped into Frank's pub both days after school but he wasn't around. And - as usual - nobody knew where he was. Shame, really because I was worried about his health, now that I was wearing the stone again.

Huck had also vanished – but there was an intriguing development. After school, on the second day, I asked Mum where he was these days. Usually, Mum just changed the subject as soon as I mentioned him but, this time, she said he'd been working in France for the past fortnight. *Then* she changed the subject.

I almost shot back a scornful response but bit my tongue instead. So, as well as stalking Frank, he was also lying to Mum. What a supreme creep! I wondered how Frank would react when I updated him.

I visited the pub again, on Saturday morning but there was still no sign of the old man. This time, I felt more worried. Again, I asked if anyone had seen him but just received the same old negative response. It was so frustrating we didn't have mobile phones. Frank didn't own one and I couldn't even afford a crappy pay-as-you-go device. Ridiculous, really.

I left a message for him, at the bar, saying I'd be around later. Then I headed into Rotney's miserable town centre to buy a couple of cheap pens for school.

There were several nasty discount stores on the High Road that sold stuff you could write with. But I had no intention of hanging around the centre so I just entered the first one I approached, a large, grotty excuse for a supermarket.

I shuffled up and down the various aisles but just as I spotted the stationery section, the stone started glowing. I felt it heating up below my neckline but it was well hidden from any nosey onlookers underneath my coat and blue sweater.

Now what? The last time it glowed I wandered into an armed robbery so was this another warning? And then, of course, the previous time the silver photo frame appeared, I had smacked my head into a door, raced down the High Street and passed out twice.

So – *basically* - the weird glowing and sightings didn't bode too well. Even the first time the stone lit up, I ended up in Room 18.

I stopped abruptly and looked around the store slowly. Nothing. Well, nothing threatening. Just a few East European mothers and their bawling babies. All the same, I remained ultra-wary.

Remember the rules, Antonia. Frank's Rules. Stay calm, don't show fear, behave discreetly and avoid confrontation. Well – good luck with that…

I was nervous, no doubt about it. My heart began thumping but I took a few deep breaths, swept my hair back and carried on walking towards the stationery section. I chose a couple of pens, glanced around again, then strolled over to the cash registers. *Just pay and get out.*

Still quiet. I stood in the first queue, waiting patiently. The old guy at the front of the queue fumbled slowly in his pockets, looking for his wallet. Maybe it was a holdup and he'd misplaced his gun. I tutted a bit too loudly and checked my watch. My heart was still banging away. Not helpful.

I considered just dropping the pens and running home – but then that really would be demonstrating fear. Giving in. I imagined Frank shaking his head in stern disapproval.

The stone remained uncomfortably warm but still below burning. I adjusted it under my sweater, relieving the pressure slightly. Then I glanced out of the store's main window at Rotney's centre. A banal, unwelcome sight but not a particularly threatening one. The only things that had changed in the last few minutes were that the stone's temperature and appearance. Come on. That was all. No reason for a panic attack.

The old man finally located his wallet and paid. Then the queue inched forward. I toyed with the stone some more and looked around. Still nothing. I breathed in slowly and looked out of the store's window again.

And then I saw something. Directly ahead. A familiar figure appeared outside the shop. He didn't notice me but I recognized him immediately. I didn't even need to see his face; the neck tattoo was enough. And the same cheap bling. It was Mr. Bully, also known as Donny.

Oh no, I thought, *keep walking, keep walking!* But he didn't. He hovered outside the window, gawping aimlessly in another direction. My queue continued its painful progression. I watched him uneasily as he took out an iPhone and started yacking. The queue moved forward again and I kept firmly behind the old lady in front. Donny hadn't looked through the store's window once and I was fairly confident I hadn't been spotted. All the same, my hands were clammy with anxiety.

Mr. Bully clicked off the phone, scratched his backside and sauntered off. I waited several seconds before exhaling in relief. The queue moved further forward again, then again. I checked the stone. It was still glowing. *Why?* Did this mean I was still in danger?

Another minute passed, then two, then I was the next one at the checkout.

A red football bounced unevenly outside, followed by three, giggling children. They completely failed to catch it and soon disappeared out of range. Then Donny suddenly reappeared outside the window, conversing intently with someone but I couldn't see who - they were just outside my field of vision.

My breathing quickened and I turned away, dropping my head. I was still sure Donny hadn't seen me but I was virtually at the front of the queue now. Dangerously exposed. Vulnerable. The old lady in front of me paid up, placed her items in a plastic bag and moved off. *Oh no.* My turn. I edged ahead *very* gradually, glancing back at Donny as my visual range widened.

Now I could see who he was with. She was staring directly at me with insane intensity. Then she drew her finger across her throat and grinned.

For a few seconds, I just gaped back. Utterly shocked.

Then it got much worse. The four massive black guys I'd see her with, also appeared. One of them pointed at me and Demi nodded. He nodded back, flexed his knuckles and strode towards the discount store's entrance.

Keep calm and *show no fear* vanished faster than a rabbit inside Frank's magic hat. I dropped my pens, swivelled round, shoved my way out the queue and bolted down the nearest aisle.

The shelved goods flashed by as I darted towards the back of the shop. I glimpsed over my shoulder and saw Demi and two of her massive accomplices pursuing rapidly.

If there wasn't a fire exit, I was a dead girl walking. No doubt about it. These guys meant business and they weren't after my lunch money.

I hit the end of the shop and veered left, desperately seeking a way out. *Come on, come on.* Then I saw it. *Thank God.* Fire exit. I smashed into it and – mercifully – it swung open.

Great. I sprinted through the doors, into the narrow alleyway running parallel with the shops. Then I accelerated, panic driving my pace ever faster.

However, as I approached the end of the alleyway, Donny and the remaining accomplices strolled casually into view. All three folded their arms and beamed with sadistic delight.

Help. Help. I wheeled round immediately and ran back towards the discount store, begging for a miracle. Instead, Demi and her accomplices emerged from the store's fire exit and slowed down when they saw I was trapped.

Then both sides closed in.

25

I didn't move.
I couldn't move.
Well, Frank, I thought, *it comes down to this.*

I'd obeyed his instructions as best as I could. Keeping calm, showing courage, avoiding confrontations. But all that remained was the final, outrageous instruction. *If you get cornered, take her out.*

How on earth was I supposed to do that, Frank? I wasn't exactly *a superhero.* Just a small, fifteen-year-old girl trapped between six of the hardest, largest and nastiest villains I'd ever seen.

Instinctively, I pulled the stone out from under my sweater and gripped hard. The heat seared and throbbed within my right palm, burning my skin. *Don't worry,* he said, *the stone's got your back.*

I snapped my eyes shut, squeezing the stone tighter, absorbing its energy. Then I opened my eyes. Something had altered. Demi and her buddies were still moving towards me but much slower. In fact, literally, in a *slow motion.*

Just as strangely, the sounds of the outside world had lowered by several tones and the overall effect was unsettling and eerie.

I stumbled backwards, forwards, confused. And then realized...I could still move at the same speed as before!

OK, now I had to think *hard* and *fast.* My impulse was to dodge all the assailants and run. I knew I could get away from them now. From my stone-enhanced perspective, they appeared unusually slack. But from where they were standing, I must have resembled The Flash.

But...Frank had given me clear instructions. *Take her out.* He hadn't mentioned anything about her pals so presumably I could just avoid them. But, then again, if I didn't make another brutal statement, her buddies would keep pursuing me. They would never stop. And one day they would catch me without the stone.

I had no choice.

I took a deep breath and then sprinted at the group that had just come out of the fire exit. There were three of them and Demi was third in line. Her new cronies reached out lazily as I approached but I dodged their lumbering arms and smashed my fist into Demi's nose. As soon as I hit her, I realized the stone had vastly increased my strength. It was like punching through straw. Her nose crumbled spectacularly beneath my knuckles whilst I drove my outstretched arm directly into her head. As she collapsed, I launched a savage kick into her chin, destroying her jaw. The force of my kick caused her head to fling backwards and her entire body rose upwards before ending up in an undignified heap on the floor. I glanced down. Demi's eyes were blank and her shattered face was covered in blood.

I straightened up immediately and turned towards the huge guy, on my left. He was holding a large, serrated blade in his left hand. I grabbed his left wrist, forcing the knife out. Then I wrenched his arm behind his back, increasing the pressure until it snapped cleanly. *How could I do this?*

The massive thug also sank back, his intimidating features contorting into a grotesque mask of pain. Then I whirled round and thrust a high kick into the second man's jaw, severely disfiguring it. As he fell away, I donkey-kicked his right knee. One brutal thrust, breaking his leg cleanly.

Now both of Demi's mates were on the ground, rolling and screeching. But they weren't screams as I knew it. More like unearthly rumblings.

Now I had a dilemma. Frank had been clear. *Take Demi out.* Did this also include her playmate, Donny? He was at the other end of the alleyway. Surely prevention was better than cure and all that?

I whipped round and sprinted back down the alley. It only took seconds.

Then I faced Donny, easily evading the clumsy groping efforts of his overgrown companions. I jumped up, pulling him down by the shoulders, then peered directly into his eyes. *Empty.* Maybe he lacked a proper brain but the nasty creep had urgently assembled a Rotney killing- crew within minutes of spotting me.

Well, same logic. If I didn't seriously disable him, *right now,* I'd be looking over my shoulder for, at least, the next thirty years. Not only that, the Year Sevens needed protecting.

I slammed his head back and twisted him around. Although, he was almost as large as his ghastly mates, it posed no difficulty. The hideous snake tattoo stretched out as I yanked his neck back, then stamped down on his left knee. It shattered immediately, fracturing the leg grotesquely. His body thudding heavily into the ground, then I kicked him savagely in the face, stomach and balls.

I thought briefly about attacking Donny's two friends but decided against it. I'd made my statement and if the stone suddenly clicked me back into normal time, I'd be in very serious trouble. Maybe Frank could control the stone - somehow - but I certainly couldn't.

Time to go.

I raced back through the fire exit and into the discount store. Then I veered right, sprinting down the nearest aisle and past the frozen queues. *No change there, then.* Out through the main entrance, swerving sharp right, then left again. I tore down the High Street only slowing down when I pulled off the main road and approached Frank's pub.

Then, suddenly, the stone *clicked off* - fading completely - and everything switched back into normal pace. A dramatic, giddying sensation.

How long had it all taken? Seconds for me. Minutes for everyone else. Or was it the other way around?

I halted completely and turned around. No one was chasing me, of course. I was out of breath and shaking from exhilaration. I knew I'd just experienced something profoundly different and overpowering. Otherworldly.

I pulled the faded stone out of my sweater and kissed it. *Thank you.* Whatever you are.

But why me? It made no sense. Frank was obviously an amazing man but I was just a hapless, stupid kid. I couldn't even buy a couple of cheap pens without ending up in a brawl.

I began walking again. There was little point in checking if Frank was back. Not now. I mean - relatively speaking - I'd only just come out the pub. Less than fifteen minutes ago. And I was driving the staff mad.

Have you seen Frank? Is Frank around? Do you know where he is? Do you know when he's back?

I headed home instead.

After unlocking my front door, I crept into my bedroom and dropped onto my dreary old bed. Then I stared at the ceiling. Intense relief and exhilaration conflicted sharply with nausea and shock at what I had done. Yes, they were villains who wanted to cut me and probably kill me but I certainly still wasn't used to seeing snapped limbs and ruined faces. If this was power, did I really want it?

No wonder *The Great Cornelius* had battered Fat Neck, a few weeks ago. Now I understood how he dodged him so easily and moved so rapidly. The old man must have known that if I was similarly threatened, the stone would perform its little magic trick. Astonishing.

I closed my eyes, snapping the ceiling into darkness. And then it struck me again.

Where was Frank?

I stayed home for the rest of the day, listening to the radio and watching television.

Of course, there was nothing in the news about a skirmish behind a Rotney discount store. That kind of thing was about as common as a person walking their dog down the High Street.

I figured I'd probably put Demi in hospital for several more days but I hadn't killed her. I'd also broken some of her friends' bones. Outside Rotney, that was considered grievous bodily harm but inside Rotney, it was only classified as minor cuts and bruises.

To make the news in Rotney, these days, had to involve death and preferably in grizzly fashion. Burning tramps was a good-crowd pleaser. But not really a cyber-bullying suicide. I think the only reason that hit the headlines was because the victim's *YouTube* video went viral. No one would have cared otherwise, apart from her family, if she had one.

Meanwhile, I should have also been sporting some nasty bruises, especially around my knuckles. After all, I'd smacked Demi and her pals with everything I had. But my right hand was completely unblemished and – in fact – physically, I felt amazing.

By seven that evening the boredom really set in, so I headed back to the pub. Frank hadn't moved any of his stuff out and there was no further news so I just drifted home again. Bewildered.

Why did I feel like he'd dumped his stone and sailed back to North Carolina? Maybe he'd gone to stay with his son or something – but he would have told me that last week, surely. And he mentioned they *weren't particularly close.*

By nine in in the evening, I was feeling very low. Life was just so crap without money, basically. Maybe, the fact we once had some made it even worse.

I had no friends, apart from an old man who kept vanishing. I couldn't go to parties, or clubs, or the cinema. I couldn't even go online because I didn't have a computer. The nearest bookstore was miles away and Rotney's charming residents had burnt their library down.

Eventually, Mum clocked my sulky behaviour. She responded by making tea and switching the TV on. Very Mum-like. Unfortunately, only *X Factor* was on. I made an ugly expression, sipped from my mug and tapped my fingers on the kitchen table.

Then the doorbell rang.

I frowned. "Who's that?"

Mum shrugged. "No idea."

"You're not expecting anyone?"

"No - are you?"

"No."

We stared at each other, motionless.

I scratched my head. "You think it's the bailiffs? Better chuck the armchair out the window before they grab it."

"No, not on a Saturday night."

"What about your friend, Huck?"

"He's in France."

"Still?"

You sure about that?"

"Yes."

I rolled my eyes. Then the doorbell rang again.

I was thinking. It couldn't be Demi, or her buddies, or the local hoodies. They were all in hospital. I doubted anyone had reported my violent antics to the authorities. So…it had to be Frank. Obviously back from his travels.

I stood up. "I'll go."

Mum nodded. I walked down the corridor, expecting the old man and preparing a big hug. I unlocked the front door quickly and flung it open. Then I stepped back in surprise.

It was Auntie Grim and Sophia.

Of course, Auntie Grim's real name wasn't *Auntie Grim*, it was Mrs. Meredith Palmer.

But *Auntie Grim* just suited her perfectly. I mean she was flipping grim, basically.

As usual her hair looked dreadful, she was wearing a shapeless, green sweater and the type of open sandals a Rotney charity shop would reject. She peered at me through her round glasses.

"Hello, Antonia. How are you?"

"Hi Auntie Meredith. What brings you here?"

I smiled at Sophia, her ten-year-old daughter but she just stared ahead, chewing gum. Auntie Grim ignored my question and strode inside.

"Is your mother in?"

"Yes…" I called after her. Sophia followed like an obedient dog.

I shook my head and closed the front door. *What the hell is my aunt doing here?* And bringing her little girl too! An open war zone was a safer environment for a child than Rotney after hours.

I turned around and wandered back into the kitchen. Mum was standing up and Auntie Grim looked impatient.

"Sophia," she barked.

Her daughter cocked her head. "Mummy?"

"Go into Antonia's bedroom and play with her. I'm sure she's got lots of interesting things to show you. Off you go and close the door. The grown-ups need to have a little chat."

Sophia looked at me impassively, still chewing.

I glanced at Mum. She nodded quickly.

"Right, then, Sophia. Come into my bedroom. Lots to do."

I walked back down the hall, my cousin trailing behind. We went into my room and Sophia sat on the bed, dangling her legs and chewing.

I slammed the door shut, then edged it open slowly.

"Mummy said you should keep the door shut!" protested Sophia.

"*Shush!!* Chew your gum."

"But – "

"*Shush!!*"

I opened the door further, listening closely. But I couldn't hear anything. They must have been whispering. I extended my neck, straining my ears but there was no improvement.

I couldn't get closer because the floorboards creaked so badly. They'd catch me immediately. I snorted in irritation and turned back.

Sophia looked at me. Her hair was cut in an ugly bob and she was wearing some ghastly pink Primark outfit. Poor kid. I closed the door, frowning.

My cousin made a face. "Your bedroom's so boring. And it's *horrible*."

"Like your face."

"Like *yours!*"

I sat down on the bed, next to her. "Why's your Mummy here?"

"I don't know. She said it was important."

"That's all she said?"

"Yes."

I tutted. "And why are *you* here?"

"I don't know. I didn't want to come. And why are *you* here? It's disgusting."

"Thank you."

"Well, it's true. And you haven't answered my question."

"I don't know, that's my answer."

Sophia didn't reply, just carried on chewing.

I played punched her shoulder. "Want to know a secret?"

"Ooooh, yes, please."

"OK – but promise you won't tell anyone? *Especially* not Mummy."

Sophia nodded eagerly, "OK."

"This a very bad place, Sophia. Dangerous too."

"How come?"

"Well, most of the people around here aren't human. I mean they look human, all right, but at midnight – when you're fast asleep – they turn into gigantic lizards and walk around hunting little children."

"Oh, shut up, Toni."

"No, it's true. The lucky children get eaten straight away but the unlucky ones get beaten and forced to perform on talent shows on ITV. It's actually disgusting."

Sophia laughed and punched my side.

"That's funny. You should be on the television. You could tell jokes for a living."

I looked appalled. "It's true, Sophia. I've seen them, massive, giant, lizards – with huge *snarling* jaws. And you know who the biggest lizard is? King Lizard?"

Sophia shrugged.

"Simon Cowell."

Sophia tutted. "Don't be silly. He's just a *man*, Toni."

I shook my head. "That's what you think. And that's what he wants you to think. Because he *looks* like a man. But this is what happens at midnight…"

I squinted, then contorted my face, then shook like crazy. I collapsed on the ground, screeching and quivering, as I pretended to change into an enormous reptile.

Sophia laughed and clapped with pleasure, bouncing on the bed as I howled in distress, clawing my fingers and wailing.

Then she stopped laughing.

I continued growling and roaring for a few more seconds before realizing my cousin had suddenly quietened. I ceased the animal noises and cleared my throat.

"What?"

Sophia pointed just below my neck.

"What's that, Toni?

"What's what?"

"That stone round your neck."

"Oh…"

My sudden movements had forced the stone over my t-shirt. *Oh no.* Frank had been very clear on this. *Don't show the stone to anyone.* At least until Tuesday evening, when we met the Professor.

I blushed, tucking the stone back quickly.

"Nothing."

This was the wrong answer, though.

"Please let me see it. It looks beautiful."

"No."

"Please, Toni, please! *Please!*"

"No."

"That's *really* mean."

I shrugged.

Sophia glared at me. "Why?"

"Why what?"

"Why can't you show me the stone?"

"Because I can't, that's why?"

"Why?"

"Because I just can't! All right?" I snapped, a bit too loudly.

Sophia looked crestfallen, then a single tear snaked down her cheek.

Oh, God, my poor cousin. "I'm sorry, honey". I sat back on the bed and hugged her. "Please understand, I just can't show it to you."

"Why?"

"Because it's a magic stone."

"Magic?"

"Yes."

"How?"

"I don't know, Sophia. Just is, all right?"

"But why can't you just show it?"

I shook my head and sighed. "I don't know. I'm sorry. It'll lose its power or something if I do. I'm not sure. Can we just leave it? Please?"

Sophia nodded sadly. "OK."

"Good."

"And don't mention it to Mummy? OK?"

"OK."

"Promise?"

Sophia nodded her head.

We hugged for a bit longer. Then I heard footsteps pacing down the hall, followed by a sharp rap on my door.

I released Sophia, stood up and opened my door.

Auntie Grim peered over my shoulder. "Right, Sophia, time to go. Come on."

My cousin jumped off the bed and immediately trotted after her mother.

"Goodbye, all!" barked Auntie, opening the front door and marching off.

I closed the front door after her and returned to the living room. Mum was back in the armchair with the television on.

I sat on the other chair, looking ahead. "Well, I think I'd have preferred the bailiffs. What was that all that about?"

Mum shrugged. "Money."

"Oh. Is she going to give us some?"

Mum sighed. "Can we talk about this some other time?"

I frowned. "*No*. Is she going to give us some? You know? Her being *family* and all? I mean, it's not like she can't afford it. Her husband owns half of Knightsbridge!"

"Don't exaggerate, Toni. He's a property investor."

"Right, that happens to own about a hundred classic cars and a house in Grosvenor Square just to keep his wine collection at the right temperature."

"Most of that is borrowed money."

"Right. Auntie's Grim's usual line."

I kept frowning.

"Don't sulk, Toni."

I turned. "You know, Mum, I think the rats in this building are better fed than us. Is she going to give us any money? I could do with a cheap laptop for a start."

Mum didn't reply.

"Well?"

"Well, what?"

"Is she going to give us any money? It must have been important. Ordinary people don't travel into Rotney in the middle of the night, you know? Mind you, Auntie Grim isn't exactly ordinary, is she?"

Still no response.

I snorted. "You know…. *whatever.*" I stood up.

Mum glanced up. "Yes and no."

"What do you mean?"

"I mean, *yes* – she's going to pay for a QC for Daddy's appeal. She's even found someone. Apparently, he's a Rottweiler with a hatred for the police. And charges about £5,000 an hour. And *no* – she's not going to give us any money until after the appeal."

I sat down, considering this. "Well, good news about Dad…. but why won't she give us any money until after the appeal. It doesn't make sense. She's *controlling* us."

"I don't know, she's a… *difficult* person. But she's still being incredibly generous, Toni. I mean this lawyer will cost her tens of thousands of pounds. Maybe even more. And it could make all the difference to Daddy."

I sighed. "I understand, I do and…you know…that's amazingly generous and all but – like – we need money *now*, Mummy. For example, I need stuff for school. I mean, it's *embarrassing*. The Romanian immigrants in my class have more than me. Can't she even give us a couple of hundred quid for a laptop? You know, just a really crap one from Argos?"

"Not for the moment, Toni."

"All right. How about fifty quid for a Tesco mobile?"

"No."

"Five pounds for a MacDonald's?"

"No."

"One pound for a lottery ticket?"

"No."

I shrugged and went back into my bedroom.

26

Then, on Sunday afternoon, I got the shocking news. Frank had suffered a stroke.

I found out from Jules, the girl behind the bar.

Apparently, while visiting his son last Thursday afternoon, the old man began complaining about a strange weakness in his left arm. His son called an ambulance and Frank was rushed to St Mary's Hospital in Sidcup. And that was all she knew.

I was *so* upset. I mean, *SO* upset.

For a start, I felt really, guilty and selfish. I shouldn't have taken the stone, it *protected* him – for God's sake! Why didn't I just say *no* and walk away? *Why?* Frank, the flipping war hero, putting my worthless backside ahead of his. *Ridiculous.*

Secondly, I couldn't bear the thought of Frank suffering in a strange hospital. It was depressing. My only loyal friend and defender in this nasty, brutal world.

I started crying. Pathetic, I know. I could imagine some tough Rotney local shaking his head and mouthing *pussy*. But, you know, I was a pussy – I missed Frank terribly and I'd let him down badly.

Jules was quite sweet, considering she was normally so unfriendly. She obtained St Mary's details and called them about Frank's progress.

Good thing too because they advised Frank had just been trans-ferred to a new hospital. Funnily enough, it was the one next to Dad's prison.

Jules phoned the new hospital and got through to Frank's ward. They reported he was comfortable and had no difficulty communicat-ing but required further observation. They also said visiting hours were between six thirty and eight, every evening, and I could see him later.

I felt a bit better after hearing this. It also helped that I knew exactly where his hospital was. Shame I couldn't visit Dad at the same time but his jailers had very different visiting hours and procedures.

I went home immediately.

Predictably, Mum's back was playing up again and she was back on the painkillers. She was groggy and frustrated but nodded sym-pathetically when I explained an old Purchester friend needed com-pany in hospital, this evening. I promised I wouldn't get back late.

Before I left for the hospital, I made a *Get-Well* card for Frank. It saved me the expense of wandering around Rotney, searching for something suitable and avoiding gangsters. It was quite a nice card, although probably decorated with too many flowers and cute ani-mals. Once I'd finished, I set off for East Acton - the hospital's nearest underground station.

Sadly, I knew something about strokes. Granny Strictness had a suffered a bad one recently and couldn't speak anymore. She was also confused. Such a shame because although she was genuinely strict, she was also really kind. Granny had paid the bulk of Dad's monstrous fine and God knows what would have happened if she hadn't.

Meanwhile, Auntie Grim hadn't helped at all, until last night.

I knew strokes came in all shapes and guises. Poor old Granny had suffered irreversible brain damage and would never regain her full mental capacity. I think she was dying too. I just hoped she was happily confused and believed her son was an exemplary member of society, not a disgraced, prison inmate.

If Frank's stroke was minor - I mean, if there was such a thing, at his age - he had a reasonable chance of making a full recovery. But I knew there a good possibility he could have a further, more serious stroke, at any time. Clearly, a big worry.

All the same, Frank possessed a *secret weapon*. The stone. If I could make him put it back on, I was sure that he'd make a staggeringly rapid recovery. Then we could both visit the Professor on Tuesday night and get some answers. I just hoped the obstinate, old warhorse would behave sensibly and do the right thing.

I arrived at East Acton station and hurried down the main road, shivering as I passed the prison, on my left. The hospital was literally *next door* and I walked through its main entrance, two minutes later.

Jules had scribbled down the name of Frank's ward on a piece of beer smudged paper and I followed the hospital's signs.

I took the lift to the fourth floor and strolled into the ward. Then I peered around, searching for the old man and praying his condition wasn't worse than described.

I located him quickly. He was sharing a dismal room with another couple of old boys but appeared comfortable enough, although he was hitched up to a couple of nasty, medical monitors.

Frank looked up and beamed. I ran over to his hospital bed and threw my arms around him.

"Watch the wires!" he yelled.

"*Silly fool*," I whispered back. "*Told* you not to give me the stone!"

Frank shrugged. "Hey, hey …enough! Have a seat."

I released my grip and sat down on the nearest chair. Then I pulled it closer to the bed and leaned in.

"I'm *so* glad to see you."

"Me too."

We chatted a bit about what happened. Frank said he felt fine but remained under observation for a few more days. Of course, I insisted he took the stone back immediately - but he refused.

"No. You'll just have to see the Professor yourself, tomorrow night."

I glared. "Err...*no!* Tomorrow's Monday night and *we're* seeing him Tuesday evening. That's you *and* me."

"Sorry, kid. I got the dates mixed up," confessed Frank. "I guess I was a bit over-excited. It's tomorrow night, actually."

I attempted a more reasonable tone. "Look, that's no problem, we'll postpone it. You've waited – what – over, fifty years to find out what the stone is. A few more days won't make any difference."

Frank shook his head slowly, almost sternly. "No."

"What? Why?"

"Draw the curtain," he instructed.

"Sorry?"

"Draw the curtain."

I shrugged, got up and pulled the hospital curtain around his bed, then sat down.

"Thanks. This is private and I don't want anyone snooping."

"OK..."

"All right. Now listen. Firstly, it was helluva job getting a meeting arranged with this guy. His secretary had a major stick up her ass about letting me see him and I had to be damned persuasive. I'm telling you, kid, if we start trying to rearrange, or postpone, or what have you, you'll *never* get to see this man, again. That's for sure.

"Secondly, he's flying back from Hong Kong today and then he's jetting back off to Greece, or somewhere, in a couple of days. The guy's hardly ever in the country. We have what you might call a *very* narrow window of opportunity.

"And thirdly, you're plain mistaken. I've waited long enough to find out what the rock is and I *sure as hell* don't want to wait a day longer than I need to. Understand?"

I was taken back. "Understood. All right – take it easy!"

"I'm sorry, it's been a rough couple of days but I need you to take the stone to this guy tomorrow evening – I'll give you the full address. Obviously, extend my apologies, explain my predicament and then show him the stone and tell him as much as he needs to know. Answer any questions."

"But Frank!" I rubbed my forehead and frowned again.

"What?"

"It means another day without the stone. You lose its protection."

"Yeah, well don't worry about me – I'm doing great. You can give me the stone back after you've seen this fella. This is much more important."

I grimaced.

Frank raised his eyebrows. "What?"

I shrugged. "Well, it's not ideal."

"I disagree. Things are just dandy. Go and see this guy and put us both out of our misery."

"But what if he asks me detailed stuff about how you found the stone, how you control its properties, what its properties really are? I mean there's *loads* I don't know."

"You know enough."

"You think?"

"Definitely. You'll ace it, kid. Just don't give me any more excuses."

I held his gaze for a few seconds in silence, then exhaled again. "You're not going to change your mind, are you?"

"Absolutely not."

I shook my head. "Stubborn old man."

"You bet."

I glared at him but he just grinned and offered his fist. "Pound it."

We knuckle punched but I kept scowling.

I changed the subject and told him about the fight behind the discount store. Frank was fascinated and kept asking questions.

"Did anyone call the cops?"

"In *Rotney*? You're joking, right?"

"You didn't report it?"

"No way. I don't want anything to do with those idiots."

"It was legitimate self-defence."

"Whatever."

Frank shuffled in his bed. "Well, I'm just flabbergasted. Genuinely so. It must have been *really*, scary. Matter of fact, it sounds like you're the real hero, not me."

I shook my head, again. "No. It was the stone, definitely. Made me brave - and strong - then completely saved me. I'd have been stabbed to death, otherwise. *Definitely*. You know, just another Rotney statistic. So many teens get knifed in the area, no one cares."

"That bad – huh?"

"No, worse. Much worse. Seriously, give me the First World War trenches over Rotney city centre any day. I'll take my chances."

Frank dropped his head. "That's tough to hear."

We looked at each other, for a few seconds, in silence, then I leaned in.

"But – thanks, anyway – it totally saved my life. You know, giving me the stone..."

Frank smiled, sadly. "Well, I had a feeling you'd need it more than me."

"Not true," I insisted. "You basically had a stroke at my expense."

"I don't see it like that. The point is..."

His voice trailed off.

"The point is?" I repeated.

"The point is we're both alive," he replied.

"I suppose."

We both considered this quietly, then Frank squinted. "So - let me get this straight - you think the stone *slowed down time?*"

"Yeah. Absolutely. I mean it's done it for you, right? What about when you were fighting in the pub?"

Frank shook his head slowly. "No, the stone massively increased my physical fitness. You know – enhanced my agility and strength and so forth. But it didn't start slowing down the clock or anything like that. I told you. I was taught how to fight, back in the day."

He thought for a moment. "Are you sure? Maybe what you really mean is it *felt* like time slowed down? It's a very common sensation when your body is on high alert. Quite a few cops report that kind of thing when they get into a gunfight. Soldiers too."

"No, no way. Time slowed down around me. Even the all the sounds were lower. I'm completely sure of it."

"Well, that's the most damned peculiar thing I've ever heard."

"What? More peculiar than turning a parrot into a leopard."

He didn't reply.

"Frank?"

"Yes?"

"More peculiar than turning a parrot into a leopard, or a stone glowing, or emitting rays, or finding silver frames all over the place?"

He cocked his head and shrugged. "No. I suppose not."

"Oh, boy..." I stretched my arms out until they clicked. "I *really* hope we get some answers tomorrow evening."

"Yeah, me too."

I lowered my arms and checked my watch. Frank noticed.

"How long you got, kid?"

"Few more minutes. I'm OK."

"That's good."

I studied the tired hospital curtain surrounding us, then turned back to Frank. "Has your son come to visit you yet?"

"Yeah, he left earlier."

"Getting on better now?"

He shrugged again. "I guess."

I nodded politely. "Well that's good."

There was a brief pause. Then, Frank beckoned slowly. I pulled my chair in, even closer.

"I need to talk to you about Huck," he whispered.

Huck. I'd forgotten all about him.

"Wait, I'll go first." I sighed. "I *meant* to tell you…according to Mum, he's been in France for the last two weeks. Not stalking old soldiers in Rotney. He's obviously a complete liar."

Frank raised his eyebrows. "Interesting. Maybe he's got a twin brother."

"Yeah, that'll be it."

Frank grimaced. "I'm pretty sure he was monitoring my internet activity and conversations from his car."

"Really? Why?"

"No concrete proof but just call it a good hunch."

"Why?"

"He's interested in the stone. No doubt about it. But he's trying to get more information before he makes his move."

"What kind of move?"

"Not sure – probably an aggressive one."

I shook my head, "well, he's definitely bad news…"

"But nothing's changed in that he hasn't *done* anything yet – and – as I keep on saying - if you confront him, he'll deny everything. Thing is, kid, I think he'll show his hand just after you find out what the stone is, so *be careful.* Your pal Demi was just an amateur, her friends too. I wouldn't worry about them anymore. But Huck is something else. Much more sinister."

"But what's the problem? I'll give you the stone back on Tuesday."

"Sure, you will, I'm just saying, exercise caution."

"But surely the stone would protect me anyway."

"Probably."

"*Probably?* What does that mean?"

"It means probably. Just stay alert, that's all."

"Stay alert? OK. No problem."

"Good girl."

We talked slightly longer before I felt it was getting late. Frank handed me a piece of paper with Professor Gibson's address. Then I kissed him goodbye and drew back the curtain around his bed. Just as I was leaving, he raised a bony, old finger.

"Hey."

"What?"

"That number you did on Demi? And her pals?"

"Yeah? What about it?"

"Outstanding."

I grinned and saluted. Frank saluted back, then I turned around and walked out of the ward.

Despite the reduced train service on Sunday evening, I got home easily.

Everything seemed fairly, quiet. I quickly checked on Mum. She was tucked up in her bed, snoring loudly and surrounded by pill bottles.

I closed her bedroom door softly. Then I sat down behind the kitchen table and checked the directions to Professor Gibson's office on an old *A-Z Map*. I could get there very easily, it was only a couple of minutes from Barbican Station. I toyed with the stone under my blouse for a few seconds, then switched on the television and caught the end of the *X Factor* results.

Then, just after eleven, the blues really smacked me. It was always the same on Sunday evenings, now.

Boy, did I *hate* Monday mornings. I seriously considered playing truant tomorrow and visiting Frank instead. After all, my appointment with the Professor wasn't until seven. However, I dismissed the thought. Probably because I had double History.

I suppose my melancholy was offset slightly by the possibility of discovering more about the stone in the evening. But *only* slightly.

Yet again, I fumed at my inability to get online. How did people survive without the internet in the olden times? I couldn't!

I really wanted to find out more about Professor Gibson. Maybe find a potential reason for his "selection". But there was no chance of that and I was sick of hunting around for working computer bays.

I watched a bit more television but it was all repeats and celebrity rubbish. I switched the box off and wandered into my bedroom. I grabbed my ancient telescope, rotated it and gazed up at the night sky for several minutes, then I sank onto my bed and stared at the cracked ceiling.

After another while, I undressed, washed and cleaned my teeth. Then I lay back on the bed, unclasped the stone's necklace and dropped it into my bedside drawer. I switched off the light and just lay motionless, gazing upwards and thinking.

The usual unpleasant noises from the surrounding streets and flats echoed through my room, as always. The charming Rotney backdrop.

I breathed in deeply and slowly, closing my eyes but it was useless. I was just too worked up again.

27

Nothing much happened at school. I looked half-heartedly for a working computer bay during lunch break but couldn't find one.

In the meantime, the stone stayed cold, I didn't find any silver photo frames, or run into classroom doors. I factored in the possibility that I might get handed a Room 18 for scratching my nose in the wrong direction – but that also didn't happen.

There was obviously no sign of either Demi or Donny and no one mentioned them. For the first time, I felt quite comfortable walking home from school by myself.

Dinner was a couple of stale sandwiches, then I set off for the Barbican.

Funnily enough, the only person I *sort of* looked out for was Dr Huck. But I didn't really understand how he could monitor our conversations. Had he planted listening bugs inside the pub? Or in my living room? It sounded like the old man was either becoming paranoid, or watching too many spy thrillers. Probably the latter.

I changed on to the Metropolitan Line at Kings Cross, just before six thirty. The station and trains were packed with commuters at the height of rush hour. Pushing, shoving and jostling. As I squeezed through the impatient crowds, I felt the stone darting around my neck underneath my black sweater.

But I still arrived at Barbican station quickly. In fact, I was a good fifteen minutes early so I inched very gently towards the Professor's office. Meanwhile, everyone shot by in the opposite direction, heading for the station and home. City people walked so much faster than Rotney dwellers but they all seemed incredibly stressed.

Despite walking ever so slowly, I turned up at the Professor's office five minutes early and rang the white bell, marked *Gibson Consultancy*. There was a good old pause, then a woman's metallic voice came through the speaker over the doorbells.

"Gibson."

"Oh, hi, I'm here to see Professor Gibson on behalf of Mr. Truesdale. Seven o'clock appointment."

Another, shorter pause.

"Third floor."

I was buzzed in and took the lift upstairs. It rose rather unevenly, clanging open on the third floor. I stepped out, glanced around and easily located the Professor's office on the right-hand side.

I strolled down the rather drab hall and pressed another outside bell. There was a bit of shuffling from behind the wall. Then a woman who looked remarkably like Auntie Grim opened the office door. In fact, for a second, I really did think it was my aunt. She had the same swept-back hair and severe forehead, although she dressed better. She also frowned like my aunt.

"Who are you, again?" she enquired, a bit sharply.

I smiled pleasantly. "I'm a close friend of Mr. Truesdale. He had a seven o'clock appointment with the Professor but unfortunately was taken unwell. I've come in his place."

I tried sounding like a Mount High prefect, not a scum bag from Rotney High. But the Auntie Grim tribute act appeared unimpressed. She raised an eyebrow and tilted her head.

"Well, this is a bit irregular, I must say. Mr. Truesdale didn't mention anything about you. I'm not sure the Professor will still see you. He's only just back from Hong Kong, you know. Very tired."

I felt like keeping the smile but responding - "well, Mr. Truesdale, mentioned you, Auntie. He said you had a major stick up your backside," - but I didn't, of course.

"And what did you say your name was again?" Same, pointed tone.

"Antonia Davidson."

"Antonia Davidson – hmmm..." She checked for something on her desk and tutted loudly. Then strode a few metres to her left and knocked on the door of an adjacent office.

"Come in!" instructed a cheerfully posh voice.

Auntie Lookalike promptly let herself in, closing the door behind her.

I craned my neck forward, listening. There was a muffled conversation taking place, next door, but I couldn't make it out. I relaxed my neck and scratched it, just under the chin. After maybe a minute, the office door opened and the lady came out. She held the door open and nodded. "The Professor will see you now. Go in."

"Thank you" I nodded back. Then, suddenly, I felt very nervous. I stroked the stone under my sweater and thought, *please help me here, I don't really know what to say.*

I walked into the office. A white-haired gentleman, in horn rimmed glasses, sat on a large, leather-upholstered chair, behind a huge, antique desk. He was *very* smartly dressed in a tweed suit, red polka dot bow tie and matching handkerchief. *Not* Primark.

Meanwhile, the office obviously formed part of some record breaking attempt to insert as many books into a single room as possible. There were books *everywhere*. All over the walls and half the floor. And not crap looking books either. They were all weighty, scholarly tomes and leather-bound volumes.

There were also loads of framed snaps of the Professor dotted throughout the room, many with celebrities. I spotted Nelson Mandela in one photo and Bono in another. Couldn't see Elvis Presley, though.

"Wow," I gasped, "have you read all these books?"

He winked. "Only the ones with pictures. Please, have a seat."

"Thanks," I settled down in a plush, old armchair and sighed gently.

"So, it's Miss Davidson, isn't it?"

"Yes, sir – I mean, Professor."

"No, no, you must call me Harry."

"Yes, Professor – Harry."

He smiled and removed his glasses. "Now how can I help you?"

"Em...well..."

I sighed again and shook my head.

The Professor kept on grinning. "Take your time..."

Posh – but nice-posh, fruity-posh not conceited-posh.

I shrugged and loosened the top of my dark blouse. Then I unclasped the black neck cord and chucked the stone at the Professor. He caught it in his right hand.

He put on his glasses and examined the stone carefully. Then he looked up. "Stunning. Absolutely stunning. What is it?"

I raised my palms. "That's why I'm here. I was hoping you could tell me."

"Really?" He raised his eyebrows and inspected the stone again. Peering very closely. Then he placed it on his desk and removed his glasses.

I leaned forward. "Do you know what it is?"

He shook his head slowly. "I have no idea. I'm afraid. Unfortunately, I'm a theologian not a geologist."

"Oh...right," I mumbled and bit my lip slightly.

"I don't understand. Why did you think I could help you?"

"Frank – Mr. Truesdale – said that the stone identified you."

"*Identified me?* What does that mean?"

I gave him some background about Frank, including why he couldn't make the present meeting. Then told him about Frank's revelatory experience while watching the Discovery channel. The Professor was shocked.

"How extraordinary! Did you see this *ray of light* illuminate my image?"

I shook my head.

"So – and I don't mean this to sound disrespectful – you just took Mr. Truesdale's word for it. After all, it's a…well, I don't know…. *remarkable* assertion."

"Yes."

I felt quite awkward at this so I described some of our experiences with the stone but the Professor just seemed very sceptical.

"Well, this all sounds rather fantastic, "he said. "Appearing and disappearing animals and photo frames and glowing stones and beams of light. I mean – and again forgive me for asking – can you prove any of this or give me a demonstration? I think I'm fairly open-minded after a lifetime of studying divine miracles but can you show me any evidence to support your story?"

I thought about this. "Not really. The stone just appears to have a mind of its own. Unless it starts glowing, I think you'll just have to take my word for it."

The Professor stared at me with a bemused expression.

I reached over the Professor's desk, grabbed the stone and fell back into my seat. Then I held the stone tightly, closed my eyes and tried to communicate with my mind. *Come on, stone, do your thing. Do it!* I opened my eyes. The stone was completely unresponsive.

I tried again but with the same result. Then I looked up.

"I'm sorry, Professor."

"Harry."

"I'm sorry, Harry. It doesn't want to play ball. You probably think I'm completely mad."

"No, I don't actually. I believe you've experienced something. I'm even grateful that you approached me – but unfortunately, I just can't see how I can help in the absence of further information or evidence. I'm sorry."

I nodded slowly, fighting back a tear. "I'm sorry to have wasted your time – but thank you anyway."

I fastened the stone round my neck. Then I straightened my sweater, stood up and turned around.

"Wait," called the Professor, as I headed towards the door. I wheeled back. He removed a card from an ornate box on his desk and handed it over. "If there are any more developments, let me know. Here are my details."

"Thank you." I took the card, glancing at it. "I will."

"You've aroused my curiosity. I'm flying to Greece in a couple of days, then travelling on to New York but you can always reach me by mobile and email."

"Thank you," I repeated.

I walked out his office, closing the door quietly. The dour secretary had gone home and I was feeling tired.

I also needed the toilet and remembered there was one at the end of the hall. I drifted through the secretary's office, turned left into the corridor and hurried into the tiny lavatory. Then, I sat on the toilet, clutching my head in my hands.

It had gone wrong. The great hope was no hope at all. Frank had either made a mistake or invented the whole thing. After all, I'd just taken his word for it and not questioned him. Maybe he'd made up other stuff as well, like the beam of light identifying Rotney on the map of London. That all sounded very dubious, in retrospect.

I didn't move for quite a while, then I started sobbing. Why did life have to be so bloody awful? After all, I hadn't asked to be born. Now I was stuck in Rotney – probably for the rest of my life – and I'd completely wasted my time coming to the Barbican.

I released my head, closed my eyes and exhaled slowed. Then I opened my eyes and glared furiously ahead. Tears were still running down my cheeks but I didn't bother wiping them away. I remained sullen and motionless for ages.

Then I realized the area a couple of inches below my neck was feeling sore. I ignored the discomfort but it kept increasing. Eventually, I shifted my position, lowered my sweater and glanced down. Then I gasped, pulled out the neck cord and unclasped it. I held the stone out, studying it carefully as it dangled down, red raw and angry.

"*Whoa!*" I exclaimed aloud.

I yanked up my trousers, hit the flush, washed my hands and burst out the toilet in less than ten seconds. Then I sprinted back towards the Professor's office. How long had I been in the toilet? I checked my watch. Almost twenty minutes! *Ugh*, he was probably long gone.

I pounded on the door. "Professor," I yelled, "Harry. Please. *Please!*"

There was no response and I kept banging away furiously but then I detected some sounds within the office. They increased in volume and eventually the Professor opened the door, looking quite startled.

"Look!" I demanded and thrust the burning stone in front of his face.

"Well I …" His eyes widened hugely, utterly entranced. "That's just extraordinary..." he bumbled, eventually. "So, it *does* want to play ball, after all! Right, bring it back into my study. Let's have another look."

We shot back into his office – and I tell you, for an old duffer, he also moved extremely quickly.

28

The stone was so hot now we couldn't touch it. Also, the Professor obviously didn't want it anywhere near his wooden desk. So, he hung it from an extended lamp stand.

We just gawped at it wordlessly like a couple of curious babies. Then the Professor jabbed me.

"Look!" he instructed, pointing.

"What?" I craned my neck forward. "I can't see anything" I peered closer. "*No!* Is that really happening?"

"Seems so."

"Whoa," I drawled slowly.

An inscription was clearly forming in black lettering on the surface of the stone. I didn't recognize the lettering. "What language is that? Is it Greek?"

"No, definitely not. Not Egyptian, either." The Professor concentrated intensely, nodded his head in disbelief. "*Astonishing,*" he muttered, "I've *never* seen anything like this before."

"Do you know what the language is?"

He didn't respond immediately, still clearly hypnotized by the transforming stone but then he emitted a small cry of triumph. "I think, I do, yes."

"Well?"

"It's Hebrew. Yes, certainly Hebrew. In fact, if you give me a second, I'll even tell you what it says."

Another pause while I waited expectantly. The Professor removed his glasses and squinted even closer. "I need to be careful, here, actually. Don't want to scald my nose!"

He kept staring.

"Yes, there we go. Five letters. I'll translate – Y-H-V-D-H."

"What does it mean?"

The Professor stepped back and tilted his head in my direction. "Y-H-V-D-H," he repeated slowly. "But, pronounced Yehudi, Yehudah or Yehuday – hmmm…"

"Didn't he play the violin?"

"What?" The Professor was barely listening.

"Yehudi – Yehudi Benjamin. My Dad's got one of his CDs. I'm sure he played the violin…"

The Professor nodded. "Yehudi Menuhin. Yes, famous fiddler. But doesn't really help us, though, sorry."

He stared at the stone again. "Y-H-V-D-H. Five letters. Red stone. Carbuncle. Five, not six. So not the six days of creation…"

"I thought it was seven days of creation?"

"Six days. God rested on the seventh day."

"Oh, sorry. My parents didn't do God. I think the most I ever learnt was God was Dog backwards."

The Professor ignored this comment and continued studying the stone.

"This has never happened before, has it? I mean an inscription appearing?"

"No."

"Well, at least, it doesn't say you've been measured on the scales and found wanting."

"What, like a weight gain plan?"

"Not exactly. It's my slightly oblique reference to the mysterious handwriting that appeared at Belshazzar's feast in the Book of

Daniel. It means impending doom – where we get the expression *the writing was on the wall*."

I nodded. "So, you think it could be a message of some sort. A prophecy?"

"Maybe."

He stepped back and scratched his head vigorously. Then he stopped and looked up. "I've got an idea".

"Yes?"

"Just hold on…"

He turned around and walked towards one his gigantic bookcases. "Now, where are you? Come on…. come on…there you are." He removed a worn book with a slight flourish.

"What's that?"

"Exodus."

"Sounds biblical."

The Professor wasn't listening. He sat down at his desk and thumbed quickly through the pages of the book. "It's somewhere here," he commented. "In *Tetzaveh*. One of the portions. I'm sure of it." He kept thumbing until he located a chosen page. "Yes, here we go. Chapter Five." He began reading quietly, focusing on the Hebrew lettering and then checking the English translation. This went on for quite a while before he looked up again. "Just hold on, Miss Davidson – "

"Antonia."

He smiled. "Just hold on, Antonia, I'm getting somewhere but I need to check some more references. Can you bear with me a bit longer?"

"Of course," I said. "Can you give me a clue?"

"Well, I think this stone is extraordinarily rare and special but – as I say – if you could just wait while I do some cross referencing, I should be able to give you a full explanation shortly."

"Of course," I repeated. "Take your time."

"Thank you, "he replied. "Shouldn't take too long. Do you want a glass of water or something?"

"No, I'm fine, thanks."

"OK. Let me know if you do."

He stood up, approached another gigantic bookcase and grabbed several more books. Then he sat down again and arranged them on his desk. I watched admiringly as he studied the open pages with astonishing focus. *Why can't I do homework like that?* Suddenly, I felt like telling him my Dad also went to Cambridge but it would have just distracted him. Besides, I didn't fancy fielding awkward enquires such as *what's he doing now?*

I checked my watch. Just after eight o'clock now. Hospital visiting hours were over. I'd have to see Frank tomorrow – but it appeared I'd have further news, at least.

I shifted my gaze. The stone still burned brightly, its strange inscription easily visible. As I gaped at it, the Professor looked up from his books abruptly. He swept a hand slowly through his hair and squinted at the stone.

"Any luck?" I enquired politely.

He didn't respond.

"Professor?"

"Antonia," he began, "To say that this is...I don't know... *astonishing*...would barely begin to cover it. But yes - I think I have a very strong idea of what this stone is. I mean, I suppose it could be an incredible hoax but..."

"But?"

"I don't think so somehow. It wouldn't add up."

He turned in my direction. "Look, I need you to tell me everything – and I really do mean *everything* you know about Mr. Truesdale. Try not to miss anything out. Something that may seem like just an insignificant detail, may be of immense importance."

"What's the stone?"

"I'll tell you that shortly, you have my word. But to help me do that – I repeat – please tell me as much as you can about Mr. Truesdale and the stone. I know you've already given me some information – and that's been extremely helpful, thank you – but I'd like to hear more. Particularly, how he discovered it in the first place and how it first manifested its properties."

I raised my eyebrows and leaned back slightly. "Well…all right, I'll try my best. Sorry, if you don't mind, can I have that glass of water, first?"

"Of course," he beamed. "Are you hungry? I think I've got some biscuits."

"No, just a glass of water, please."

"Sure."

He popped out of his office and reappeared, a few moments later, holding a glass of water and a plate of assorted biscuits. "I thought you might change your mind about the biscuits," he said and passed over the glass and plate.

I smiled back. "Thanks."

I sipped the water and munched the largest biscuit. "Might as well start at the beginning," I mumbled, as I chewed. "A few weeks ago, I was walking home from school, one afternoon, when I saw a poster advertising a magic show in the pub, just down the road from where I lived…"

And so, I told the Professor pretty much everything I could remember. He just sat there listening very carefully, occasionally scribbling in a moleskin notebook.

I described Huck's shifty behaviour in plenty of detail, including Frank's final warning. Once I'd finished, the Professor checked some stuff on his laptop, scribbled some more, then removed his glasses.

"Interesting," he remarked slowly, "all very interesting indeed." He pressed his fingers together and stared ahead, then blew out. "You want some answers now, don't you?"

I checked my watch. Almost half past eight.

"Don't worry about it," I said casually. "I need to get back for *EastEnders*. Just give me a shout when you're ready."

The Professor frowned, before realizing I was joking. He grinned. "Well, I wish I had more graduate students like you," he replied, "all very sombre, you know, theology students."

I smiled back and raised a palm. "Over to you…"

"Well, look, I'll do my best," he promised. "Let's start with some background. If you look in the second book of the Old Testament, Exodus, you essentially have an account of how the Hebrew people, the Israelites, were enslaved by the Egyptians and then redeemed by Moses. Moses, by the way, is an Egyptian name."

I nodded. "It's OK. I've seen the cartoon."

"The *cartoon?*"

"Yeah, you know, *The Prince of Egypt.*"

The Professor laughed. "Of course, the cartoon! I'm afraid I haven't seen it. I'm sure it's very good, but anyway back to Exodus. It relates that after the Israelites received the Ten Commandments, they were instructed by their God to build a Tabernacle in the desert. This was designed to be a portable dwelling place for the Divine Presence. What they called the *Shechinah*. Exodus also contains lengthy instructions about how to build the Ark of the Covenant that contained the Ten Commandments. Again, this was also portable so they could carry it across the desert."

I nodded attentively.

"Now, look, this is the essential bit. In Exodus, the High Priest of the Israelites is very carefully instructed as to what he should wear during the divine service and how it should be designed. One of the items that he's told to have is a Breastplate. And Exodus is very specific in this regard. However, there is also a lot of commentary about the relevant verses. Some of it, contradictory, in fact. But, cutting to the chase, the Breastplate contained twelve jewels, mirroring the twelve tribes of Israel."

I kept on nodding,

The Professor turned his laptop round.

"In this instance, I'm breaking a golden rule of academia. This is the relevant *Wikipedia* entry. You can see the reconstruction of the Priestly Breastplate and how the twelve stones are set out."

I studied the screen intently as the Professor continued.

"Somewhat grudgingly, I admit *Wikipedia* is quite helpful on this. It says here, under the section relating to The Jewels:

The twelve jewels in the breastplate were each, according to the Biblical description, to be made from specific minerals, none of them the same as another, and each of them representative of a specific tribe, whose name was to be inscribed on the stone. According to a rabbinic tradition, the names of the twelve tribes were engraved upon the stones with Naxian stone, or what is also called emery.

"All right, well that's all very well – but the crucial stone, as far as we're concerned, is this red one on the second row. In fact, you might recognize the lettering."

He pointed to a stone on the screen and I leaned in closer.

"Same lettering!" I exclaimed.

"Yes."

"But what does that mean? What are you saying?"

"Well, what *Wikipedia* doesn't tell you is that there are many ancient stories written about this particular stone. It is, without any doubt, the most important stone in the breastplate and has phenomenal power."

"What is it?"

"It's the stone of Judah. Judah was the leader of the twelve tribes and the most powerful. The stone is also known variously as The Red Sunshine Stone or just The Sunshine Stone. It has been compared to burning coal and there have been various classical disagreements whether it was actually red or blue turquoise but the consensus opinion appears to be that it was a carbuncle."

"Isn't that a boil?"

"Yes, that's one meaning. However, a carbuncle can also be an extremely rare and precious stone. It's also considered to have magical properties, although, these are not specifically defined."

I listened in silence.

"Now, look, there's more – and as I say you won't find this in *Wikipedia*. But you will find it in here…" said the Professor, pointing at the opened books.

"The stone of Judah has other mystical properties. Firstly, whoever holds this stone cannot be defeated in battle. The stone protected the tribe which led the other tribes in war. This explains – on a simple level – for example, why you and Frank won your physical fights. But – on a more profound level – it means, while you have the stone, you defeat all physical enemies – for examples, viruses, or even the negative effects of ageing. That's why, for example, Frank's health improved so dramatically after he started wearing the stone around his neck."

I started gawping at this point. "Wait! Professor - you're saying this is the *original stone?*"

"Yes, I am – and I'm pretty sure of it too. Now look there's more.

"According to certain Eastern European traditions – I hesitate to use the word, mythology, as it connotes historical inaccuracy – the Sunshine Stone appears every thousand years to an extremely worthy person. Someone who has demonstrated incredible integrity, wisdom, leadership or courage. It's a mystical indication to that person that they have the ability to redeem their world."

"*Redeem their world?* What does that mean?"

"It means they have the potential and power, should they choose to exercise it, to alleviate current suffering, misery, injustice and hunger on a global scale. To stop wars and bring universal salvation. Like a Messiah, although I'm not fond of that word."

"Why?"

"Again, religious connotations. Jewish tradition, for example, teaches that the Messiah will descend from the tribe of Judah. In fact, the Judeo-Christian concept of the Messiah is largely based on the idea of a divine or supernatural redeemer. However, this is fundamentally opposed by Gnostic ideas which – "

"*English*, Professor, please."

The Professor stopped and removed his glasses. "Miss Davidson – Antonia – what I'm trying to say is that this stone appeared to Frank for a specific reason and at a very particular time. Every time the silver photo frame appeared it was a reminder of why he'd received the stone."

"Because of his actions in Korea? Why he received the Medal of Honor?"

"Yes."

"And why did the stone pick you? I mean obviously you're incredibly knowledgeable about this subject but is there any other reason? Anything I don't know."

"I think so, yes."

"Really, what?"

"William Frederick McFadzean."

"Who's that?"

The Professor turned the laptop back and tapped a few keys.

"Here we are…" He replaced his glasses:

The night of June 30th, 1916 found the 14th Battalion Irish Rifles in their assembly trenches at Elgin Avenue in Thiepval Wood.

It was here in the trench, in darkness, before the morning attack that Billy McFadzean would sacrifice his life and be posthumously awarded the Victoria Cross.

The battalion war diary records, "heavy bombardment, great trouble in keeping the candle alight," In the trench Billy was singing his favourite song "My little Grey Home in the West" and keeping his comrades spirits up with his jokes and banter.

The trench was about seven feet deep and boxes of Mills bombs were being distributed prior to the attack. As Billy lifted a box, it overturned, spilling the bombs onto the floor of the trench and dislodging the pins in two of them. Knowing full well what would happen, Billy threw himself flat onto the bombs just as two of them exploded. Billy lost his life instantly however this heroic act saved the lives of dozens of others and incredibly only one other man was injured.

William McFadzean's Victoria Cross was gazetted on September 9th, 1916 and once again his name is remembered on the Thiepval Memorial for all those with no known grave.

His commanding officer Lieutenant Colonel FC Bowen wrote to Billy's father on September 16th.

"Dear Mr. McFadzean,

It is with feelings of great pride that I read the announcement of the granting of the VC to your gallant son and my only regret is that he was not spared to us to wear his well-earned decoration.

It was one of the finest deeds of a war that is so full of big things and I can assure you that the whole battalion rejoiced when they heard it. Your gallant boy, though gone from us, his deeds will forever live in our memories and the record will go down for all time in the regimental history to which he has added fresh and great lustre."

The family also received a letter from Buckingham Palace on December 18th, 1916.

"It is a matter of sincere regret to me that the death of Private McFadzean deprived me of the pride of personally conferring upon him the Victoria Cross, the greatest of all awards for valour and devotion to duty."

Signed George R I

The Professor looked up and removed his glasses.

"George V?" I asked.

"Yes,"

"Who was the soldier?"

"My great uncle. My family were originally from Ulster. His VC was the first to be won at the Battle of Somme."

"That's amazing," I said. "So, the stone was kind of reaching out to your family as well?"

"I think so, yes."

"But I still don't really understand. I'm sorry for being thick. Are you saying that the stone – that appears only once every thousand years or whatever – appeared to Frank because he was incredibly brave and now he can make the world a better place?"

"Yes, I am. Of course – as in the case of my Great Uncle – there have been other supremely brave and incredible men in history but the stone has obviously decided that Frank is the most meritorious. It's chosen Frank to receive its favours – for want of a better term."

"But Professor, "I protested, "even assuming that's true – and it's very hard to believe, surely it's too late. Frank is a very old man. I mean, I know he's in great shape or *was* in great shape. Maybe, that's my point. He's eighty-one years old and he's just suffered a stroke. He's hardly able to start going around the world being Nelson Mandela or Mother Theresa or whoever. I mean, for a start, he's in hospital."

"You're wrong."

"I'm *wrong*?"

"Yes, you're wrong."

"How can I be wrong? I saw him yesterday evening and he was wired up to a bunch of hospital monitors."

"You're still wrong."

"I am?" I thought about this. "How?"

"According to the Old Testament, he's at the correct age. Abraham didn't receive his divine revelation until he was seventy-five – the age, by the way, that Frank said he attained when the stone started to manifest its powers. Then, if you recall, these powers increased and became revelatory when Frank turned eighty. The same age as when Moses received his divine revelation at the *"bush that burned but was not consumed."* A bit like the stone, don't you think?

"There are other interesting comparisons. Rabbinic commentary states that Moses was beckoned to the bush by his dead father's voice and amongst the signs he received his staff was transformed in to a serpent. Frank reported similar miracles."

"Well, no, not really – I mean I think you're stretching the point a bit. All right he said he heard his Dad calling him but he turned a rabbit into a monkey, not a stick in to a serpent."

The Professor nodded. "Same thing. Transformation. And then he learnt how to do it, at will, after that point. But he just didn't pick up on the clues. For example, why his photograph kept appearing."

"But you're talking about *revelation*. Frank's not religious."

"No, I was talking about revelation in the context of the Old Testament. Personally, I believe in God, or the concept of God – but what I think of as God is the greater power of the universe to manifest itself, not a Father Christmas lookalike sitting on a throne in heaven. However, what is clear, is that Frank has received both *revelation* and *revelatory experiences*. He has received a greater calling – and I don't exactly know who's made that calling. But it's a calling, all right."

I brushed my hair back and shook my head. "Whoa – this is *very heavy stuff*, Professor."

"It is."

"Frank thought it was like a Superman thing."

"It is. Same principle. Superman was invented as a messianic figure by two young Jewish men just before the Second World War. It was their creative response to the growth of evil and Nazism."

"Whoa."

"All the superheroes are Messianic figures to one extent or another. In fact, how does Captain America – another response to Nazism – prove he is meritorious enough to receive his superhero abilities?"

"I don't know."

"He jumps on a grenade to protect his fellow conscripts. Sound familiar?"

I nodded. "But…I still have loads of questions."

"All right, I'll try my best."

"Thank you. Well, first question. I understand why Frank was chosen or selected or whatever. I even understand why you were too now. It makes sense. But why me? I'm nothing special – that's not false modesty, or anything – it's the plain truth. I'm just a stupid teen trying to get by."

The Professor inhaled sharply. "It's a good question and I have to say – and I don't mean this disrespectfully at all - it's not immediately evident. The reason may become clearer in time. I'm not implying you're not a special person, quite the contrary, in fact. It's just you're still a very young girl and your special talents and abilities haven't fully manifested. Indeed, they might not for some time. The important thing is the stone has identified something within you – maybe an enormous potential – and so, to borrow your expression, you've also been selected.

"In fact, your expression isn't quite correct. According to some of the references, one very special person – Frank, in this instance – is identified, or chosen, or selected and the stone appears to them. It not only provides them with a message but guides and assists them. Its powers are adapted to that person's special abilities or personality. So, in Frank's case because he showed an interest in creating illusions, it made the illusions real. But because people in the twenty first century can't accept miracles, no matter how spectacular they are, they either rationalize them away or become actively hostile. That's the primary reason why the pub spectators descended into violence. They couldn't deal with what they were seeing. But you could. And there's a reason for that.

"The special person receives what's called *enablers*. Someone that helps them achieve their ends. In Frank's case, there are numerous *minor* enablers – for example, the pub landlord that accommodates him, the doctor that treats him, and the pilot that flies him – the list is endless – but there are rarely more than two *major* enablers. Major enablers play a critical role in helping the special person achieve his or her potential and are actively selected by the stone. The reason for the selection may not be immediately apparent – for example, in your case."

"But not in yours?"

"No, I think it's pretty clear why the stone selected me. Don't you think so?"

I nodded, "yes."

I thought about this again but another question surfaced quickly, "and what do you think all this business with Dr Huck is about?"

"I'm afraid that's also not entirely clear. I think you'll just have to wait and see on that one."

"Do you think he's something like Satan in disguise trying to collect the stone and stop Frank from saving the world?"

"No, I don't. I think his role is somewhat subtler than that. It really sounds like you've been watching too many movies."

I half-smiled. "Do you think he's actually a good guy. Maybe he's a descendant from an ancient race of people that have sworn to protect and monitor the stone whenever it appears?"

"No, I really don't think that. Try and get away from this clichéd Hollywood way of viewing the world. I know it's hard for young people, they're constantly fed on this entirely unrealistic and simplistic, cinematic vision and structure. Real life is not Harry Potter. It's infinitely more complex, not something that can be contained in a two-hour narrative. This is not about Goodies versus Baddies or Cowboys versus Indians, this is about a realistic shot at making this imperfect world a better place."

"But how?" I asked – and then suddenly I remembered I'd asked Mr. Shaw a similar question only a few days ago.

"Well, in Frank's case, the stone will guide him and assist him and give him the required strength and power. How exactly it will be achieved, I have no idea."

"And could he fail?"

"Of course, he could. By inference, the last person the Sunshine Stone appeared to, didn't succeed - maybe a thousand years ago. Otherwise, the world wouldn't still be in such a bloody awful mess. Ordinary people can only try and improve the world by tiny steps, one at a time – but Frank now has the potential and ability to take an enormous step forward."

I nodded again. "I understand. So, what should I do now, Professor?"

"Get back to the hospital, this evening. Don't wait until tomorrow. In the first instance, Frank needs the stone so he can physically recover."

"Visiting hours are over."

"Doesn't matter. You're a major enabler, remember? It's an enormous privilege and responsibility. Get back to the hospital and break down the door if you must. Keep out of Dr Huck's way and if he confronts you, treat him with extreme caution. He remains an unknown quantity. Instead, find Frank, as quickly as possible. Tell him exactly what I said and give him the stone back. It doesn't belong to you. Then, let the stone take him to the next stage of his development and direct his destiny. If you need me, you have my details."

"I do. Thank you *so* much." I stood up and turned towards the office door.

"Hey, Antonia," called the Professor.

I turned around, "Professor?"

He motioned towards the lamp. "Don't forget the stone."

29

As soon as I grabbed the stone and marched out of the Professor's office, the burning glow faded away but the Hebrew inscription remained clearly in place.

I took the Metropolitan line from Barbican to Liverpool Street. Then I changed on to the Central Line and headed towards East Acton Station.

It was after nine o'clock now and the crazy Central London rush hour had eased. I wondered what I'd say when I got to the hospital. I imagined a stern lecture from the ward sister about visiting hours followed by a sharp kick up the backside.

I presumed responding about World Redeemers and Enchanted Stones wouldn't help all that much. I'd probably ended up getting admitted, then placed in a strait jacket. It was funny how quickly our society associated miracles, prophecy and a Messianic complex with mental illness. No wonder Frank worried so much about the men in white coats!

The tube train passed swiftly through the stations on the Central Line – Lancaster Gate, Queensway, and Notting Hill Gate. But not fast enough. I was flipping *desperate* to see the old man now. I could finally give him some answers, although I had no idea how he'd react.

I tutted, shuffled in my seat and checked my watch repeatedly. Every now and again, I snorted through my nostrils for added effect. It didn't make the train go any quicker, of course.

I glanced around the carriage. Same stressed-out faces, as before. Tired, suited, overworked commuters on their way home. In fact, I recognized their haggard expressions. Jailbird Daddy had sported the same look for years.

At last, the train reached East Acton Station and I sprinted through the station and out through the ticket barriers. It was quite cold now and Acton was hardly the most charming area of London. But I didn't care. I slowed to a jog and pounded briskly down the main road, barely noticing the Victorian prison on my left.

I arrived at the hospital, hardly out of breath and strode through the main reception and into the lift. I pressed the button for the third floor but the doors remained open as two orderlies wheeled an empty bed in. Slowly.

I bit my lip and eventually the doors closed. The lift ascended ever so gently, finally arriving at the third floor. Then the doors open lazily and I sprung out, swerved left and bolted towards the ward.

I hit the security doors, seconds later. They were firmly locked so I hit the buzzer on the left. There was no reply whatsoever so I kept pressing the bell. Again, and again. I was so frustrated that I kept stepping backwards and forwards, cursing, circling and mumbling *come on, come on.*

Eventually I spotted a male nurse through the window and beckoned wildly. He approached cautiously, looking slightly bewildered.

"Visiting hours are over now," he announced through the doors, "you need to come back tomorrow."

"I know but it's an emergency," I said.

He frowned. *Could he hear me?*

"*Emergency,*" I pronounced again, firmly. "Open up, please."

Maybe it was a quite naughty saying it was an emergency in the middle of a hospital but - aside from giving Frank some very pertinent information - I knew that the faster I could return the stone, the quicker he'd recover.

The nurse opened the door, still looking bewildered.

"Who are you here to see?"

"Mr. Truesdale."

"Mr. Truesdale?"

"Yes, William Truesdale, admitted a couple of days ago, suffered a stroke. He's in one of the rooms on the left."

"Oh, I see." He sighed wearily. "You'd better come with me."

"Sure."

I followed the nurse towards the ward reception about twenty metres down the aisle. But as we walked, I noticed he was acting awkwardly.

"You, all right?" I asked but he didn't respond. Then I began sensing something was wrong. For a start, he hadn't asked me what my emergency was which I thought was strange.

We got to the reception and another nurse, sitting behind a computer monitor, glanced up.

"She's come about Mr. Truesdale," said the male nurse. *Boy*, he really did sound miserable.

"Oh," said the other nurse. Now they'd both said *oh*.

"What's your name, please?"

"Antonia Davidson."

"And what relation are you to Mr. Truesdale?"

"Very close friend."

"But not a relative?"

"Not exactly."

The nurse nodded, slowly. "Do you mind just sitting in the waiting room? It's just on the right, a few metres further down the hall."

"Of course," I mumbled – but I was spooked. "Everything all right?"

"Please just have a seat in the waiting room someone will see you in a minute."

"See me? OK... "

I walked unhappily through the hall and into the waiting room. It was a simple affair with a few worn chairs, grotty paintings of flowers on the wall and some ancient magazines on a low coffee table.

I sat down on the nearest chair. Something bad had happened. That was extremely obvious. Poor Frank. Best possible scenario, he'd suffered another stroke and they were operating on him, loosening the blood clots in his brain or whatever. Worse possible scenario, he was dead.

I hated feeling frightened – and when I was wearing the stone, I felt much more protected. But now the stone was cold and I felt terrified. I couldn't even bear thinking through the implications if Frank was dead. Not just for me – but for the whole world.

I fancied seizing the stone and holding it tightly in both hands. But it was too risky. Someone was going to walk through the door, any time now. Instead, I clutched it through my blouse.

I closed my eyes. *Stone,* I prayed, *or God or Jesus or Allah or universe or whoever's out there, if anyone's out there...* I grasped the stone tighter. *Don't let Frank die...please, please...don't let him die! Please!*

Oh no, I thought. Maybe when the stone glowed earlier in the Professor's building, it wasn't *revealing* itself but warning that Frank was in trouble. And I misunderstood the sign. Instead of running back towards Professor's office for a diagnosis, I should have headed for the hospital. Immediately. Returned the stone to the Frank and saved his life.

In fact, I should never have taken the stone. *This was all my fault.*

Then, I was seized by an even more alarming thought. Maybe the Hebrew lettering had appeared at the point Frank's soul left this earth. *Signifying his death!*

I'd really failed, hadn't I? I sniffed loudly and a tear ran down my cheek. I brushed it away and waited.

Still no one came. *Torture.* I checked my watch. It was after ten now. *What was going on?* It was just ridiculous. What was causing the delay? The longer it continued, the worse I felt.

I shot up, clenched my fists and paced around the waiting room. Then I sat down and checked my watch. I knew Mum would be worried now. Fretting about where I was because I didn't have a mobile *like every other human being in the country.* Poor Mummy. Poor Daddy. Poor Frank. Poor me. *Oh, God.*

I checked my watch, yet again. Six minutes past ten. Right, I'd go back to the ward reception in four minutes and find out what the hell was going on. They'd obviously forgotten about me, the disorganized, uncaring idiots.

I bounced my legs up and down, faster and faster, exhaling loudly and gritting my teeth. It didn't help so I studied the flower paintings instead. They looked like they'd been painted by someone with a bad sense of humour. I was about to start pacing again when a small, bald doctor, holding a clipboard, walked in.

You could see it was bad news just by the way he carried himself. He stared ahead with a deeply unhappy expression, then glanced over.

"Can I sit down?"

I nodded, bracing myself.

"It's Miss Davidson, isn't it?"

I nodded again, too nervous to open my mouth.

"Not a relative, though?"

I shook my head, slowly.

"Em…" he looked down at his clipboard and then up at me, "I'm afraid – well, there's no easy way of saying this – em…"

I looked at him, sadly. Waiting. Fighting tears.

"Mr. Truesdale suffered a massive cerebrovascular accident at around seven thirty this evening and we were unable to save him. We tried everything – "

"A stroke?"

"Yes, a cerebrovascular accident or CVA is a medical term for a stroke. Technically, it was an embolic stroke. The clot moved up from his arms to his brains despite the medication we were prescribing and – "

I swallowed. "Did he suffer pain, or fear?"

"I don't think so, no, it happened very quickly. Extremely quickly, in fact. We performed an emergency carotid endarterectomy but were unable to save him. I'm so very sorry."

I stared at the doctor for a few seconds and then I started crying. I probably cry a bit too much for a fifteen-year-old girl – it's been a hard couple of years – but I'd never cried like this before. At first, I sobbed silently but intensely, then I began to howl in anguish. I curled up in the chair in a foetal position and grabbed my chest as my body throbbed violently.

I think the doctor watched for a few moments before mumbling something about a nurse. Then suddenly there were a couple of nurses and an orderly surrounding me. I'm not quite sure what happened for about an hour after that, my memory comprises just a few random images. I remember one of the nurses stroking my head and another one giving me a glass of water. There was also a fervent conversation in the background about contacting mum, or getting a cab and how I was in no condition to get home.

I don't suppose I allayed their concerns my making the odd statement about how we'd lost a world saviour and were doomed for the next thousand years. God, I wish I hadn't said that stuff - I really do - but I was already feeling like I'd *seriously* blown it. Why did I accept the stone? *Why?* Selfish idiot.

But the awful guilt was still small compared with the sheer agony of losing my best friend and protector. It *physically* hurt like I'd swallowed a massive parasitic squid, which was pulling and consuming me from the inside.

I think one of the nurses mentioned that Frank's son had left just before I showed up. I'm also pretty sure she said that if I phoned the hospital, when I felt better, they'd give me his contact details.

I calmed down around eleven. A few minutes later, I just wanted to go home. I popped into the toilet and studied my reflection. Unsurprisingly, I looked awful. My eyes were raw from crying so much.

I drenched my face in water, tidied myself up and thanked all the nurses. Then I walked back through the ward's hall. An elderly black orderly let me out and I took the lift down. I think I was moving like a zombie, although, obviously I had no interest in feasting on the flesh of the living. My overwhelming desire was to get into bed and curl up forever.

Once outside the hospital and in the cold, dark air, I began to cry again and sobbed all the way back to East Acton Station. I didn't even notice the prison.

I passed through the ticket barriers, still wiping my eyes with a sodden tissue and snivelling loudly. Then I made my way onto the platform. I was the only person standing on it and the digital clock on the station notice board read 11:32.

The train arrived four minutes later and I boarded as soon as the automatic doors slid open. There was only one other person in the carriage, a huge, snoring lady. I sat down and watched the train doors close, then remained immobile and dazed as the train headed towards East London.

Very few people got on and off. Meanwhile, the fat lady woke up, just after we passed Liverpool Street Station and tumbled out of the train at Bethnal Green. She stank of stale alcohol and body odour.

Then the train moved off, bumbling along slowly before finally stalling. I heard the engines whirring down and a couple of shouts from outside. Then nothing. The train just sat silently, dropping in temperature.

I was completely cried-out for the evening so I just sniffed loudly every few seconds and dabbed my nose with wet tissues. My carriage was completely empty now which was probably just as well as I didn't much fancy company.

It hit midnight and then the train started up again, croaking and puffing into Mile End Station. It stalled again and the train doors opened. No one got on and the train showed no signs of continuing its journey.

God, I thought, *the tube really is a disgrace. Absolutely not what I need.* I sniffed loudly and checked my watch. Then the carriage doors snapped shut. I waited patiently but the train still didn't move and I shook my head slowly in disbelief. More delay.

Then, incredibly, the train doors opened again.

"Oh, this is ridiculous!" I said aloud to the vacant carriage. Then I heard slow deliberate footsteps approaching, gradually increasing in volume.

I turned my head in the direction of the noise but couldn't identify the source. The steps got louder and louder and then the mysterious pedestrian appeared to the left of my carriage, walked down the aisle and sat directly opposite me.

"Hello, Antonia," he said.

30

I looked down.

"I thought you were supposed to be in France?"

"Well, I was – for a few days, anyway."

I snorted. "Whatever."

Huck straightened himself in his seat and pressed his fingers together. He was unshaven and still wearing the same crappy suit.

"I'm really sorry about Frank, "he said, "He was a truly good man. A great man, in fact. But he didn't suffer in the end and if it wasn't for the stone he would have died many years ago. The injury he suffered ripped out his insides, you know. That's what happens when you smother an exploding grenade. It's not very pretty. Poor man. He barely functioned until the stone did its thing. But the magic shows gave him a new lease of life."

I looked up and shook my head sadly. "What do you want, Huck? I'm really not in the mood for this."

"Of course, you're not. You're distraught and in shock. Plus, you've had to absorb Professor Gibson's quaint little theories."

I stared at him. "How do you know about that?"

"We pretty much know everything, Antonia. We have to."

"Did you bug his office, like I presume you bugged Frank? Sounds like he was right after all."

Huck didn't reply but his raised eyebrows answered my question.

"*Idiot*," I muttered.

Huck still didn't respond.

I sniffed loudly and dabbed my eyes and nose for about the hundredth time. "Who are you, anyway?" I guess you're not really a scientist. Frank said you were a private detective. Is that right?"

"Actually, I *am* a scientist."

"Yeah, of course you are." I shook my head and snivelled again.

"Well I am, Antonia, it's just that I work for a government department now and they do things slightly differently."

"How about that!"

Huck leaned forward. "Antonia, look at your stone."

"It's not my stone."

"All right, look at Frank's stone."

I didn't move.

"Go on. Look at it."

I glared at him with disgust, then unbuttoned the top of my blouse and withdrew the stone. It lay cold and passive in my palm.

"What do you see?"

"Nothing."

"Exactly, it's not glowing."

"So?"

"So - if I'm the baddie or the supervillain or whatever you imagine I am - it would be glowing by now. In your case, the stone glows for two reasons. Firstly, to warn others not to mess with you and secondly, to warn you of impending danger. Think about it. The only exception was with Professor Gibson when the stone glowed in a different kind of way. To reveal its biblical lettering and give the Professor a helping hand."

I gawped at him. "How do you know this?"

"We've monitored everything, Antonia. We have to."

I looked down at the stone. It remained unresponsive.

"If you don't believe me, you can at least trust the stone," said Huck. "I'm not your enemy, never have been. I'm here to help you."

I looked up at him. "Well, never mind the stone, *I* don't trust you. I think you're a sinister little creep, Huck. You approach me at my lowest point, spouting a load of crap and think I'll believe everything you say. And I'm not the only one who doesn't trust you. Both Frank and the Professor told me to be really careful when you made your move – which is what I assume you're doing now."

Huck leaned back. "Fair enough. Frank saw me sitting in a car outside his room for an hour and made certain assumptions – and based on what he said to you and what you repeated to the Professor, you were similarly cautioned. A simple chain of events. Except Frank didn't have a clue what I was doing, much less the Professor and to use an old mathematical analogy, they put two and two together and came up with five."

I didn't reply so Huck continued.

"What Frank and the Professor came up with were only *theories*, at the end of the day. But there was a difference. The old man finally worked out the truth before he died but the Professor was off the mark. That's the problem with academics, you see, they don't live in the real world – especially theologians, they're a breed apart."

"I have no idea what you're talking about. What truth?"

"Frank wasn't the selected one, the redeemer, Messiah, saviour – whatever you want to call it – but he was still chosen. The Sunshine Stone appeared to him so that he could fulfil a task of extreme importance."

"What?"

"You weren't the major enabler. Frank was."

"*What?*"

"He was tasked to locate the next person, the person with the ability to save our rotten world, the person that appears only every thousand years or so and give them the stone."

I kept gawking

"Well, who's that?" I demanded, eventually.

Huck should his head. "You know what my favourite Americanism is?"

I frowned at him, "no, what?"

"Dumbass. It's such a great word, don't you think?"

I shrugged, then sniffed loudly.

There was a pause and I suddenly realized how tired I was feeling.

"It's you, dumbass," said Huck.

"I *am* a dumbass," I replied sadly.

"No, I mean, it's *you*, dumbass."

"Me? Me what?"

Then suddenly I understood what he was saying. "Rubbish!"

"Absolutely not, Antonia. Her Majesty's Government is now fully aware of this and wishes to assist you."

I sniffed and looked at him wearily. "You know, Dr Huck, it's been a really long day, a really *awful* day and I'm tired of listening to you. With the greatest of respect, please get off at the next station, get lost and never appear in my life again."

Huck didn't move. "Of course, you're distraught and now you blame yourself for Frank's death – but that's why we decided we had to approach you immediately before your guilt swallows you up and destroys you. Your old friend realized what his true role was in the end – it took him long enough, by the way – and made sure you had the stone and that it remained with you. As I said, the stone gave him, at least, an extra ten years of life, anyway – and he appreciated this and was happy to die in the knowledge that by giving you the stone he had achieved something of incredible importance."

I shook my head. "It's rubbish, Huck – *rubbish*. Even I'm not that naïve. Sorry. The stone appeared to Frank, not me and I was just try-ing to help him out."

"So why did it direct it to him to Rotney?"

"I don't know...to help him in his quest for the truth about the stone, or whatever."

"No, to locate you. Even Frank realized that eventually. The mag-ic tricks, the silver photo frames – it was all to bring you in."

"No, Huck, what brought me in – whatever that expression means – is that he was the only decent human being in Rotney and kept saving my backside."

"No, what helped you jump over your natural barrier of scepticism and begin to understand the importance of your mission was the supernatural events you started to encounter and couldn't explain away. Fifteen-year-old girls can't suddenly learn to fight like Stephen Seagal and send four villains into intensive care in about three seconds."

"Oh, you know about that too?"

"Of course, I do." He leaned forward again. "Now, look, I know you're tired and deeply upset and all your defences are up but I need you to listen very carefully to me please, Antonia.

"I'm going to get out at the next stop. You're right, you've had an extremely difficult day. There's only so much information you can take in before your head feels like it's going to explode. I know you don't trust me, right now and that's wholly understandable. But I want you to take your time and think very carefully about what I'm about to say.

"We know about the stone. We've known about it for a few years, in fact, since the Americans alerted us to its presence. I can't reveal how we know what we do – not yet, anyway. However, there's a few things we didn't know until very recently – for example, who the stone's intended target was – that's you, by the way. And now we know, we want to work with you. You have no idea what you and the stone are capable of. The stone is not about just a few magic tricks and fancy kicks. It's an object of supreme potential and power. But we can't harness that power without you – and we need you to assist us.

"I'm not talking about highfalutin ideals such as world peace and redemption but I am talking about making the world a very much better place, reducing war and starvation and poverty and injustice. You can help us and we can help you. This is most certainly not about giving a few pounds to charity or winning a charity badge for looking after sick animals, I'm talking about genuinely alleviating global misery."

I stared at Huck, wiping my eyes.

"In return, as I say, we can help you. I'm sure you'd like to see your father come out of prison, maybe even get his old job back, move out of Rotney, get back to Purchester and High Mount. It's really not as difficult as you think."

"So, my Dad *is* innocent?"

Huck sighed. "Your father made some serious errors and unintentionally broke the law but due to over-zealous policing and a vicious, self-serving regulatory body - plus I have to say some despicable conduct in the populist media - his situation was made very much worse. Nevertheless, we can still get some redress and assist him."

I frowned. "Well, why me?"

"Why you? Do you mean why've you been selected?"

I nodded.

"Well, you won't be surprised, we've looked at you very closely. The Professor was a bit harsh. You're an exceptional individual with great potential. Due to your personal circumstances, you also possess a keen sense of justice – and there's no doubt you have balls too. Also, what you don't realize, is that because of your exposure to the stone your *intellectual* capabilities have also increased. Your IQ has probably gone up a couple of points just on this train journey! At High Mount, you were, at best, a middling student. Now you're beginning to run rings around your teachers and if you carry on wearing the stone you'll probably end up at Cambridge, like your father. We need you, Antonia. Will you help us?"

I looked over Huck's shoulder. We were pulling into Leyton.

Huck leaned in, even closer, "well?"

I sat back, firmly. "*No.* I still think you're full of crap. The stone appeared to Frank, not me. It's *Frank's*, not mine."

I sniffed loudly. "You know, once upon the time, when I was just a little girl, I used to trust the police, think they were the good guys. Cheer them on, you know? Especially, in the movies. Now I know a lot better. I'm not quite so naïve. They're just a bunch of thugs – and I don't trust anyone, or anything, to do with the authorities. They're all liars and connivers. People who'll say and do whatever they want just to get their way.

"So, listen up, Huck. I *certainly* don't trust you, or your ridiculous story, or the Government - if that's who you really work for. The stone and its powers aren't mine to give, or yours to take. If the stone had appeared to me, maybe we'd be having a different conversation. But it hasn't, it didn't and you're still full of crap – although, I admit, you almost had me going with your little story about my Dad. So please, Huck, I repeat, get out at Leyton station, get lost and leave my Mum alone. She's gone through enough already. If I see you again any-where near her, I'll break your jaw. And I'm getting very good at that. All right?"

Huck shook his head, exhaling slowly. "I'll stay away from your Mum. In the meantime, look after the stone, please. Think very care-fully about what I just said and if you change your mind, don't worry about contacting me, I'll find you."

The train slowed down to a resting stop and the doors sprang open. Huck nodded slightly and disappeared. Then the doors closed and the train rumbled on towards Rotney.

When we finally got there, I started sobbing again. It was almost half past twelve and eerily quiet. I'd never walked through the town so late. The ticket office was firmly locked up and the ticket barriers were open.

My flat was less than ten minutes' way but I just couldn't handle going home immediately. I walked aimlessly out of the station and headed towards the lake which ran almost parallel with the High Street. You could occasionally see the odd duck in its murky waters but I assumed they'd all be tucked up and asleep now.

Of course, normally, I'd be terrified of wandering through Rotney at such an ungodly hour. But I was wearing the stone and felt protected. I noticed a few sad drunks singing and belching raucously on the other side of the road but I ignored them.

A few seconds later, I felt a sharp familiar heat under my sweater.

"Oh, *now what?*" I asked aloud. "I've really had enough this evening."

I glanced around but there was nobody. It was completely quiet. The drunks had wandered off and I was quite alone. I stopped walking and considered my next move. Lake? Or home?

I stood there, sniffing, for a few seconds. Then, I shrugged and carried on towards the lake.

With about two hundred metres remaining, I turned a corner and passed two men sitting quietly on a wooden bench. I just kept going without looking at them. Predictably enough, I soon heard footsteps walking behind me. This continued for a few moments, then I wheeled round.

There was no one there. I stopped walking, scratched my head and glanced around again, Nothing, nobody. I checked the stone again. It was still burning. *What was going on?* Was it an alert, or something else now?

I continued walking, reaching the lake a few moments later. It was completely quiet. I peered into the darkness and inhaled slowly. Then I sat down on the ground. I knew I was acting irresponsibly but my head was blown. I just need a moment by the water, then I'd head home.

After sitting calmly for a few minutes, I stood up slowly and headed back towards the station. I speeded up slightly and adjusted the rock that was getting uncomfortably warm.

I turned a corner but found my path blocked by two large, white men. Both had shaved heads but were dressed smartly in suits, loosened silk ties and Oxfords. Still threatening, though.

I stopped and sighed. "Do you mind? I need to get through, please."

"Isn't it a bit late for you?" asked the man, on the left. Quite well-spoken.

"Yes, it is, which is why I'd like to get home as soon as possible. So – for the second time – *do you mind?*"

They didn't move. "No, I don't buy it," replied the first man, "I think you're looking for a bit of action. Pretty little girl, like you. Not getting much at home, are we?"

I shot him a look of hatred. *"Excuse me?"*

The first man grinned. "Oh, don't be like that, darling. We're here to help. So how about it?"

I kept glaring. "How about *what?*"

The second man, still grinning, raised his fist slowly and snapped open a large blade. *Click!* "A little bit of action, darling". Also, well-spoken.

I sniffed and shook my head. "Gentleman," I said slowly, "I have had the *worst* day and I've just lost my best friend. Please let's not do this now. Just turn around and walk away. Please. I'm asking nicely."

They exchanged glances and laughed. "Polite, isn't she?" commented the first man.

"Very polite," agreed the second, "but we're not going anywhere, love. Not until we've had a bit of fun. And I'm sure you'll enjoy it too."

I shook my head, sadly. "OK – but just remember I did ask you nicely."

The first man nodded to his colleague who lurched in my direction, thrusting his knife forward. I kicked it neatly out his hand, dodged back and slammed an elbow into his forehead. It stunned him badly and he wavered giddily in the middle of the path.

I stepped forward, grabbed his tie and drew him forward, then I thrust two fingers into his eyes, broke his jaw brutally with my fist, then kneed him in the balls. He screeched like a pig but I held the tie taut, supporting his weight and preventing his collapse.

I hoisted him up with my right hand and stared directly into his eyes. "You didn't have to do this," I said, calmly.

The second man looked beseechingly at his companion. "Help me, Joe. Get this mad, fucking bitch off me!"

I glanced over at the first man but he was just standing there, shocked. While Joe thought through what to do, I punched his friend on the right side of his head and released him. He sank into a messy, unconscious heap in the middle of the path.

Then I turned around. "Walk away, Joe. Leave it."

Joe stumbled backwards, regained his footing and then his composure. He dipped his head and widened his eyes. His whole face appeared consumed with rage and venom. "*You are fucking dead*," he hissed.

Then he snorted, emitted a bizarre war cry and darted forwards. I swivelled quickly and donkey kicked his thigh ferociously, snapping his leg cleanly. He dropped onto the floor, screaming hysterically and rolling around.

I watched him for a few seconds, then took a step forward and dropped onto my haunches. Joe convulsed violently just underneath me. His trouser leg was already soaked in blood and I think he'd also wet himself.

I shook my head. "Why didn't you just walk away, Joe? I didn't want to do that. I really didn't."

Joe spluttered in agony, "Bitch," he groaned, choking on his tears and struggling for breath, "you *fucking* bitch! I'm going to kill you! I swear to God I'm going to fucking kill you…"

I exhaled in resignation. "Really? You're the one lying on the floor, Joe. Why don't you think about that?"

"*Bitch!*" he spat back again.

He writhed on the floor for a bit longer, continuing to curse violently, then also passed out.

I turned around and walking back towards the lake, exhausted and repelled. When I finally reached the bank a few moments later, I felt unbelievably distressed and tired. I dropped my head and closed my eyes. Branches to my left rustled and a thin breeze stroked my cheeks, teasing and chilling.

I opened my eyes and reached under my sweater. The stone was cold. I unclasped it from around my neck and held it in my palm but I could barely see it.

I stood there for ages, numbed and motionless. Then I took an enormous breath and threw the stone as hard as I possibly could into the lake. It sailed high into the night, smacked the water in the distance and disappeared.

31

I made my way home as quickly as possible.

Losing the stone's protection was obviously unsettling but I felt strangely relieved of responsibility. The stone was Frank's, not mine and I wasn't going to piggyback off its properties any longer.

I thought about what Dr Huck had said - but not all that much. It just seemed obvious that if I really was the special one, I would have found the stone, not Frank. Huck had obviously done a lot of "homework" but I just wasn't persuaded that he worked for the government, or could really help.

No doubt he, or whoever he really worked for, knew, or would find out, that I'd chucked the stone in Rotney Lake. If they wanted the stone that much, they could send in some divers. It wasn't a huge lake.

Of course, there was nothing in the papers about the two guys who attacked me in the park. No one was interested in that kind of thing, least of all the police.

There was no more news about Donny and Demi, either. They certainly didn't return to Rotney High. But I think the pupils suspected I had something to do with their disappearance because I was treated with even more caution and respect.

I tried contacting Frank's son but got nowhere. The hospital misplaced his telephone number but supplied an email address instead. I emailed him twice from a school computer but didn't receive a response. Then I gave up. I suppose I could have tracked him down, if I had really wanted to. I found out his name was Jack Truesdale and obviously I knew he lived in Sidcup but... I didn't, in the end. Maybe I will, one day.

Frank's body was flown back to America and he was buried in North Carolina. There were several obituaries on American websites but obviously nothing about the stone. One of the websites mentioned he was a keen amateur magician, and another one said he'd suffered a fatal stroke in Kent.

Huck kept his word. I didn't see him again after our midnight chat. Then, shortly afterwards, Mum told me her firm had settled his legal case and he'd taken up a new position in Europe. I just shrugged and mumbled, *good riddance.*

I started making a few friends at school but not close ones. I even got invited to a couple of parties but they were dull. The pupils just got stoned and high.

A month after getting rid of the stone, there was a major development. My Dad's appeal was partially successful after his QC produced compelling evidence of police malpractice. He wasn't acquitted but his sentence was halved and he was transferred to an open prison.

Although, it wasn't quite the ending I wanted, there was one very good piece of news. The massive fine was "reviewed" in our favour. Auntie Grim cleared the new amount immediately and then gave Mum a check. Mum didn't tell me how much it was for but it was enough for us to get out of Rotney and move into a spacious, two-bedroomed flat in Purchester.

Leaving Rotney was just *wonderful.* The funniest thing was packing to go "home". Mum and I had so little stuff that it only took a few minutes. We left the furniture in the flat but I took the "Rat Sign" with me as a memento!

Tyrese gave me his number and asked me to call him. Maybe I will, one day.

I returned to Mount High for the second term. It was like swapping a medieval torture chamber for a five-star hotel. Meanwhile,

Mum reduced her working hours to two days a week and used some of Auntie Grim's money to pay for private medical treatment. Her back improved gradually and she began smiling again.

Sadly, Granny Strictness didn't improve and finally passed away in March. She left nothing in her will – Dad's fine and legal costs swallowed up her entire savings.

The funeral was held on a Sunday afternoon and Dad was given permission to attend.

Then, during the summer holiday, I stayed over at my friend Amy's house. We spent all evening watching crap films on *Netflix*. Then we went upstairs to her bedroom. It was a very warm night and we chatted to about four in the morning before she finally fell asleep. But I just lay in bed, thinking about Frank and wondering if he was looking down on us.

I couldn't sleep. I felt high. About six in the morning, I got up and stretched. Then I peeped through Amy's bedroom window. Her garden appeared really inviting so I slipped on a t-shirt and padded barefoot down the stairs, as quietly as possible.

Amy's room was housed in the upstairs extension so there were two flights of stairs. At the bottom of the staircase, I turned right, tiptoed through the kitchen, and unlocked the back door. Then I stepped out into the garden.

It wasn't very large but very pretty and well-tended. The rectangular lawn was cut short and there were plants and flowers on both sides and at the back.

I closed my eyes and inhaled deeply. I could never breathe properly in Rotney; it was suffocating in every way. But this was beautiful, perfectly peaceful and refreshing. I opened my eyes, remaining still on the grass, experiencing nature with all five senses

Then, I became aware of a quite different, more powerful sensation. *Pain.* The sole of my right foot was heating up. Slowly, at first, then rapidly.

I yelped in surprise, shifted abruptly aside and looked down. There was a small, burning patch, shining brightly in a small circle within the lawn.

I dropped to my knees and dug quickly into the ground with my fingers. Moments later, I extracted the Sunshine Stone and even though it was glowing so brightly, I held it in my palm and cried.

Made in the USA
San Bernardino, CA
11 March 2018